5/9 ▷ 5/4/97 26 T
07/08 JBD

GEOFFREY REES

SEX WITH

STRANGERS

Farrar Straus Giroux · *New York*

Copyright © 1993 by Geoffrey Rees
All rights reserved
Printed in the United States of America
Published simultaneously in Canada by HarperCollinsCanadaLtd
First edition, 1993

Library of Congress Cataloging-in-Publication Data
Rees, Geoffrey.
Sex with strangers / Geoffrey Rees. — 1st ed.
p.   cm.
1. Gay men—United States—Fiction.   I. Title.
PS3568.E415S4   1993   813'.54—dc20   93-1242 CIP

A special thank you to H. Richard Quadracci, whose
friendship and support helped make this book possible.
—G.R.

IN MEMORY OF

JOSEPH SMALLEY

How should we like it were stars to burn

With a passion for us we could not return?

—W. H. AUDEN

CHICAGO

I had a thousand foolish, romantic reasons for taking the train to Chicago, but most of all I wanted to savor every inch of every mile of the distance that would separate me from my hometown. I could have flown, but in an airplane the distance exists mostly in the mind, the distance between the sky and the earth not felt, while the body remains cramped in a thin foam-backed seat, barely aware of any motion whatsoever. It seemed pointless to me to deliberately travel so far from home and get there so easily. I wanted to be inconvenienced, to arrive tired and exhausted, worn out from a long, hard journey but still unable to suppress my excitement at being somewhere new. The train seemed just the right speed for me; anything faster and I might forget where I was headed or why I was leaving. I pictured myself in a black-and-white film, waiting in the dead of night at the depot in a desolate prairie town for the one train a day headed to the big city, and I was that innocent, bright-eyed farm boy who had saved up my pennies and was leaving the family homestead to seek fame and fortune in the great metropolis. The train would give me the time I needed to reinvent myself.

So on an unendurably muggy September evening I packed closed the last of my boxes, crammed the acquisitions of a last-minute spending spree into the engorged black nylon set of suitcases my father had given me as a high-school graduation gift, and prepared to begin my new life. My father clucked loudly and pretended to look around confusedly when we pulled into the train yard in Worcester twenty minutes later, as if he had never been to a train station in all his long years, as if he couldn't believe such places still existed, as if the squalor and desolation surrounding us were somehow personal. It was indeed a depressing sight—no soaring gateways capped by Winged Victories, no terra-cotta vaults lined with murals of the American Landscape, no grand clock tower under which to nervously anticipate a cherished lover's arrival. Box cars stacked three high against a barbed-wire fence trailed off farther than the eye could see, burnt-out hulks of automobiles littered the side street, rotting warehouses and loft buildings lurked embarrassed in the shadows of their wealthy overbearing near-relations, the limestone-and-glass towers of the rejuvenated down-town, and a canal of blue-green sludge that must have stopped flowing years ago cut right through the heart of the railyard. There were no train tracks anywhere in sight, and the station itself hid behind a chipboard-and-steel-tube scaffolding, like some long-forgotten movie star, the most glamorous and beautiful of her time, who hides her head in old age behind a screen and bitterly refuses to be photographed.

One set of tracks remained, and we waited by a rusting shed for the train to pull in, its whistle in the distance finally breaking the silence between myself and my father. He walked me onto the train, where he again looked around in amazement, as if he were entering the cabin of an alien spaceship that was about to remove me to another planet as part of some intergalactic exchange; he appeared far more confused and mystified than disapproving or worried, and for the first time that whole summer he seemed unsure of himself, reluctant to let me go and probably more reluctant to try to keep me. Then bells clanged, my father waved to me from

the receding platform, and the train rolled heavily under me:
the long journey was begun.

I settled into my seat. I pulled a novel from my overnight
bag and pretended to read, all the while staring above the
top edge of its pages at the vanishing points of the skyline of
the city as the train traced a slow circle around it until we
were speeding through the suburbs and the sunlight was fading fast and the tops of the trees were blurring into the edge
of the purple sunset and an occasional back porch or treehouse
shot out at me through the speed and the darkness to suggest
the mysterious presence of alien life all around me before
falling back into the unattainable distance, while in my mind
I could almost count the railroad ties heaving and buckling
one after the other in endless succession on their beds of
granite gravel. Before long we had reached the Berkshires in
western Massachusetts, the blackness of the mounding hills
reflected by the luminescent darkness of the night sky, and
I felt very alone and very happy.

Now I took the time to explore the dingy length of this tired
old train; my car was almost deserted and I headed back to
the café. I strolled through two cars of almost empty sleeping
compartments, where an older couple, the woman wordlessly
knitting, her husband working a crossword puzzle, sat visible
through the open door of their sleeper and an overweight man
with a handlebar mustache who smoked heavily chatted with
a conductor about the train journey and commented on the
terror of flight which confined him to such a means of travel.
A group of gray-haired black men played cards and drank
beers at one of the plastic orange tables in the café, and
another group of old men sat around just drinking beers and
not talking much at all. Almost everyone looked at me
strangely for a second and then seemed to lose me altogether—I felt like the youngest person on that train by at
least fifty years.

I bought a soda and a bag of pretzels and made small talk with the bored clerk, who told me what to expect for the stages of the journey, Albany rapidly approaching, then the cities of upstate New York throughout the night—Utica, Rome, Syracuse, Rochester, Buffalo—Cleveland before dawn, then Toledo, South Bend, Gary, and finally Union Station in Chicago sometime late the next afternoon. I pocketed my change and walked forward to my seat near the head of the train, and as I meandered through the rows of sleeping compartments, peering discreetly, I hoped, into any that happened to be open, I noticed a young conductor sitting expectantly on the edge of his downturned mattress staring out into the corridor. He smiled at me as I passed, and when I looked back as I exited the car, the blond-headed man was peering after me, leaning languidly in his red-and-blue uniform against the thin frame of his compartment door.

I had resumed my seat and picked up my book again before it occurred to me that I probably had an admirer on board; I felt restless, unable to concentrate, sitting there wondering what I should do about this man who I felt sure was watching me. We pulled out of the Albany-Rensselaer station and crossed the Hudson River; the train was fuller now, mostly with older people, but there were also a couple of younger women with children crossing the great Empire State. I decided not to bother about the conductor, and succumbing to the numbing boredom of the trip, counting the hours that had passed in comparison to what still remained and realizing I had not covered even one-eighth of the destined distance, I settled back in my seat and began reading in earnest.

Midnight rapidly approached, passed, and the lights of the car dimmed; I was left with nothing but the narrow stream of an overhead light, too weak for reading; but I was not yet ready for sleep, so I put on my shoes, buttoned the top of my

shirt, and went to sit in the café. I paused on the way back
by a side door in the train that had been chained open. The
night air was warm and heavy from the mist off Lake Ontario
and the train rocked from side to side gently; looking out into
the blackness at the bobbing lights in the distance I could
almost have been at sea, and I pictured for a moment the sun
rising over the water and the distant shore magically appearing
with the daylight. Only the noise of the calm lapping of the
waves was missing, replaced by the wooden clatter of the
creaking rail bed, returning me to my musty third-class
surroundings.

I ordered a tea and sat by myself at the far end of the
almost empty lounge; a group of four or five men sat together
at the other end, silently playing poker, occasionally breaking
the stillness to curse their bad luck with the cards or gleefully
rake in the small pot collected at the center of their table. I
slurped my tea and read, looking up every now and then to
follow the progress of their game, when I was surprised by a
voice speaking at me from behind, and the conductor who
had smiled at me earlier laid a hand on my table and in a
low, calm voice asked if he might sit down and join me for
a moment.

He was definitely a young man, not older than twenty-six
or -seven, and pleasant if rather ordinary-looking, with dirty
blond hair, solid square features, yellow-brown eyes shaded
by thick, well-defined brows, and a barely perceptible field
of razor stubble evenly coating two ruddy cheeks. He smiled
at me sweetly, invitingly, evidently trying hard not to leer,
and though my heart began beating a little faster as I considered the possible consequences of conversing with this
stranger, the idea of adventure on a train (hadn't it indeed
been my secret purpose?) overwhelmed the potential sleazi-
ness of it all, and so I offered him the seat across from me.

"I noticed you pass my sleeper earlier this evening. Did you get on at Boston?" His fingers traced the edge of the table.

"No—Worcester."

"How far are you headed?"

"Chicago; that's the end of the line, isn't it?"

"Yup. My name is Dennis," he said, offering me his hand; his fingers were short and thick and well scrubbed, and he did not greedily keep hold of me or grimace knowingly at this touch. I began to like him a little.

"Thomas Hobart," I responded. "Pleased to meet you."

"Well, Thomas, will you be in Chicago long?" He struggled to keep his voice low, to not sound lecherous.

"I'm going to school there."

"Oh." This seemed to stump him, as if my going to school meant there was something peculiar or dangerous about my age, and it occurred to me that I was probably much younger than he realized, not that I thought there was anything young about myself at eighteen (I certainly felt old enough and ready for anything), but the revelation of my youth seemed to increase his consideration for me. He looked at me quizzically for a minute, then pulled a scrap of paper and a pen out of his pants pocket. He wrote down his full name, followed by the address of a residential hotel in Chicago, and handed it to me.

"Listen, Thomas, this is where I stay in Chicago every Thursday night—the train gets in Thursday afternoon, we leave again Friday morning, so any time you'd like to come and visit me, this is where you can find me. I'd like it very much if you would come and see me there. You can leave a message if you want, and then I'll know to expect you." His manner was polite and sincere; I felt flattered by his offer, relieved I was not forced to make a decision about acting impulsively on a moving train in the middle of the night in

upstate New York, and pleased I now had a friend in Chicago
and an open invitation to a bit of adventure.

I yawned, and he rose and apologized for bothering me,
assuring me he would not pay me any more attention on the
train, only pausing to say he hoped I would remember to visit
him. I thanked him and said I thought I probably would. He
left the café and I returned to my book for a few pages before
heading back to my seat and trying to sleep. The train had
just pulled out of Rochester and I noticed Dennis had left
the door to his sleeper open; I could see him writing in a
little notebook, but he paid me no attention at all, as if we
had never spoken and I just didn't exist, and I eased back
into my seat and slipped off my shoes, confused by the mysterious discretion of his advances yet grateful after all for his
thoughtfulness.

The train had just begun picking up speed, the lights of
Rochester quickly disappearing in the gloom, when I rose to
brush my teeth in the bathroom at the front of the car. As I
headed back to my seat I passed a tall, dark-haired, very
serious-looking young man who had evidently just got on and
was headed to the front of the train. He looked at me as I
squeezed to one side to let him pass through the aisle,
weighted down as he was by a heavy suitcase and overstuffed
shoulder bag. I smiled at him and he scowled meanly back
at me in the darkness, irritated at my blocking his path and
anxious to get beyond the obstacle I posed. He was a funny-
looking character, tall and deathly thin and slightly stooped,
and I could swear he was talking to himself as he pushed
down the aisle and into the forward car. I dropped to my seat,
and as I drifted into a restless sleep, I thought about his
strange, ghostly, white face cursing me in the darkness.

I awoke in Cleveland to the light of the sunrise over Lake
Erie, breakfasted in the café before we reached Toledo, and
spent the rest of the morning wondering at the flatness of

the unchanging Ohio landscape, until it finally became the unchanging Indiana landscape. Not long after lunch we pulled out of South Bend, and checking my calculations, I figured I was within three hours of my journey's end. The shore of Lake Michigan soon became visible in the distance, noticeable not from any signs of water or boats but because of the solid wall of factories which lined the water's edge like the whimsical constructions of an Erector set. Smokestacks billowed tall columns of congealed black exhaust, other buildings simply sweated steam off their rooftops, and an occasional steel tower mysteriously spewed fire at the industrial-gray sky. I had reached Gary, Indiana, and was awed by the sulfurous smell of the city; the pollution seemed to be seeping through the cracks in the rail car and slowly poisoning me.

Now the lake itself, which I had never before seen, came into full view, and I stared at the taut black surface somewhat amazed—the word "lake" seemed such a feeble description to me of the vast inland sea, covered with a flotilla of barges and steamers and freighters, that stretched away into the infinite distance. The surrounding flatness of the landscape that had so bored and mystified me became meaningful in relation to the appearance of the lake, as if the monotony of the land were a necessary reflection of the vast level surface of the water, and I wondered that the lake didn't just spill over its edges and wash away the shoreline in a swampy mess, the two seemed so perfectly wedded together in their flatness.

The factories receded, replaced by looping highways and the grid of regular city blocks, and the train turned away from the shore and headed inland, the view of the water replaced now by the distant shimmer of the skyscrapers of downtown Chicago. Their indistinct, muffled mass quickly dissolved into the individuated peaks and valleys of the tall and then taller and yet still taller buildings which formed a fence around the center of the city, until I was almost beneath the crushing height of the most enormous tower of them all, and then I was immersed in the darkness of the train shed as we pulled to a slow halt in Chicago's Union Station. Twenty-one hours had passed since I left home, a thousand miles had rolled by, I had traced a barely perceptible curve on the arcing surface of the earth rotating beneath me. Beyond the exhaustion and terminal boredom of my journey I felt a tremendous sense of accomplishment—I had arrived.

Bold shafts of afternoon sunlight shot through the decaying roof and filled the cavernous station with a religious light. I rose and stretched, tied my shoelaces tightly, as if assuring myself that I could stand alone on my two independent feet. I descended the three metal steps to the platform and took my first deep breath of the Chicago air. I hailed a porter and proceeded to the end of the train, passing Dennis as I did so; he stood in one of the train doors fussing with a box of electrical switches. He smiled and saluted me, nimbly raised his hand from the fuse box to his brow, then bounced the tip of his index finger off his temple as if to signify he was thinking of me and wished I would do the same. It was a goofy gesture, just silly enough to make him appear affectionately clumsy and sentimental, and I wondered, would I ever see him again.

In no time at all I had gathered my bags together and piled into a taxicab and was immersed in the downtown Loop; through the shadows of the El train tracks overhead I could make out the long rectangular blocks of the city stretching east and west, north and south, in a Cartesian grid of precise coordinates. My taxi emerged from the darkness of the trains and the block-long brick buildings and pulled onto Lake Shore Drive. While the driver raced south away from the city I craned my neck and turned in my seat to gawk at the skyline as it pulled into focus with a little necessary distance. The shore of the lake was lined by a bright ribbon of green, which sharply divided the expansive horizontal plane of the water from the sparkling vertical plane of the rising curtain of the city's skyline.

Several miles must have passed and the lake and city had almost merged behind me when we pulled off the drive into a neighborhood of old-fashioned high-rise apartment buildings. We turned west away from the water by the Museum of Science and Industry, passed under a wide set of train tracks onto East Fifty-seventh Street, then turned again onto South Blackstone Avenue, the block lined with attractive, well-kept stone row houses, each house faced with a deep front lawn and a black wrought-iron fence. In the middle of the block was a five-story Gothic concoction of brick and limestone, a sort of fanciful old residential hotel heavily decorated with trefoils and menacing gargoyles, and the street in front of this funny-looking building was crowded with station wagons and miniature moving vans full of students' belongings. A multitude of sullen-looking adults and even more sullen-looking young men and women milled about the front walk, some carrying milk crates full of record albums or winter sweaters, others seeming to direct the flow of traffic in and out, while still others watched in helpless despair. This curious, dungeon-like building, which seemed to frown down at the otherwise smiling streetscape, its name, "Blackstone Hall," carved portentously above the front entry, was my new residence.

I spent the afternoon unpacking my things, attempting with a heavy heart to make my cramped room cozy while ignoring the frantic exchanges all around me of families scolding and arguing and wishing each other goodbye and good riddance. I searched in the blizzard of young faces storming around me for one who looked interesting, for any potential companionship, or at the very least the possibility of interesting conversation, but I saw nothing to entice me or make me feel hopeful.

The next morning I rose early and set out to fuss with all

the bureaucratic business attendant on beginning college. I passed under the high Gothic arch at Fifty-eighth Street and University Avenue and headed straight across campus for the bursar's office; I was eager to cash a check for several hundred dollars, my first weekend in Chicago only hours away, and dismayed to discover that an enormous crowd had formed. I took my place at the end of one of the many long lines. The morning was hot and muggy and the air conditioning was no match for the pressing heat of the human throng; I stood sweating, fighting to hold my place in line, tapping my foot impatiently on the linoleum and thinking already about escaping back to my room for a second shower, when I was startled by the feel of a hand on my head gently fingering the spiky mess of my hair. I was just then recovering from a disastrous experimental hairdo, having dyed everything black the spring before, then chopped most of it off in disgust at the dismal result; the tips were still tinged with purple highlights from the black dye while the brown roots were rebelliously sprouting in protest against the assault they had endured. The overall effect was a rather chic wildness, an endearingly messy look which shamed me but appealed to others.

"You have remarkable hair—it's a very unusual style. Where did you have it done?" To my amazement, the man standing there virtually fondling me uninvited in this huge crowd of people was the same tall, pallid individual whose face had haunted me in the middle of the night on the train the previous Wednesday. I stammered back at him and blushed; I felt nothing but total embarrassment at his attentions, as if he were stamping me with the mark of Cain in front of this huge crowd, assuring I would never make a friend or find a sympathetic companion to share this new life with me.

"I'm sorry; I only meant to compliment you." He retracted

his outstretched fingers but continued to stare at me with a peculiar mixture of longing, self-satisfaction, and humor. Then he screwed up his eyes at me in mock seriousness and asked, "You look very familiar. Do I know you from somewhere?" Was this man a total maniac, or was he playing games with me? Did he really have only the vaguest memory of our encounter on the train?

I trembled somewhat pathetically from the heat, embarrassed at what I felt sure was becoming a spectacle, and answered him, "This is a mistake." I held in my hand, along with the check I was waiting to cash, the necessary identification in the form of my driver's license; with an easy boldness and not a moment's hesitation, this stranger grabbed the license from my hand and read the name out loud to himself. I watched in helpless amazement as he compared my picture on the license to my presence there before him, then handed it back to me as if I had just dropped it and he were performing a valuable service by honestly returning it.

"You're much more attractive in person, Thomas. It was nice talking to you. Goodbye." He sauntered through the crowd; I watched him disappear through the double glass doors of the entry. I felt sure the eyes of everyone around were fixed on the spot where my unwelcome friend had just been standing, and I felt more uncomfortably conscious than ever of the growing heat and the completely alien nature of my environment. I wanted to swoon from the shock, I felt so painfully self-conscious, but my legs held steady beneath me and I instead waited patiently for my turn at the cashiers, all the while studiously working to avoid eye contact with any of my university neighbors.

Classes began the following Monday, the first week dragged on, and the heat that had seemed so unusual at my arrival lingered indefinitely over the Chicago campus; a late-summer heat wave had descended and cast an oppressive pall over

the city. In the afternoons I would walk back to my room,
toss my heavy, mostly unopened books onto the bed,
change shirts, and then continue a quarter-mile past the
train tracks to the lake, where a grassy triangular plain, known
to neighborhood residents as "The Point," ended in a rocky
prominence, from which vantage a miniature view of the
downtown skyline was perfectly visible in one direction and
the barest outline of the steel mills was discernible in the
other. Here I would sit and marvel at the monotony of the
lake's surface, the curving easiness of the shoreline, the absence of dramatic confrontation in the meeting of the two,
and sink for an hour or so into the frustration of my own
boredom.

In my room before going to bed each night I opened the
front cover of the paperback novel I had been reading on the
train and since finished, where I had copied down the address
of Dennis the train conductor, and before falling asleep I
repeated to myself, "The Hotel Madison," and wondered,
would I pay him a visit. Thursday approached more rapidly
than I had anticipated, my last class ended early in the day,
and as I walked back up Fifty-eighth Street to my room I was
still uncertain what I would do. I walked slowly, weighing
the near-certainty of disappointment and self-disgust against
the cherished possibility of pleasure and excitement. I
stopped for a moment to chat with one of the students on my
floor, and when he confidently waved to me as I passed on,
calling out some reference to our anticipated shared meal, I
knew for certain I would be dining out that night.

The Hotel Madison was a modest residential hotel several
blocks north of the Tribune Tower and a block west of Michigan Avenue. A tall red neon light draped the front fire escape
and flashed the building's name at regular intervals. From
the outside I could already imagine the somewhat seedy interior, where the glow of the neon blinking on and off through

the dusty venetian blinds lit up the lonely lovemaking of the hotel's patrons like a strobe light, and my initial impressions were confirmed by the subsequently matching reality. I was rather pleased by the old-fashioned, run-down seaminess of the place, as if I were acting out a role in a movie and this was the set especially designed for these scenes. It seemed to me if I was going to have an affair with a train conductor, this was definitely the place to do it.

Dennis did not act the least bit surprised when I showed up unannounced, only apologetic that he was not more ready to see me. I arrived late in the day, just at the time when afternoon officially becomes evening, marked by a subtle shift in the settling western light, the gradual softening of which over the course of several hours accelerates by a rapid and exponential increase, until the sun has all but completely set. Dennis had been napping when I disturbed him, sleeping off the exhaustion of his long day's travel in preparation for whatever he did to occupy his free weekly night in Chicago, and he stood before me in his T-shirt and stocking feet, his belt unbuckled and the top of his pants hanging open.

"You surprise me; I thought you might not come." I stood in the doorway and he beckoned me in. "I was just making up for last night's lost sleep. Come on in and sit down." He closed the door, gently rested his right hand in the small of my back, and steered me to a lumpy brown chair by the window on the other side of the bed in the small, L-shaped room. My body tingled at the feel of his hand and I stared at his neck and shoulders; they were square-shaped and fairly thickset, his skin glowed slightly orange in the cheap yellow light, and a few stray brown hairs sprouted vagrantly at the back of his neck. He leaned over me, balancing himself on the arm of the chair, and kissed me on the forehead.

"Hungry?" He smiled. "I was just going to take a shower. Why don't you make yourself comfortable, and when I'm ready

we can have dinner." He reached into his suitcase, which
lay open on the floor at the foot of the bed; after taking out
a clean undershirt, shorts, and socks, he disappeared into
the bathroom, pushing the door behind him until it snapped
shut. A moment later the rushing explosion of the shower
filled the room. I didn't move from my chair; I contemplated
rifling through his suitcase or the desk drawer next to the
bed, but decided I would rather not know anything more than
necessary about him—even his last name I wished then I
could do without. I regretted the necessity of ever having to
leave this room with him, and wondered if instead we couldn't
just drop all pretense and stay there, restricting our dalliance
to this limited patch of private territory. I wanted to go to
bed with him, but I dreaded the necessity of having to talk
with him, of any other sort of expectation rising between us.
I found him sexy, easily recognized his attractions, but that
did not mean I necessarily liked him or in any way wanted
to be his friend. My desire was offset by the fear I felt at the
possibility of not being able to manage this encounter.

The shower stopped and I could hear him grunt slightly as
he vigorously dried himself before emerging in his clean shorts
and socks, the T-shirt tossed over one shoulder. He stood
before me in his underwear, as if allowing me a preview of
what to expect, and I liked what I saw. His chest was pale,
broad, and muscular, and only a little hairy, his legs sturdy
and well shaped. Before pulling his pants on he grabbed his
crotch in one hand and playfully cradled the indistinct bundle
hiding inside, for the first time revealing to me a look of
unambiguous desire in his eyes. He didn't say anything, not
needing to, for he had captured my complete attention, and
confident that he provoked in me the desired response, he
finished dressing.

We hurried out of the room, as if to stay there a minute
longer were to risk completely losing control of ourselves. It

occurred to me, as we climbed down the two flights of stairs to the hotel lobby and my pulse recovered its more normal pace, that I was enjoying this postponement of pleasure; I felt as if he had teased me with the glimpse of himself, and I liked it. I looked forward to the time when we would return to his plain little apartment and finally undress, but in the meantime, knowing that moment was only a couple of hours away made the interval all the more exciting. He didn't need to say much of anything to me; just having him there next to me, his physical presence a marker of what to expect, was enough to keep me from feeling bored.

We walked several blocks north out of the commercial neighborhood surrounding the hotel, just crossing over into Old Town, and I did not question his choice of restaurant for dinner. We did not talk much over our meal; he hardly asked me any questions about myself, for which I felt grateful, and he did not offer much information about himself in return. We seemed to watch each other eat under a microscope, as if every action at the table were to have a corollary in bed for which we were obliged to study and prepare. About three-quarters of the way through the meal he reached out to me across the table; brushing his outstretched fingers across the back of my hand, he whispered, "I feel like I'm about to explode."

"You will," I answered, and he grinned at me as I withdrew from his touch. Food could no longer hold our attention, so we paid the check, he accepting without argument my offer to split the cost, and marched back to the hotel in a holy silence, neither of us daring to even look at the other, as if to communicate in any way during this delicate time would jeopardize the success of our inevitable coupling. We raced up the hotel stairs two at a time, panting heavily before the apartment door while he fumbled with the key, his fingers jittery from anticipation. He slammed the door closed behind us, and standing in the middle of the room, we embraced, squeezed each other so painfully hard we seemed to hope through force of will to dissolve into each other's bodies and thereby forgo the necessity of having to disrobe, which we somehow in the darkness, despite our impatient desperation, still managed to accomplish without ever having unglued ourselves one from the other until, without knowing how we got there, we were lying naked, locked together on the soft, narrow mattress, while the red neon of the exterior light reflected just as it was supposed to on the bedroom wall, and the autumn breeze rolled through the open window and tugged at the frayed edges of the dirty canvas blinds.

Hours later, in the deadest hour after midnight, when the last rowdy remnants of the nearby Rush Street crowds had completely disappeared and the insomniac city itself seemed finally to have fallen asleep, I disentangled myself from Dennis's sleepy embrace and showered, determined to spend at least the waning hours of the night in my own dormitory bed. Dennis sat up, woken by the light from the bathroom, and watched me bathe through the door, which I had failed to close properly so that it drifted open. When I emerged naked from the bathroom, with just a towel wrapped loosely around my waist, Dennis switched on the bedside lamp and sat up straight against the flimsy Formica headboard. He dragged the sheets up over his waist but was unable to hide his erection in the folds of a green wool blanket.

I felt uncomfortably conscious of his lustful gaze watching me as I dripped a soggy set of footsteps on the carpet, prudish and awkward now after my period of abandonment, but also pleased with myself for possessing the power to arouse him, happy that I was desirable in his eyes. I sat beside him on the bed and let his strong hand wander knowingly through the fold in the towel which remained wrapped around me. I kissed him and attempted to rise, but he held on to me with a firm grasp.

"Don't go. Why are you leaving?" And with his hands he attempted more eloquently than with words to make the argument for my staying, but much as I responded to his touch, I felt determined to leave. More than ever he seemed a total stranger to me, and the loneliness of his company and his room seemed unbearable in comparison with the possibility of being truly by myself; I needed that solitude to recoup from the loneliness of the hours we had spent together. I did not attempt to explain to him my mixed feelings, the contradictory pull I felt between physical desire and the horror of his company.

"I have a busy day tomorrow—everyone will wonder what happened to me. I should really go home." Of course there was no one in the world at that moment who cared where I was or what I was doing, but somehow that made returning to my room seem all the more important.

"Will I see you next week?" I assured him he would, and he responded by loosening his grip on me, allowing his fingers to trail down the back of my leg as I stood up. Dennis watched from the bed while I dressed. When I had almost finished he rose to use the bathroom, as if wanting to make sure before I left to provide me with a good full glimpse of his nakedness. He returned and draped his arms around my shoulders: "You promise to come?"

"Sure." I shrugged, tired and anxious now to effect my escape. He handed me my jacket, which somehow had gotten hung on a wire hanger in the shallow closet, and standing behind the front door as he opened it, modestly assuring that any lonely sleepwalker who might be out prowling in the hallway at this ungodly late hour would catch no glimpse of his undress, he couldn't resist groping me one final time. He

pressed my hand in his, and after reminding me that he would
be expecting me the next Thursday, he pushed me out the
door and swiftly slammed it shut, so before I fully knew it,
in my sleepy exhaustion and the confusing lingering physical
sensations from our time together, I had walked to the corner
of Michigan Avenue and hailed a taxicab to the South Side.

I stopped the taxi in front of the museum at Fifty-seventh
Street and the lake, now wider awake than before and no
longer in such a hurry to return to Blackstone Hall. I was
enthralled by an incipient drama unfolding in the eastern
distance of the lake, so shocking and enormous I doubted
the truth of my vision and suspected myself of hallucination.
The taxi circled away from me, the light traffic along Lake
Shore Drive hummed steadily, but my vision was held by the
miracle I witnessed: facing straight out over the water, I
noticed a tiny yellow flame flicker at the edge of the sky, and
while I stood watching in confused fascination, the fire grew
until after only a few short minutes the sun, like an enormous
disk of molten orange steel bubbling at the bottom of a black
pit, was dangling dangerously close to the water's reflective
surface, and I held my breath, uncertain whether this huge,
heavy, dripping star of light would manage to rise safely
into the sky or whether it would stagger under the force of
its own unfathomable weight and splash into the lake, sub-
merging me in an eternity of darkness. The suspense was
unbearable—never before had the world seemed so fragile
and so indeterminate, the possibility of apocalypse so completely real; the whole spectacle of the uncertain universe
was unfolding before my puny vision.

Not until the sun had shrunk to an unimpressive yellow
ball of indistinct light, painful to look at for its ugliness as
much as for its brightness, did I turn, and confident that the
day had securely begun with myself its necessary witness, I
traced my steps back to Blackstone Avenue and my drab little

room. Already a handful of the most diligent of my fellow students were wandering the hallway, none of them taking notice of my presence in the lobby as I waited for the elevator to deposit me in a turret of the tower. In the peace and quiet of Room 506, where I lay fully clothed on my bed staring out the window, I felt my face burn in the streaming morning light, and with an anxious, grateful prayer for having narrowly survived the apocalypse, I began to recover from the terrifying discovery that my own life hung by such a slender cosmic thread, and prepared to sleep into the distant afternoon.

The quarter passed quickly, and before I knew it the lingering summer heat was long gone, replaced by the violent early winds of autumn off the lake and the short gray days of standard time. I settled into a solitary pattern of existence, attending classes in the morning, napping in the afternoon, studying alone in the evening, exploring the city on the weekends, the whole week regularly punctuated by my Thursday-night excursions to the Hotel Madison. I sometimes swore to myself after seeing Dennis that I would not return again, but by the time the next Thursday rolled around I forgot whatever condition had made me loathe myself and I once more succumbed to the strength of my desire. I was always certain to return to my own bed before dawn, but the lengthening of the encroaching winter nights left me with greater and greater latitude to exercise my options for escape, and Dennis seemed to philosophically accept as a part of our trysting my regularly fleeing his company at some unexpected hour, which, by virtue of its unpredictability, soon became fairly predictable.

The weeks meanwhile passed with no further sign of my disturbing admirer from the bursar's office; not in the library or anywhere else on campus did I see him again, until one Wednesday afternoon only a week before Thanksgiving, after finishing my last class of the day, I headed for a change to the Coffee Shop at the corner of Fifty-seventh and University, a bustling hangout which I generally avoided, not having made any friends.

I was feeling inexplicably more hopeful than usual this afternoon, hopeful I might at least observe a bright face in the crowd to attract my attention and draw my thoughts away from myself. I followed the slate paths through the cloistered quadrangles, piercing one high limestone wall after another, crossing lawns now dead and brown from the nightly frosts, and entered the paved courtyard farthest north and east on the campus, which the thick lead-paned windows of the Coffee Shop overlooked. The tables were crowded with ruddy, glowing faces and I felt instantly disheartened by the noisy reality of the place; I doubted there was any distraction for me there, but ashamed of my cowardice I ordered coffee and a doughnut, and proceeded to the back of the room; almost immediately I noticed my tall, pale-faced, mysterious friend sitting in a booth. I approached and hovered above him, saying nothing. After a short, startled moment he looked up at me, interrupting the animated conversation of his companions, and his eyes opened rounder with pleasure and surprise.

"Thomas Hobart." He remembered my name. "Won't you join us?" He slid over in the booth and patted the narrow leather bench with his hand as an invitation for me to sit down, which I gladly did. "Look, Jane, my victim from the bursar's office." He turned to me. "Jeepers, Tommy, where have you been all these weeks?" He called me Tommy in an easy, possessive manner which I wasn't sure I liked but which I felt unable to resist.

"Michael, control yourself," Jane scolded him, then assured me, "You've no idea what Michael's imagination has already made of you. You apparently made quite an impression."

"I guess I could say the same, although we only met for a minute." I wondered what he could have been saying about me, and I decided I didn't want to know.

"A minute's usually all it takes." A second woman, squashed into the corner of the booth by Michael's making room for me, spoke now in a loud, clear voice. She reached her hand out, waved it in front of Michael's face, and introduced herself. "I don't want you to think I would tolerate any unfair advantage—I'm Chris. A pleasure to meet you, Thomas."

The fifth and final member of our party, a short, mousy character who rocked forward sleepily in the opposite corner next to Jane, making what seemed a Herculean effort to open his eyes, nodded at me across the table, and simply said, "Hello."

"That's Mark," Jane explained. "He's trapped in outer space."

"He's what?" I thought I heard her correctly and understood what she was saying, only her words made no sense.

"Hallucinating wildly. It's just something he does every now and then. We may look like we're having a kaffeeklatsch, but actually we're babysitting."

"Would you like to help?" Chris asked.

"Impossible," Michael interrupted. "Thomas is clearly just a child in need of protection himself."

"Michael, people pass laws to keep you away from their children," Jane sarcastically commented.

"Thanks, but no thanks." I declined Chris's offer. "He does look pretty sick, though. What do you do with him?"

"We just take turns and let him follow us around wherever we go," Chris said. "He's fine as long as he's holding on to someone. But he starts to panic when left by himself."

"Like the rest of us," added Michael.

"He'll come down eventually. Let's go check out my new

apartment." Jane stood up and the rest followed. I watched
them pull on their coats and held back as they headed toward
the exit. Michael and Chris turned to me and each took hold
of one of my arms, then asked in unison, "Aren't you coming,
Thomas?" I allowed them to escort me to the street, where a
light snowfall had begun. Michael kept a gentle hold of my
arm and we headed north on University Avenue into the
surrounding neighborhood, the four of them shouting and
hitting each other and running in circles on the sidewalk
while I responded to the occasional comments they tossed in
my direction, none of them seeming to question my sudden
appearance in their company; by the time we had turned east
on Fifty-third Street I felt as if I had known these people for
years without realizing it and they had only been waiting
patiently for me to find them.

Jane, who had run ahead of us, stopped at the corner of
South Dorchester before a greasy storefront where heavyset
black women in hairnets stood behind two-inch plates of
bulletproof Plexiglas and squirted hot sauce onto platefuls of
chicken and Wonder bread. On the peeling sign over the
entry a grinning chef in apron and toque swung a meat cleaver
at a frightened, red-faced chicken.

"Look—conveniently located only seconds from Harold's
Famous Fried Chicken." She proudly gestured at the spotted,
dirt-encrusted plate-glass window.

"Chicken sandwiches, anyone? My treat." Michael held
the door open and we huddled into the cramped restaurant;
pine-veneer paneling lined the two far walls below huge mirrors which had long ago ceased to reflect anything in particular
through the hazy film of grease which coated them, and a
bright orange Formica counter supported the sheets of Plexiglas. Michael ordered several chicken sandwiches with hot
sauce without asking any of us whether we were hungry or
what we wanted to eat, while entranced I watched the me-

chanical motions of the women steadily frying batches of poultry. I had never seen such food before; I was utterly fascinated by the newness of this diet, and rather pleased with myself for so easily experiencing what struck me as "the real thing," this strange concoction of chicken on the bone like the nutritional equivalent of emotional experience.

Jane settled into a blue-and-white lawn chair, the only place available to sit; Michael stood behind her and ran his fingers through her messy chestnut hair, smoothing the top and sides, which had been tousled by the friction of the dry wind. Chris stood next to me and talked knowingly of Harold's fried chicken; she gave me a sort of lecture on where to find the best bad food on the South Side of Chicago: Harold's was at the top of her list. Mark clutched the sleeve of Chris's jacket as we talked, Jane having somehow detached Mark from herself during our walk. He floated between us, his eyes flickering open wider in recognition of his surroundings before he returned again to the interior of his mind. Chris looked past me at the traffic piling up at the streetlight outside, seemed not to hear some question I was in the middle of putting to her, shouted, "Oh my God, she's back!" and ran out the door, rushing at a shiny black car stopped at the corner. She waved her arms wildly until the driver, a dark young woman with enormous silver hoops in her ears, rolled down her window, and the two kissed with astonishing passion out there in the middle of the street. The driver slid over, allowing Chris to ease into her seat, and in an instant she was speeding away toward the lake without ever having looked back.

"She's such a slut." Michael spit out the words in disgust. "You know what the girls call Melinda?"

"No."

"The vulva." They burst into knowing hysterics, filling the smoky interior with the sounds of their animalistic cackling.

Mark in the meantime, not at first having realized that he was left without anyone to hold on to, suddenly came to his senses and panicked. He dug his nails into the top of my arm, locking my shoulder in place.

"Looks like it's your turn to babysit." Michael paid for the chicken, now almost ready, and Jane too approached the orange counter. The cashier wrapped our sandwiches in heavy-duty foil, stacked them in a brown paper bag, placed them on a turntable, and rotated them out to us through the Plexiglas.

"That was Chris's old girlfriend," Jane explained to me as we headed around the corner. "She left the country ages ago without a word to anyone. We think she's dangerous. We're not even sure we like her." I wondered for a moment if she was speaking with the royal "we," if she was even aware of what she was saying, until Michael made it clear to me that they often spoke for each other in this way.

"Frankly, we hate her guts." He held open the door to Jane's building, a typical red-brick block of prairie-style flats, rectangular bays zigzagging away from the street into a dark, narrow courtyard. Changing the subject completely as we climbed the stairs, Michael continued: "There's a wonderful house by Louis Sullivan just around the corner—a regular paean to the prairie in yellow brick and limestone. Remind me to show it to you later."

Jane's apartment was one long corridor of room after room; at the front was a sun porch piled full of boxes and milk crates, and at the other end, beyond what seemed like an endless succession of darkened, empty bedrooms, was a huge dining room, completely empty except for a flimsy, fake-crystal chandelier which swung in the draft seeping through the cracked windowsills, the dangling crystals faintly singing to themselves. We sat on the floor, Mark still firmly gripping my jacket, which I tried to remove, only to find him sneakily attach himself to my shirt-sleeve, while Jane fetched some beers from what appeared to be an equally empty kitchen and switched on a radio.

The tinny music filled the room. Michael sprawled the plates of chicken in a little circle, and enticed by the hot aroma, I tore into my sandwich. The hot sauce, which had looked so innocuous streaming from the red squirt bottles full of the stuff, exploded in my mouth. I had had no idea what to expect and was not prepared for this scorching sacrament. I gulped at the beer Jane handed me, its sole effect to fan the fire in my mouth and sinuses, so that the only remedy was to continue feeding the flames until they eventually died down; I consequently picked the bones of my sandwich clean, surprised to discover when I was finished that the burning which had driven me on completely evaporated with the last bite of the bread soggy with chicken fat, and I recognized what a transcendent, transporting experience that simple piece of fried chicken had been.

"The apartment is great, Jane—and so much space!" Michael pecked at his chicken, teasing Jane about her total lack of furniture. "I assume you're at least hiding a bed somewhere in this cave?"

"What for?" Jane giggled at herself.

"Don't be fooled by Jane's modesty, Tommy. The woman knows exactly what I'm talking about." Michael appeared to take pride in his knowledge of Jane's sexual habits.

"I wish I did." I uttered the phrase with no ironical intentions and only a glimmering awareness of my own obtuseness.

"Your boy wonder shows immense possibilities, Michael. How fortunate for both of us." Jane took my comment for a discreet dismissal of Michael's smutty imputation against her character.

"Remember, Tommy, your innocence is always your most charming defense." Michael spoke seriously, as if he were

explaining to me the code of conduct which should regulate
our relations.

"What are you talking about?" Jane poked a finger in his cheeks while he chewed another bite of his sandwich.

"I think I know perfectly well what he means." This comment on my part apparently gave Michael great satisfaction, because he returned his chicken breast to his plate, nodded emphatically in my direction, and said, "You see, Tommy and I already have a special understanding."

Jane yawned at Michael's vagueness and we all fell silent. The radiators hissed and the pipes banged so loudly Mark jumped from his stupor to turn his head in terror, as if he were fighting a war inside his head and desperately searching for a safe place to escape the bombs. The winter draft blew down the back of my neck, and through the diptych of dining-room windows I could see the wooden back porches of the opposite row of buildings, a green trelliswork pattern against the maroon bricks.

Mark began to loosen his hold on my arm; his hand slipped almost into my lap before he limply raised it again, searching for some place to rest in contact with me. Jane and Michael had finished their sandwiches by now, and looking at the darkening sky overhead, I said, "I think he's falling asleep."

"Let's put him to bed and get out of here." Michael and I pulled Mark to his feet, then dragged him down the hallway after Jane, who turned into a small bedroom; a bare mattress with a blanket and a box of books were pushed against the wall under the window. We laid Mark out on the mattress and Jane carefully wrapped him in the thick wool blanket. I felt like an Egyptian priest of the dead presiding at my first mummification. While Michael and I watched from the doorway, Jane knelt at Mark's side and held his hand in her own and whispered quietly to him to relax and go to sleep, assuring him he was safe and everything was all right. She laid the back of her free hand against his cheek and kissed him on the forehead. Sitting by his side, coaxing him into sleep, she was a completely different person, a mothering angel of comfort and rest; like the independent observer who is accidentally brought under by the hypnotist, I fell completely under Jane's spell. She relaxed her grasp of Mark's hand, allowed it to drop with a dull thud on the mattress. After brushing her fingertips across his brow one more time, she motioned us out of the room, being careful to leave the door slightly ajar and the hall light on. None of us was allowed to speak, and our silence prolonged the undisturbed potency of Jane's magic, until midway through our descent of the back stairway, exposed to the rapidly dropping temperature and the wind whipping through the chute of the alley, she broke it herself.

"If we're lucky maybe he'll wake up and remember to throw himself out the window this time. It would save us all a lot of trouble. Too much acid, my ass."

We hit the pavement and slithered through a damp passage in the basement of the building, emerging on Dorchester at the entry to the courtyard.

"Where do we walk you, Tommy?" I had only been with them for a couple of hours, but they had adopted such a knowing tone and attitude that it startled me to be suddenly reminded they actually knew nothing about me, not even where I lived.

"Blackstone Hall."

"Oh my God!" Michael began in a low moan. "Not the 'Dungeon of Hyde Park.' I once slit my wrists in the bathtub of 506. My roommate was devastated by the failure of my suicide attempt. He was all set to spend the quarter in Mexico—you know the university has a policy, if your roommate kills himself, you get automatic As for the quarter."

I gulped hard and looked at him as we crossed Fifty-third Street and walked south along Dorchester. "I live in 506."

It occurred to me after saying this that Michael was perhaps playing some sinister game with me; after all, there was no reason in the world, since he had taken such an immediate interest in me, that he shouldn't have already learned where I lived, although I wondered, if that were the case, why he had never tried to contact me. "Are you serious?"

"Of course, that was over eight years ago. Michael was still despairing over the loss of his first love." Jane confirmed the truth of Michael's claim, filling in the details of the episode while we walked, Michael occasionally chiming in additional bits of information.

"The first is always the hardest." He threw great tragic weight into his voice. Jane continued as if she were relating the plot of some cheap operetta.

"Michael had been sounding his swan song for weeks. Joe finally decided to leave town, he became so frightened that Michael would do something and everyone would hold him responsible."

"Of course, it *was* all his fault."

"Well, try as Michael did, he just couldn't separate Joe from his trousers, and finally we thought perhaps the prospect of some other young man would lift his spirits. So we attended a big party downtown at the Art Institute, where the boys tend to be cute and easy and not especially bright—"

"Which is basically how we like them—"

"—but Michael proceeded to get so pitifully drunk we found him at one point, not aware of what he was doing until we pointed it out to him, making out with an apparently even drunker young woman. And then he just disappeared out the front door, all the while screaming about how he 'just wanted to lie down and die.' It wasn't the first time he'd had too much to drink and turned morbid at a party, and we expected he would just pass out in the hallway."

"I tried but I couldn't do it."

"When he didn't show up for breakfast the next morning
we knew something had to be the matter. By the time we got
to Blackstone they were loading him into the back of the
ambulance." Jane spoke in a cheery, undramatic voice, seemingly unaware of her effect on me. "Well, here we are."

We had turned the corner at Fifty-seventh Street, and the
building loomed in the glare of the streetlights ahead of us.
Michael kept quiet as we approached, until we were standing
together at the end of the front walk, when he spoke again.

"Perhaps we'd better leave you here. I'm sure we'll see
you again very soon, now that we know where to find you";
with these words, keeping his hands securely in his coat
pockets, Michael modestly pecked me on the cheek. Jane's
warmer kiss followed. They watched me enter the lobby and
wait for the elevator, but when I turned to wave a final goodbye, they had disappeared into the darkness, and alone I
ascended to my now thoroughly haunted attic.

I had parted from Jane and Michael with no definite plans
to see them again, only a vague reassurance that they would
soon seek me out, and I began to feel suspicious thinking
about them alone in my room that night, remembering their
conspiratorial attitudes and whispering; I wondered if they
had some secret plans in store for me. I had made no reference
to my having sighted Michael on the train, nor did he, and
I began to doubt myself on this point also—was the figure I
had passed in the night merely a hallucination, a ghostly
presentiment of the suicidal character who had previously
inhabited my room? I began to feel I was caught in the eye
of a storm raging around me, these strange new people swirling
like a cyclone through Hyde Park, wreaking devastation on
the innocent lives unfortunate enough to fall in their path.
Was I to be their next victim, the object of one or the other's
passing fancy, to be dropped or pursued in relation to the

frustration or pleasure my responses provided? I was, in short, overcome with a newfound sensation of paranoia.

The next evening I spent with Dennis, and never before had I felt more comfortable with him. I had always found satisfaction in his bed, otherwise I would not have kept returning, but this evening was altogether new and different. We did not talk any more than usual, which was not very much, but the awkwardness evaporated from our conversation. There was so much that I knew I did not want to share with Dennis about my life, but absorbed as I was by my own self-consciousness, I had not been fully aware before that he was so obviously keeping his own secrets close. As I thought about him on the bus heading downtown, it occurred to me that I didn't know his age, the town where he lived, what sort of education he'd had, if he had any family. Dennis, for whatever reasons, had been guarding his private life as closely as I had been guarding mine, and this realization freed me to think of him on equal terms. Until then I had felt cheap in my own eyes for holding back parts of myself, for mostly being interested in the sex, but the thought that Dennis was only interested in the same encouraged me to accept the terms of our arrangement more fully. I was still careful to leave before dawn, but now rather than feel sullied, as if I needed to slink home defiled before daylight should catch and expose me, I thought of my leaving as necessary to the preservation of our arrangement, as the demarcation of the special line I crossed when I entered that third-floor room at the Hotel Madison, a precious foreign state that existed nowhere else but in these nocturnal sensations and which was much too delicate and fragile to risk exposure to the damaging rays of the sun.

Friday passed with no signs of my newfound friends, and I waited unsure whether they would seek me out or I must look for them, and whether I even wanted to see them again.

My uncertainty was laid to rest Saturday morning, when I was woken by a sharp knock on my door, followed by the gruff voice of the husky bodybuilder who lived down the hall informing me I had a telephone call. I jumped out of my bed frightened and astounded—I had not in the over eight weeks of living in that dormitory received a single call. Once every Sunday night I telephoned my father back in Worcester, and then always from the library, and I was only vaguely aware that a hallway telephone even existed, sometimes hearing the echo of its ring but never giving it any further thought. In my bathrobe I padded down the hall past the open doors of several rooms, most of the students looking at me as I passed as if they had never seen me before, those who did know me marveling that I had received a telephone call. I felt certain it was my father on the line and took a deep, calming breath before lifting the receiver.

"Hello?"

"Aren't you coming to breakfast?" It was Michael, and he sounded slightly annoyed, as if I were late for an appointment and he was calling to complain about my standing him up.

"I don't know, you tell me." I knew he was going to tell me anyway, and waited for my instructions.

"Of course you are. Hurry up and get dressed. We're at the laundromat around the corner. We'll meet you downstairs in five minutes. And don't bother to comb your hair." I raced back to my room, frantically brushed my teeth, and sorted through a pile of clean clothes wondering what was appropriate attire for such a breakfast invitation. In my haste I chose a mismatched pair of socks and a sweatshirt to go with my good shoes and trousers, which combined with my tousled hair and dirty overcoat must have made me quite a disheveled sight, but this apparently was exactly what Michael was hoping for, because when I emerged into the bleak daylight and

greeted him and Jane at the end of the concrete walkway, he
took my hand in his and exclaimed with delight, "You look
perfect. A picture of disarray."

I had no idea what he was talking about but I was completely intoxicated by their presence; since I'd dropped the
phone five minutes before and hastened to dress, all traces
of paranoia or doubt had been erased from my mind, and I
was filled heart and soul with the desire to please. I lapped
up every last bit of attention they lavished on me and wished
and wished for more. I had postponed hoping they would seek
me out for fear of becoming unused to my settled loneliness,
but now that they had proven their interest in me, I desperately wanted to become their friend, and gladly, willingly,
submissively allowed them to take me arm in arm and lead
me where they would.

Jane and Michael seemed as happy to see me as I was to
see them. Michael kept pinching me in the side, Jane crossing
her eyes at me affectionately in an attempt to communicate
something. We walked north along Blackstone with a bright
spring in our step, the chill air heightening the rosy blush
on all our cheeks, so that we looked like three cherry-cheeked
angels with the tears from the whipping wind at the corners
of our eyes the symbols of our joy.

I had no idea where we were headed until we reached Fifty-
third Street and crossed over to a steamy glass-fronted
cafeteria-style restaurant with an enormous sign overhead
reading VALOIS—See Your Food. The window was dripping
wet with condensation, but through the mist I could see the
restaurant was bustling with hungry young patrons. Michael
held the door open and we assumed our places at the end of
a long line.

"Brace yourself," Jane began. "This is your official in-
auguration into the primitive social life of Hyde Park."

"Think of this as a kind of deflowering. You may feign innocence, but after a Saturday-morning breakfast at Valois you've sunk to the lowest depths of Hyde Park society."

"Just where I've always wanted to be."

"And more important, just where we want you to be."

We had reached the counter. There was almost no food to be seen anywhere, only a steam table with a container of sausages floating in hot water and a steel shelf covered with bowls of Jell-O, cottage cheese, and containers of chocolate milk set over ice, yet plate after plate loaded with stacks of pancakes and potatoes or omelettes and toast or pork chops smothered in gravy kept flowing over the counter and coming to rest on the assembly line of orange-and-green plastic trays. I stood there confused about what to order, my moment of hesitation instantly marking me as a virgin to the system as well as creating a highly visible disruption in the line. The cook in his dirty blue-checked apron instantly began snarling at me, mocking my ignorance, while groans of exasperation began to rise from the crowd behind me, until Jane stepped in to rescue me from my confusion.

"Two poached eggs on pancakes with bacon, jelly, potatoes, and a Coca-Cola," she confidently barked, then turning to me said, "It's always a little overwhelming the first time, isn't it?"

I opened my eyes wide and tilted my head to one side. "I trust you completely."

"Tommy's doing just fine." Michael scanned the room as he talked, like an eagle searching from its soaring height for the barely discernible movement of its prey, circling effortlessly overhead before swooping in for the kill, rushing headlong across the room, the tray in his hand lifting on the rush of air beneath it. He staked a claim for three seats in a patch of emerging sunlight near the wet window.

I followed Jane at a snail's pace across the room, our

progress impeded by her stopping to talk with the couples and groups assembled at almost every crowded table. She seemed to know everyone in the room, and they all seemed to be looking at us. Jane smiled at some of those who called out to her, and waved to others, while to still others she made the effort to stoop and exchange showy little air kisses, occasionally pausing long enough to say a few words and even make reference to my presence. She did not introduce me to any one of this throng of acquaintances, but she signaled by her glancing in my direction—stuck as I was behind her in the narrow passage and dependent on her to lead me through—that certain of these people deserved my attention and were being placed on a similar alert. Michael watched our progress from his closely guarded aerie, noting whom Jane stopped to talk to and whom she passed up completely, clucking his approval at her discretion. By the time we reached him, the whole room had been effectively made aware of our presence: Jane and Michael were sharing their breakfast with a mysterious young stranger, a curious newcomer to the scene, fodder for the feeding frenzy of speculation and gossip which obviously kept this room spinning on a Saturday morning.

"That should certainly give them something to think about." Michael waved a strip of crisp bacon like a baton as he spoke.

"We seem to have made quite an impression." Half the room was watching us eat, and when they weren't looking, the other half assumed the guard.

"You deserve all the credit, Tommy." Jane shook her hair back over her shoulders and her eyes twinkled.

"The real question," Michael speculated aloud, "is who do they think slept with whom? Let's keep them wondering."

The buzz filling the room was now intelligible: "See Your Food" was the place to be seen on the morning after. Michael and Jane had deliberately brought me with them as a kind of trophy to show off, to leave everyone wondering how I had been won and where I would materialize next. One apparently scored big points in the competitive social game of this claustrophobic community for making a so-called discovery, and I was the valued game piece being maneuvered across the playing field. The spotlights were all on me. I loved it.

We chuckled over our breakfast, all of us satisfied with the impression we had made. From our little corner we practically presided over the room, regally nodding hello or goodbye to people as they passed us, studiously avoiding eye contact with others, Michael and Jane each whispering juicy tidbits of gossip as they pointed in different directions. I had made it less than halfway through my stack of pancakes when Mark, the mousy little man who had passed out on Wednesday, drifted in with a hefty, Eastern European–looking woman about three times his size, swathed in a fake leopardskin coat and black tights much too close-fitting for her full figure. Mark stood chatting with her at the end of the line before he noticed us, then left her and approached. He removed his coat, tossing it over the back of a chair across from mine, and invited himself to join us for breakfast.

He looked at me and spoke. "Don't I know you from somewhere?"

"Last Wednesday. You were clinging to me for dear life." He thought for a second.

"That's right. Was I well behaved?" He grinned, and I laughed too, because the question so suited his preposterously juvenile appearance.

"Are you ever?" Michael interrupted.

"What are you doing with that heap of tie-died kielbasa over there?" With an easy familiarity Jane insulted the woman now waving to us from the line; I noticed she was indeed wearing six or seven layers of tie-died fabrics under her coat,

some of the pieces trailing down to her knees, none of them
appearing to comprise an actual garment.

"You know how it is. Another Friday night home alone.
Katrin and I figured we might at least pretend we had sex,
maybe give someone who doesn't know better a nightmare."
I was beginning to catch on to the game being played all
around me.

"You're not kidding anyone." Michael waved limply back
at Katrin and gagged over the table.

Mark resumed his place in line while Jane and Michael
continued to make disparaging remarks about assorted char-
acters scattered throughout the room, the presence of "Miss
Pirogi 1957" having sparked a surprising show of salty in-
vective. I began to wonder if beneath the smiling nods and
laughing façades all turned in my direction there was not a
well of bitterness waiting to be tapped.

Mark left Katrin to make her own way and took up his seat
across from me, having given up the game early on in favor
of satisfying his curiosity regarding our own confident troika.
He prattled on and on in a stream of consciousness between
bites of his breakfast, revealing a remarkable consistency in
the tenor of his thoughts. Drugs and sex were all he talked
about, and according to him, everyone in the room was on
something and doing someone. With no explanation of where
or how he acquired all this information he confidently assured
us it was all true. Pointing to one rather scruffy-looking young
cock of a man surrounded by a cackle of doting hens, he
assured us that the same man had been turning tricks at
Belmont Beach all week long. He was full of such information,
compulsively spitting it up as he spoke, unable to resist telling
what sounded like outrageous and very dirty lies.

We had finished our meal and become exasperated with
Mark's stories, Jane and Michael constantly interrupting and
insulting him, when Michael made a proposal.

"I'm dying for a box of Frango mints."

"What's a Frango mint?" I had no idea what a sensation my ignorance would cause. All three gasped in pretended horror and looked at me as if I had just announced I had only one day left to live.

"Poor Thomas," Jane moaned. "Never had a Frango mint!"

"Is that such a disaster?"

"Something must be done immediately." Mark was in a regular panic.

"We're heading right down to Marshall Field's to get this over with." Michael stood up and began pulling on his coat, like a field marshal who has just received news of a surprise attack and feels that to sit still a moment longer is an unforgivable shirking of duty.

"Is it really such an emergency?"

"Child, you speak from ignorance." Michael pulled me out of my seat, and not more than two minutes later we stepped onto the express bus at Fifty-third and Lake Park Drive, Mark having chosen to leave this necessary ritual of Chicago initiation in their trustworthy and experienced hands. Michael dragged us through the Saturday crowds on Michigan Avenue and State Street until we had safely arrived at a counter of chocolates in the heart of the department store, where he charged an enormous box on his Marshall Field's card. He handed me the candy, then just as quickly ripped it out of my fingers and greedily, like an addict only seconds away from his next fix, tore the plastic wrapping open and popped one of the dark chocolate squares into his mouth, pushing one between my lips also. Jane helped herself to a handful, which she inhaled one by one. We were drunk on the mint flavor and silky texture of the chocolate, huddling near the escalator while harried shoppers pushed past us, groaning with satisfaction, until I began to feel embarrassed by our decadent indulgence.

"It's almost better than sex." Jane's teeth were brown with
milk chocolate dissolving in her mouth.

"I wouldn't know." Michael clutched the box to his chest
and feigned an innocent glance at me.

"You wish," I answered. I caught a fleeting look of hurt
in Michael's eyes, indistinctly sensed my words had pinched
some emotional nerve and betrayed my own instinctual war-
iness; already a great deal seemed at stake between us.

Michael stashed the box inside his coat and we coasted on
the wave of people pulsing through the store and out the
revolving doors. We spent the day wandering through the
city, Michael and Jane lecturing me on the architecture and
history of Chicago, reveling in the grand hopes and failed
images the former hog capital of the world had once held for
itself. Despite the bitter wind we walked a complete circle
around the Loop, then headed up Michigan Avenue to Oak
Street Beach, where we finally came to rest, exhausted from
our struggle against the elements and the excitement of our
rushing downtown. We sat atop a concrete barrier, ignoring
the traffic behind us, and marveled at the wicked, turbulent
lake.

In between the architectural history and anecdotes I was
able to piece together a clearer picture of who Michael and
Jane were. He was a graduate student at the Oriental Institute,
who had arrived at the university sometime in the distant past
and had never left. I was fascinated to discover that this
flirtatious man who had taken such a liking to me could read
cuneiform and conjugate the verbs of Assyria and Sumer. It
seemed incongruous that anyone should still know such
things, but I at least imagined those with such knowledge to
be single-minded, hermit-like geniuses who hid in their stud-
ies behind thick doors and forgot, in the concentrated effort
of their communications with the dead, how to converse with
the living. I wondered if he ever dreamed in Sumerian, but

Michael made light of his erudition and even more so my respect for his learning.

Jane too was a graduate student, younger than Michael, though likewise of indefinite age and origin. I couldn't actually figure out what work she did except that it was biological and very esoteric. Michael teased her when she tried to explain to me the aims of her research, implying they were at least partially related to an affair she had been conducting with an elderly, Nobel prize–winning biochemist in her department. I did not so much ask questions about their lives as listen carefully for meaningful markers in their conversation to which I could refer back and demand explanation. It had already been established as a ground rule of our conversation that direct questioning was not allowed. Rather, we were like three trial lawyers, each waiting and hoping one or the other would introduce a topic into the conversation, thus clearing the way for further inquiry without objections. I was in this respect granted an automatic advantage, Michael having decided early on that I was far too young to have any secrets, and I was happy to leave him with his illusions. Together we seemed to negotiate an image of myself which we were both duly obligated to maintain.

The lake had begun to blacken in the fading afternoon light when we returned to Michigan Avenue to wait for the bus to Hyde Park. We stopped one final time at the bridge over the Chicago River to stare at the Tribune Tower, now exploding with light like a firecracker, before squeezing together in the back of the bus. Michael drew out the half-empty box of chocolates and slowly, with the satiated calm and confidence of those who enjoy plenty and want not, we picked the chocolates from their crinkled white paper wrappers, nibbling them corner by corner instead of sucking them whole, relishing their delicate, subtle flavor instead of desperately searching for a quick, overpowering explosion of taste.

They rode with me to Fifty-seventh and Lake Park, and walked me down to the corner of Blackstone. We said goodbye on the street, the three of us exhausted and at a loss for words, not quite sure at this moment of parting what to make of the day we had spent together. I still wondered, was this all a fluke, or were these people really my friends? Michael held me fixed for a moment with a mournful gaze that I had not yet seen but with which I would eventually become painfully familiar. Jane seemed already well acquainted with this new mood; she slipped her arm into Michael's and quietly kissed me goodbye, assuring me I would see them very soon, intimating we had begun something grand together that day, while Michael watched, for once at a loss for words, grateful for Jane's intervention.

Standing there on the street corner in the trailing darkness, with Michael suddenly eerily quiet and otherworldly, I felt an overwhelming sense of familiarity and sadness, as the strange portrait of the pale-faced, uncomfortable-looking young man who had haunted me on the train unexpectedly returned. I had really begun to think that the man on the train had been another person or a ghoulish phantom of my imagination, but I knew now that whether phantom or reality, that ghostly face I had seen in the middle of the night presaged some mysterious harsh truth. Something was happening, some secret purpose not yet revealed to me was driving my frenzied connection with these two; I felt I had known them for a long, long time and would know them for many years more before we all reached our pitiful conclusion. I compulsively kissed Michael goodbye full on the lips, not meaning to but somehow impelled to do it. Without looking back, without asking when we should meet again, without thanking anyone or expecting anything, I rushed to my lonely little room and crawled into my bed and hid under the blankets, wishing I could cry but unable to find the tears, uncertain for whom or what I wished to cry, instead staring blindly at the wall until, I don't know how many minutes or hours later, I fell into a dreamless, heavy sleep.

I spent Thanksgiving in Wisconsin, at the home of a wealthy distant relative on the wooded shore of Lake Geneva. Final exams were rapidly approaching, my first quarter coming to an end; the days piled one on top of the other in such rapid succession I hardly missed not seeing Michael or Jane. Nor did I see Dennis, although I found myself unexpectedly thinking of him (it was Thursday, after all) while my overfed cousins carved the turkey and doled out the dressing. I stayed away from Chicago for five days, my first excursion beyond the bounds of the city since my arrival, and was surprised at how relieved and happy I felt upon returning, the neighborhood seemed so new in my eyes, the people so foreign, my horizons so greatly expanded. As I walked from the Illinois Central station along Fifty-ninth Street, I was struck by the promise and hope lurking in the Midway, the broad swath of desolate meadow (a relic from the Columbian Exposition of 1893) that divided the university from the surrounding community like a mine field. All around me, now that I cared to look, were signs of a past full of hope, of a generation of dreams which remained unfulfilled. What incredibly grand and ambitious dreams the Chicago titans of commerce and industry had had, to create whole neighborhoods of millionaire mansions and then abandon them, to hire the most famous architects in the world to build a temporary World's Fair grounds, confident something even more magnificent would rise in its place, a future that never did materialize. This wide, open hollow of mud and grass seemed all that remained.

I saw Michael only once more before returning home for the Christmas break. I thought of seeking him and Jane out, of ringing her doorbell unannounced, of lurking in the Coffee

Shop or scouring the halls of the Oriental Institute, but I knew I would do none of these things. I felt certain fate would draw us together at the proper time, that to actively search for something was a violation of the whole ethic Michael and Jane had introduced to me. To use their moral terms, it would be rude to make anything happen—the only polite thing to do was to wait for whatever came next, and that was exactly what I did.

I finally crossed paths with Michael during the week of final exams, literally bumping into him as I scurried along one of the narrow slate trails which cut diagonally across the quadrangles, my eyes glued to the ground in defense against the brutal cold, he crossing on the opposite diagonal, clutching a thick stack of Xeroxed material in his bare hands. Neither of us saw the other approach in the dreary winter gloom under the gray Chicago sky, which arrives sometime in mid-November and hovers in its varying shades until April, until we were standing facing each other. I was unable to conceal the excitement I felt at my finally, fatefully encountering him. His hair, black and straight, blew wildly in the wind, and he kept reaching up to pull it from over his eyes as we spoke, his lips glistening with moisture in the dry air. Neither of us said anything the least bit clever, and this I took to be a sign of a new turn in our acquaintance, an easing of our previous dependence on repartee. Michael shivered; he wore only a thin sweater and was obviously running some errand, rushing to wherever he was expected. I asked to accompany him, and we hurried to the Oriental Institute, the building separate from the rest of the campus across University Avenue, antiquated and imposing by itself on the corner.

Michael had a small office on the third floor; the hallways were barely lit, as if bright light would disturb the intense study of the resident scholars. He did not invite me to inspect his cramped attic space. Instead, he tossed the stack of papers on a chair, grabbed his coat and hat from a hook on the back of the door, and as quickly as we had ascended the stone stairs we descended them again. We hovered in the shelter of the porticoed entrance. I waited for him to suggest what should follow.

"Let me show you that Sullivan house I told you about." Michael wound a long black scarf around his neck and shoulders as he spoke, experienced preparation for a walk in the cold. I followed him north, neither of us able to speak much because of the fierce wind. We had crossed Fifty-third Street when he quickened the pace, gesturing excitedly at an indistinct structure up the block on Woodlawn, and shouted, "Do you see it?" We stood directly beneath a streetlamp before a distinctive, temple-like structure of prairie-style domestic architecture, a faded jewel almost not noticeable from its lack of polishing in the middle of a block of nondescript row houses.

"How depressing," I said, struck by the pervasive, sad aura of faded wealth and glory surrounding the house.

"It's criminal," Michael began, "the way they let such a monument just fall apart, slowly die from neglect."

Michael unwound his scarf enough for him to speak and gesticulate comfortably, pointing out to me the unusual massing of the structure and the distinctive terra-cotta cornice, a cornucopia of corn husks and wheat grasses. The house was a high, solid rectangle of yellow brick stretching back quite a distance from the street, the bulk of it hidden within an open rectangular box so that the only sign of inhabitability was a strip of thin, lead-paned windows directly below the cornice, the whole structure capped by a wide, flat brim of concrete. The house was extraordinary, as much for the decay into which it had been allowed to sink as for its testament to an era of architectural innovation. We crept along the concrete side path which led to the front entrance and provided a glimpse within the boxy exterior. Michael traced horizontal line after line with his finger in the air, every so often dropping a sparse vertical through the accumulated strata. A dog appeared from the back alley, a tough-minded mongrel bitch which would not be placated and vigorously barked us back to the sidewalk; she persisted in her attack until we retreated beyond the streetlight to the other side of Woodlawn, where we hesitated, shivering, for one last guilty look.

We dashed around the corner and into a supermarket, seeking respite from the cold. My toes and fingers ached miserably. Michael grabbed a cart. Gathering up his courage, he asked, "Are you hungry?"

"What do you mean?" His words had sounded ambiguous, and I sought clarification, but he took my comment for a form of flirtation that seemed to make him uncomfortable, set him on edge, as if he were nervous and shy and trying not to appear too interested in me or care too much about my response.

"It was just a question. I need to do some shopping; you're welcome to join me if you'd like." Then, reflecting on his own hesitancy and thinking better of himself, he continued: "Would you like to have dinner with me?"

I had always been aware of the interest Michael took in me, from the moment he first approached me in the bursar's office, his expression a peculiar form of admiration and desire combined with mockery and self-deprecation, but I had never felt this desire to extend beyond a complex form of flattery, a neat, undemanding formula for titillation without real lust or commitment or pain. I felt that Michael was struggling desperately as we strode down the aisles of the supermarket not to break this easy illusion he had so carefully constructed around me, the illusion that he was curious but not really interested, desirous but not covetous, worthy yet somehow not deserving, as if preserving an emotional balance sheet where acceptance and rejection carefully tabulated their totals and each made sure the other was never at an advantage. My own responsibility in this complicated scheme was to not feel myself desirable; a simple enough task, I thought.

I accepted his invitation. He looked ridiculous, endearingly harmless, almost childlike, as we stood by the fruits and vegetables in the last aisle near the checkout. He sniffed a head of broccoli.

"It's not supposed to smell like anything." I laughed at him.

"Then it must not be any good, because it smells like something." He put down the broccoli and lifted another to his nose, determined to discover the smell of the vegetable anyway, then returned that to its place, and lifting a head of cauliflower instead, he abruptly spoke to me, the white blossom of vegetable shining through its plastic wrapping like an enormous, organic microphone designed to amplify his words not in decibels of sound but in some other, earthy dimension.

"Are you taking the train back East?" He spoke as if we had already discussed our encounter on the train, as if there was nothing peculiar about this reference, which perhaps needed to be aired before we could advance to some state of greater intimacy; as if he were trying to adjust our relationship, lift it to some other plane, thread together the loose ends of our acquaintanceship in the solidifying acknowledgment of this early fateful meeting. I must have looked at him blankly, because he continued.

"Did you doubt that I remembered? Of course I noticed you; I'd have noticed you anywhere." He rambled on hypnotically, compulsively, seemingly unaware of the strangeness of his words and the otherworldliness of his expression, the look that had first haunted me so completely. "I wondered earlier, should I say something, but then you made no ref-

erence yourself, and I'm afraid I am never very good with
first impressions. I thought you didn't appreciate my attentions that morning in the bursar's office, so I assumed it was
better to pretend it hadn't happened. You looked at me as if
you'd seen a ghost. I don't look like a ghost to you now, do
I? I don't frighten you, I hope?"

I felt a hole open in the pit of my stomach through which
all my courage and self-esteem dropped like an anvil, pulling
me toward the scummy linoleum underfoot; I blinked, amazed
to find myself still standing solidly, listening to Michael's
words. Some peculiar, cruel conspiracy of timing caused me
to remember, just as Michael so pathetically, almost psychotically sought my approval, that this day was Thursday,
the last Thursday before I returned home for almost a month,
and Dennis would be expecting me any minute now in his
room at the Hotel Madison.

"Oh God!" I felt terrible, but I knew the instant the memory
of Dennis came to me, followed by a wave of physical memory
marking the pleasure I experienced in his company, that I
would have to leave Michael standing there alone with his
shopping cart full of groceries.

"Now I've really gone and said something awful, haven't
I?"

"No. No. Only I just remembered I was supposed to meet
someone downtown. I can't believe I totally forgot. I'm sorry,
I really am sorry. I'm late already. God, I'm sorry; I'll see
you later," and quickly tapping my hand on his shoulder in
goodbye, I raced out of the store. Michael stood watching me
in a daze, perhaps suspecting me of having executed a hastily
planned escape. I ran all the way to the bus stop, determined
when I had settled panting into my seat to block the episode
from my mind, not to think about it at all, not to worry what
Michael would be thinking of me that moment. I ran again
from the bus stop on Michigan Avenue to the familiar seedy

little hotel where I had already spent so many nights. Breathless, I knocked on Dennis's door. He answered in a bathrobe, evidently relieved I had finally shown up. Not wasting a single moment, I pushed him down onto the bed and attacked him with a hailstorm of passionate kisses, bowling him over with the strength and force of my approach. At first he was so overwhelmed he could only laugh and push me away and urge me to stop, then finally catching the fire inside me, he responded in kind. I thought briefly of Michael as I rolled through the tangled sheets with Dennis, Michael's image projected for a moment like an airy hologram in the room before slowly and permanently fading into the darkness, until I was glad he was gone and all I could see or think or feel or smell was Dennis beside me and on top of me and beneath me and all around me, sleep descending afterward like the final dream in a series of long dreams that had composed the whole three and a half months just past.

By late Saturday afternoon I was safely settled in my old bedroom in Worcester, sleeping off the last bit of exhaustion from final exams, my father having picked me up at the airport in Boston that morning.

The city lay under a foot of snow when I returned in the middle of January; the lake seen from the air formed a frilly border of ice on the sloping collar of the shoreline. I descended into an enormous scale of gray, spanning from the lightest shades in the impermeable cloud cover through the dirty snow and ice covering every available surface beyond the reach of necessary human contact, to the median value of the deteriorating freeways and the dull aluminum of automobiles—no matter what color originally, red, blue, yellow, green, black, all had turned the same shade of salted earth—to the matte gray skyline, the flinty gray unshorn shrubbery and trees of the parks, the exhaust from the buses and the heating plants of the housing projects along the highway heading south from the airport; the incomprehensible sprawl of the metropolis, so green and abundant when I had first rolled into town the previous autumn, was now one monotonous composition in black and white, awesome in the consistency of the winter's gloom that had taken possession of the land. I was unspeakably happy to be back in Chicago.

I had been afraid to think much about the city while away, my new life felt so fragile and improbable. I doubted, once I had returned home, where nothing seemed to have happened in all the months I had been gone, whether Chicago still existed, as if the university and Blackstone Hall and the neighborhood of Hyde Park and the people I had met were mere products of my imagination: I narcissistically fantasied them all away as my selfish creation. I was infinitely relieved to discover that my fear that none of what I had experienced had been real evaporated as I recovered a full awareness of my surroundings, the unifying gray of the atmosphere evidence of a mystical cohesion which existed only within the bounds of this city and of which I was an essential part.

I was confident, as I stretched out on my bed in Blackstone Hall and fiddled with a transistor radio I kept by my side, that my life was about to be transformed, that somehow by returning I was automatically promoted to a different, more democratic plane on the social scale, was confirmed a peer with Michael and Jane and the rest. I continued to suffer a twinge of guilt over my abandonment of Michael that day in the supermarket, but it occurred to me as I wondered how and when I should see them again that that episode would if anything have elevated me in their eyes, proved to them I was as insane and fickle and as much like them as they had hoped, as capable of behaving erratically, as likely to panic, startle, or charm, and—what probably mattered most to them as well as to myself—as capable of providing grist for the mill of gossip and scandal and talk that kept this small world turning.

These thoughts were confirmed my first evening back. Anxious to preserve my feelings of excitement and privacy, I avoided my noisy, depressing dining hall and instead walked around the corner to Venuto's, a hopping pizza joint on Fifty-seventh Street, thinking I would wallow in the loneliness of a solitary meal. I had barely set foot in the door when Chris, only faintly recognizable in innumerable layers of black, exclaiming loudly to get my attention, invited me to join her in a big wooden booth near the entrance. I had not seen her since the day she fled from us at Harold's, yet she seemed eager to have me at her table, as if the woman in her company

would be impressed by her knowing me. I quickly discovered
she already knew who I was, Chris announcing while I hung
my coat on a hook, "Tommy's the one who fled Michael at
Kimbark Village."

They looked at me amazed, admiring, and squeezed together in one half of the booth. I shrugged and sat down
opposite them. "It was nothing, nothing at all."

"Ha," Chris snorted. "That's what you think. Michael
doesn't generally handle rejection well."

"You've already got yourself quite a reputation." I recognized Melinda as the driver of the car that infamous first day.

"Nothing to match your own, I'm sure." She laughed at
my response, apparently pleased with the mutuality of our
impressions.

"So what are you going to do about Michael?" Chris
sounded serious and concerned, as if I were lost in a maze
and she hoped to help me discover the exit.

"Must I do anything?" I began to feel this situation was
more out of control than I realized: had I perhaps waded into
too-deep waters, risked being dragged out to sea by the un-
forgiving undertow, eventually to wash ashore bloated, cold,
and purple? "Anyway, it's not like I stood him up at all. I
just forgot I had an appointment. It was nothing more than a
case of bad timing."

"Sounds like excellent timing to me."

"That all depends on your point of view." I was ready for
a change of topic and declared my intention of procuring
something to eat. Their table was one huge combination ash-
tray and coffee cup; cigarette butts, piled recklessly in bun-
dles, seared off the cheap varnish, their ashes borne aloft by
the winter draft, settling over the table like a fine layer of
volcanic soot while the two mugs of coffee Chris and Melinda
sloshed formed a pair of seismic lake basins, abysmal black
pits of unplumbed prehistoric depth. A busboy cleared the

filth from our table, leaving in its place a thin, smoky film of dishwater.

"I never apologized for abandoning you in Harold's that day," Chris began.

"Oh please, everybody's doing it," I joked.

"It's something we have in common." Chris and Melinda sat together unnecessarily close in their half of the wide, deep booth. Melinda's hands were under the table, and Chris occasionally pretended to slap in protest at whatever was happening below eye level. Periodically they turned to each other and French-kissed; each opened her mouth wide and allowed her tongue to glide visibly over her teeth before their lips formed a perfectly sealed seam. After carefully disengaging themselves they would look around to see if anyone had been watching, unable to hide their disappointment if no one smiled approvingly at them. All the while they maintained a coherent, surprisingly normal conversation, interspersing stories of Michael and Jane with tales of the university and great moments in their own recurrent love affair.

"Michael's been in Hyde Park forever. He was one of those university whiz kids who never bothered to finish high school, just came right here when he was seventeen. That must have been ten or eleven years ago," Melinda speculated. "Way before my time." My pizza had finally arrived and I gladly let them ramble on, revealing piecemeal what I considered valuable information.

"Jane's been around as long as I have," Chris continued. "Incredible as it may seem, she was my first girlfriend." Melinda smiled at this admission, after which they kissed, as if to squarely consign Jane to her place in the past. "The big scandal with Jane is that she started sleeping with men about three years ago, and ever since she can't seem to get enough of them. We can't figure out why she ever thought she was a lesbian."

"Who wouldn't want to be a lesbian?" Melinda sounded genuinely convinced of her sexual superiority and shocked at the thought that there were people in the world whose ultimate desire was not to scale the erotic heights with which she herself was so familiar.

They both looked suspiciously at me, noiselessly devouring my supper, as if they had simultaneously experienced the same disquieting thought and were unable to proceed until their doubts had been laid to rest.

"Is something the matter?" They were staring down their noses at me quite severely.

"Go ahead, reassure us, make us happy." I raced through my mind, retracing the trail of our conversation, trying to figure out what they must have been wondering, until I finally hit on something.

"Most of all I would like to be a woman so I could love a woman as a woman." I took another bite of my pizza and prayed I had answered them correctly. They both breathed deep sighs of relief, kissed again, and turned to me.

"Whew! You had us worried for a minute." Chris attempted to make light of their interrogation.

"You know, you gave Michael quite a scare." Melinda explained the source of their doubts. "It occurred to us that maybe you didn't, you know . . ." Melinda reached an impasse, stopped short at a surprising loss of words, before Chris picked up the slack.

"Have sex with men." Their mutual thoughts now became completely intelligible.

"Thanks, Chris. I shudder at the thought of saying those words." Melinda laughed and pretended to shiver, rubbing her arms around herself as if from fear as much as from cold, then shook her head in an attempt to rid her mind of the contaminating image that had arisen there.

"I assumed it was obvious." I pictured Michael's self-doubt

and embarrassment at the thought that I was much more than simply not interested; our flirtation was already complicated enough. "Anyway, you've got nothing to worry about." I established a new basis with them upon uttering these words, allaying any incipient fears they had and at the same time widening my prospects in their eyes for social achievement. I had overcome the biggest hurdle I faced before being allowed entrance into their inner sanctum, and all of Michael's ambitions for me, all the credit he had been giving himself for discovering me and bringing me out, all of this was now confirmed.

I lingered satisfied over the remainder of my meal before saying good night to this pair of acquaintances; our parting was infused with knowing familiarity. Already we seemed to share an important, somehow definitive sensibility. If asked, I couldn't have yet explained the idea that I felt drew us together, but I recognized its formative influence—Michael and Jane the source from which the current flood of my own intellectual sensation had stemmed—and like an overconfident actor who has just auditioned for a leading role, I had, as I walked home in the clear cold night, already begun to rehearse my lines in preparation for the inchoate drama that was about to unfold.

When I passed under the arch at University and Fifty-eighth the next morning, the campus was transformed. The previously alien scores of figures shuffling along the stone paths looked comfortingly familiar; the hardness of the Gothic limestone, so imposing and heartless and deadening before, now seemed brought to life in the cold and the snow, while an oblique, tough sunshine only brought the final touch to a complete and satisfying picture of an appropriately harsh landscape. Besieged by sheets of ice and drifts of snow, the outrageous, fortress-like stance of these buildings made perfect sense, thick-walled bastions of the intellect bravely facing the brutal elements of nature.

Armed with my newfound sense of possession I confidently headed for the Coffee Shop after lunch. I slipped quickly through the double doors, a draft of wind pushing me along, swirling the tail of my overcoat about my knees; where I had so recently been swimming upstream against an over-powering current of strangers, I found myself wading in a calm, shallow pool of familiar faces. Jane was alone in the same booth where we had first met, and as I sat down across from her I wondered, now that finding her seemed so abso-lutely effortless, why so many months had passed without our knowing one another.

She leaned across the table to kiss me before beginning: "I thought I might find you here. When did you get back?"

"Yesterday afternoon."

"That explains why you weren't home Saturday night. We stopped by to invite you out. Someone always has a big party the weekend before the new quarter begins."

"I'm sorry I missed it." I couldn't at that moment remember ever having been invited anywhere I had actually enjoyed myself, felt I was welcome; I craved the opportunity, and Jane was quick not to disappoint me.

"You didn't miss anything." She waved a hand dismissively in the air. "But this Friday we're hijacking you for twenty-four hours, no excuses allowed." Michael appeared in the entry, and his face lit up when he saw me. He raised his arm to wave hello while Jane wriggled, startled for a moment, in her seat, as if she were the bait on a hook and Michael were reeling us in, and I were the catch on which they hoped to feast. He made a beeline toward us.

"Mark is having a slumber party at his parents' house in Wilmette," Jane continued. "It should be an intimate little affair; just fourteen or fifteen of us in our pajamas."

"You do own a pair of pajamas, I hope." Michael slid in next to Jane.

"A nightshirt, actually." A whim of a purchase I had made at the last minute, my father having urged me to acquire a pair of pajamas, exhorting me assuredly without explaining why that I would regret not having them, and I wishing neither fully to comply with his advice nor totally to ignore it, had happened upon a nightshirt instead. Its wide red stripes and long tail caught my fancy, appealed to my old-fashioned fantasies (I pictured myself bunking down for the night on the train as I sped across the continent). I began to consider that my father knew a thing or two more about the life of young people than I had been willing to credit.

"You are eccentric!" Michael clearly looked forward to the sight of me in my nightshirt. "Now all you need is a big brass bed and a nightcap to go with it." I laughed at the picture he painted.

"I'd rather have a four-poster with night shades and a hot toddy to put me to sleep." I listened to my words echo across the table. "That sounds like something dirty, doesn't it? Ringing your manservant for a 'hot toddy' before bed?"

"I can think of dirtier." Jane's announcement did not surprise me.

"Is there a reason why everything either of you says ends up sounding sexual?"

"It's the unfortunate disjunction we experience between saying and doing, words and action," Michael began to explain, and I realized, as spontaneous as my question had been, that their well-considered answer constituted a carefully constructed summation of years of experience.

"We talk about sex all the time because we never have sex in real life." Jane easily followed the train of Michael's thought.

"That's a lie. We do have sex, but only with people we

hate." They both burst out laughing, evidently pleased at the
witty truth of Michael's analysis.

"I think I understand." The image of Dennis's naked, almost orange body floated briefly through my mind.

"We fall in love, but not with the people we desire sexually."

"And we have sex, but not with people we love personally."

"We suffer the traumas of postmodernism."

"Our love lives are the victims of literary theory."

"How pathetic!" I exclaimed.

"Exactly!" They answered in unison, happy their message was getting across. Amazingly, they wanted me to see them as pathetic, as deficient, and more strange, their pathos and deficiency were so immensely appealing, made such immediate sense to me, neatly seemed to describe so much of my own measly limited experience, that I wanted to be like them.

We continued talking, spinning out the fine points of their theories of love and sex and postmodernism, when Michael finally decided, "We need a slogan. Why bother defining an incipient political movement if you don't have propaganda?"

"Technically, we are postmodernist homosexuals." I had rapidly advanced to equal status as a theoretician.

"True, but we need something snappy, something to get the juices flowing, you know, like . . ." We waited silently, expectantly, as Michael drew a long, deep breath, gathering his thoughts together in the pause until he caught the proper words securely in his mind and spit them back out at us: "Pomo-Homos!"

"That's brilliant. We're the Pomo-Homos. Now we really know who we are." We all three rolled the word around in our mouths, practiced saying it until we had convinced ourselves that was who we really were. Michael was not yet fully satisfied.

"We still need a slogan."

We were stumped. We had long since run out of coffee, and the excitement and satisfaction surrounding the discovery of our secret identities dissipated in the frustration of not having a catchphrase to succinctly express the fundamental beliefs of our philosophy, a bold motto to live by. Jane thumped the table nervously, Michael started as if he was going to stand and leave, the tension too much for him, until effortlessly, Dennis smiling at me from over their shoulders like a happy ghost mouthing the words I had searched for, immediately confident I had found the necessary phrase, I announced: "I've got it."

They stared at me like two hungry wolves who hadn't eaten in a week and were on the verge of capturing a prey they had been vigorously stalking since before dawn.

"Love without lust; lust without love." I drew out the pause between this pair of independent clauses, to highlight the palindromic symmetry of the word sequence and the antonymic equation of the thought expressed. They were entranced, bedazzled, dumbstruck by the perfection of my slogan. We spent most of the afternoon sitting in our booth, holding forth as a host of people passed through, each person inaugurated into our new philosophy and identity. We experimented with the words and how to present ourselves, practiced spreading the gospel. By the time the light had begun to fade into a purple gloom reflected in the limestone courtyard, we had been transformed, individually and as a unit.

We had put on our coats and were heading out the door, myself sandwiched between them, all of us almost touching, when Jane joked: "We should touch like this forever, the three of us."

"That's impossible." My rational response provoked them.

"We are a trinity," Michael chanted. "Three in one and one in three. We belong to each other."

"Separate yet eternally inseparable." We were clinging to each other now in the freezing cold, the daylight dead and gone, the darkness palpable, the thin winter atmosphere choking our lungs.

"One indivisible being, yet three separate individuals." I was having trouble following the religious inspiration behind the metaphor they had adopted and instead struggled to fit this newly defined plane into the geometric framework which had so far diagrammed our relationship.

"Three bodies, one spirit?" I quizzed myself, working to piece together this strange new puzzle. "Love without lust; lust without love. Three in one; one in three." We walked east on Fifty-eighth Street toward the lake, Blackstone only a short distance ahead. I was anxious before I left them to gain a clearer picture in my mind of the relationship they were describing.

"Of course," Jane answered my query. "The two fit together beautifully." I was eager to hear her explanation. "The spiritual union we experience with the people we love precludes any sexual contact, and the physical union we experience with the people we desire precludes any love or even sympathy."

"This," Michael pronounced with a dramatic, final gesture, as if explaining with a wave of his arm the meaning of life, the question to end all questions and the answer of all answers, "is the dilemma of our lives." Once again we had reached the front pavement of Blackstone Hall in a resounding moment of truth.

"What better way to say goodbye." They loosened their grasp, the three of us simultaneously kissed, and without a further word they were gone and I was alone in my room, free to contemplate the strange meaning of the attachment I had just formed. I did not, however, dwell on the thought, allowing it instead to casually drift in and out of my mind like a seabird flitting across the foamy waves of the ocean, only occasionally descending far enough to just dip its pronged toes into the cresting surface of the water, always hovering just above the surface but so lightly coasting on the sustaining breeze that it makes only the tiniest, least obtrusive tear in the rippling fabric of the deep.

With Friday night's slumber party already an infamous event in my mind, the week flew by in a flurry of tedious academic activity, the burden of the schoolwork become more onerous now that I had other thoughts to occupy my time. Before I knew it I was showering and changing clothes in preparation for my first visit to the Hotel Madison in over a month. I had not given any thought at all to Dennis during the period of our separation, nor did I begin to think of him again until I had hopped off the bus a few blocks early and walked northward on blustery Michigan Avenue, not wanting to arrive too soon for the date we had made for the resumption of our affair. In contrast to our generally more casual arrangement of arrival and departure, this evening we had agreed on a time, and having to force myself to slow down, to postpone briefly our meeting, I was left with the memory of Dennis in the last moment I had seen him previously; I struggled to conjure an image of him, any image, so I should have some imaginary standard to hold the reality in its place, and when my mind drew a blank, when I could paint only the vaguest, most blurred portrait of him, even the physical sensation of our lovemaking indistinct, I felt terrified, doomed, repulsed by the prospect of his cold, unknowing, and unknowable flesh, his hollow voice, his blank meaningless stare. I stopped above the frozen water of the Chicago River and considered the consequences of turning back, of heading home and never seeing him again. I almost hated Dennis at that moment, hated my somehow needing him; I

did not want to have to look at him, to have to speak to him,
to have to say his name or hear him speak my name, to give
one fraction of an ounce of myself to him, but I wanted him
to touch me, to lose myself completely in the expert manip-
ulations of his fingers and his lips and the tip of his nose and
the rest of his cool body, enough so that I conquered my
revulsion and fear and continued walking north on Michigan Avenue, neither willingly nor unwillingly, consciously
or unconsciously, but propelled forward by entrancing, all-
encompassing desire.

When I returned to my room before dawn on Friday morning
I found a short note under my door, a triangle of white peeping
out from above the threshold: "Pick you up at 5:30 o'clock
p.m. Friday evening." I reread this sentence several times
while pulling off my boots, struck by the triple positive of
the "o'clock," "p.m.," and "evening." Michael didn't seem
to be taking any chances. I lay on my back and began to feel
irritated that my Thursday night's absence had been at least
obliquely noticed. I was not prepared to share my secret with
anyone, and as I dozed I thought of plausible excuses to
account for my whereabouts during the time in question and
wondered, would I tell the truth or not, should anyone ask.

My slight anxiety over facing the author of the note was
confounded when I woke from my afternoon nap, having
rushed back from school to rest up for what I was hoping
would be a busy night, to a knocking at my door. Jane had
come to fetch me.

"Were you sleeping? You did get my note?" She searched
my room for clues to my personality as she spoke, following
me into the bathroom with her eyes when I went to brush my
teeth and wash my face, as if the color of my towels spoke a
world of information to her.

I got myself ready and out the door, and the two of us were descending in the elevator before I thought to ask, "Where's Michael?"

"He went with Mark and some of the others. Melinda wanted you to ride with us." I was troubled by Michael's absence; we were a trinity, we belonged to each other, this was supposed to be our transformative night together, and I felt guiltily alone in Jane's company, as if she and Michael had conspired somehow to betray me.

Melinda's familiar, sparkling black car was parked out front, its passengers not visible through the defrosting windows. I recognized the voice of a popular female rapper blasting from within. Jane pushed me into the middle of the front seat and climbed in after me. The music was deafening and Melinda merely smiled hello before abruptly whisking us away. In the cramped back seat Chris and three other women eagerly mouthed the words to the song, sometimes slapping the low leather ceiling for emphasis. We had safely reached Forty-seventh Street and turned onto Lake Shore Drive when the song ended and Melinda reached over and snapped off the radio, eliciting shouts of disappointment and protest from the gang of four trapped behind us.

"Everybody ready for the Pomo-Homo slumber party?" Melinda hurled this question at us as if she was attempting to incite a riot.

"Is everyone a Pomo-Homo already?" I questioned Jane, surprised and a little unnerved by the pervasive influence of our afternoon of theorizing; I was quickly becoming bound to this new identity.

"What can I say? We've obviously tapped a ground swell of political feeling. Give yourself some credit." Jane waved at Chris in the back seat.

"You're a genius, Tommy." Chris yawned.

"It's just all happening so fast." I thought for a moment.

"Although I guess that's sort of the point." We passed Soldier
Field, the football stadium wedged curiously in the middle
of the drive, and sped north on the wide, straight stretch of
road running alongside Grant Park. Melinda barely slowed
down as we headed into the series of curves that teetered on
the dangerous edge of the city, until we were safely brought
back again at the Oak Street Beach to the other end of Michigan Avenue's Magnificent Mile. The striving skyline rapidly
receded behind us, its inverse image like the high-pitched
whistle of an approaching train which breaks into a low moan
when it finally passes.

"I'm a Pomo-Homo with a car," Melinda joked, and honked
the horn.

We continued between the uninterrupted wall of apartment
houses and the lake. The wide stretch of roadway turned
inward and ended, replaced by a narrower local street. Only
once before had I been this far north of the city, and while
I had always known Chicago was large, still it seemed to
stretch on and on without end before we finally passed a large
cemetery and clearly entered the better reaches of what I
knew to be called Chicagoland.

"Where the hell are we?" We seemed to be driving through
one huge monotonous suburb.

"No need to panic; we're almost there." Melinda turned
off the main road and steered us through a web of wide, dark
streets. The land here was not as interminably flat as it was
in the city, and we descended into a hollow, densely wooded
and barely lit. It was almost like being out in the countryside
back home, the warm lights of the houses hidden at the ends
of long drives; I felt like a child returning from a day's excursion to the big city. We turned onto a gravel lane, passed
through a thicket of maple and pine, and were greeted by the
bright shining face of a tall, grand old lady of a house set on
a rise overlooking the lake, two sets of extraordinarily high,

narrow windows framing the doorway on the big front porch.

We tumbled out of the car and up the porch stairs and drifted inside without knocking. The living room opened to the right, where Mark and Michael and several others lounged on a sofa and drank from coffee mugs.

"Welcome!" Mark did not bother to rise from his seat, instead shouting his greeting to us.

Michael rose and came to kiss me meekly on the cheek. "I hope you weren't doing anything naughty last night." He looked at me with an intensely curious gaze, but mercifully chose not to follow this line of questioning any further.

"Nothing a self-respecting Pomo-Homo couldn't be proud of, anyway." I smiled.

"Mark and I were just about to make a run for pizza. Come with us."

Mark led us out to the garage and we piled into the front of a beat-up old station wagon. A dog appeared when the electric garage doors opened and whined to get in, and Michael popped open the rear door so it could join us. We drifted through the suburban darkness. Mark pointed out familiar landmarks to us as we drove, aiming a finger at a blank spot in the darkness and explaining that was where his best friend in third grade used to live, gesturing in another direction to indicate the location of his junior high school. Michael sat quietly next to me, his elbow jabbing my side. I wriggled free of his awkward touch and listened politely to Mark's rambling monologue. Our indistinct surroundings slowly became visible with regular streetlights as the avenues straightened out, until we reached the radiant intersection of two broad boulevards, each corner a huge competing strip mall ablaze with neon, the intersection itself aglow from the fire of at least a hundred ever-changing traffic lights. We parked before a vast plastic palace of pizza and left the dog curled in a ball on the back seat.

When we returned to Mark's house everyone had already changed into pajamas and was sprawled on the sectional sofa or stretched on the deep-piled carpet watching television in the family room. I put on my nightshirt and sat with Michael on the floor, picking at the now cold pizza. His thin profile glowed like some strange phosphorescent mineral formation in the flickering blue light of the television, and I remained by his side throughout the evening, impervious to the incessantly mindless surrounding chatter, concentrating instead on the changing channels on the screen.

I had risen to use the bathroom and was returning to my place when Jane grabbed my hand and pulled me down next to her on the sofa. She wore a pair of beige striped cotton pajamas, the top button of the shirt carelessly left undone, and I could just make out the shape of her breasts in the shadows. We squeezed together in a corner of the sectional. I could feel her soft brown hair brush against the side of my neck and the firm, fleshy resistance of her hips pressed against my own skinny legs. She felt warm and soft, and when I put my arm around her waist, drawing her even closer, she whispered something in my ear which I failed to understand, so intoxicated was I by the seductive sensation of her soft voice reverberating against my eardrum, the fold of my earlobe like a funnel which directed the wide, vague message of her words into a trickle of focused physical sensation captured by some hypersensitive vessel at the center of my brain. I was on the verge of kissing her when the lights switched on and I realized that I had slipped a hand into her pajama top and grabbed hold of her bare waist. I secretly extricated myself from this embrace, embarrassed by the ignorance of my desire.

"Bedtime, everyone," Mark announced.

Michael emerged from the rising crowd and offered a supporting arm to Jane and me. "Can I show you all to your room?" The real slumber party now seemed set to begin.

Ignored by the others we slipped upstairs, Michael leading the way down a damp passage to a wing of the house over the garage. Our room was cluttered with the accumulated debris of a past generation; I felt spooked, caught in a seventies time warp, the titles in a rack of cassettes and a moldy CB radio mysterious artifacts from another era in the history of civilization. I imagined myself in the funeral hall of some deceased ancient prince, his worldly possessions perfectly preserved, ready for that expectant moment when his eternal soul would return from the world of the shades and he would resume his earthly life exactly at the tasteless, tacky moment where he had left off. Michael had chosen Mark's old room for ourselves.

"Frightening." I couldn't suppress my thoughts.

Jane and I collapsed together on the bed, only to discover the mattress was old and sagging in the middle. When Michael lay down on the opposite side of Jane we all three rolled inevitably toward the center, Michael and I smothering Jane in between us. We lay there for a while, a human triangle on a lumpy bed, and talked.

"Here we are, the original Pomo-Homos." Michael waved one of his long arms in the air above us as he spoke, and the floppy pajama sleeve fell almost to his shoulder, revealing his pale white skin; his arm flashed like a fluorescent wand. "This definitely makes it official."

"The world's only one-night stand of a political movement." It seemed like the perfect summation of the political philosophy we had so far developed.

"Love without lust; lust without love." Jane recited our motto. "Tomorrow it will all be history."

"That's the beauty of it," Michael began to explain. "As the physical experience diminishes, the spiritual bonds deepen. In the end we are all reduced to a hopeless dependence on a handful of memories."

"Don't be so morbid." Jane shuddered beneath us. "I'm
in no rush to become anyone's memory."

"Patience," Michael patly responded.

"Are you hopeful for the future?" I asked him.

"What do you mean?" He answered me with the same
question I had once posed him. I thought for a moment to
decipher what I did mean.

"I mean, are you afraid of dying?"

"Are you?"

"Terrified."

"I'm not. I think of myself as simply falling asleep for a
very long time, and when I wake up, I'm in heaven." He
spoke calmly, as if he were painting a pretty picture in his
head and admiring the handiwork of his creation.

"I plan on living forever!" Jane burst from between the two
of us and hopped out of the bed. "Come on, let's snoop."
She pulled a tape from the rack and put it into the dusty
cassette player. She mouthed the lyrics to the song while
Michael and I tore through the dresser drawers in search of
incriminating evidence from the past. We turned next to the
closet, where Michael found a hideous blue corduroy suit
with foot-wide lapels. He slid into the jacket, the sleeves
barely reaching beyond his elbows, then worked his way into
the pants, unable to zip the fly. Jane found an accordion on
the closet shelf and took up the loops around her shoulders,
and we danced in a circle around the middle of the room.
Jane's pajama top came undone, the expanding accordion all
that covered her exposed breasts, and Michael spun in a
series of disco pirouettes until our party was disrupted by the
roar of the seam splitting right up the middle of his blue
pants, causing him to stumble back onto the bed, his legs
high in the air, his face bursting red from the excitement.
He wiggled free from the torn trousers. The tape ended; I
turned off the overhead light, and we climbed into the bed,

Jane once again filling the hollow in the center of the mattress, Michael and I balancing precariously on the higher sloping sides.

I dangled one arm near the floor, loosely hanging on to the bed frame in order to maintain my balance, but in a wave of exhaustion I began to relax my grip and slowly slid toward the center, where Jane seemed to be awaiting me, her arms outstretched and inviting; in a moment I was secure in her arms, the inertia of my fall arrested by the attainment of its goal. I was in a trance, outside my own body, with no control over its actions, Jane leading the way down a primrose garden path I had never yet walked. We had been engaged for many minutes in what seemed like one long, slow kiss when I knew that at least this night's adventure would soon have to end, and as I was about to shift my body slightly in preparation for sleep, now only a few seconds away, I recognized Michael's hand reaching into the gap which had opened between Jane and myself. But he had waited too long to attempt to insert himself, for within the next instant I had fallen into a narcotic trance and any hope he had had of seducing me evaporated in my unresponsive though not completely unconscious state. They whispered to each other in the night, the calm, reassuring, delicate murmur of their voices a lulling comfort in this strange bed after an episode of exotic sensation.

In my sleep, I dragged my limp body, like Sisyphus forever pushing his stone, to a precarious perch on the high slope of the mattress, only to roll once more into Jane's unyielding presence and begin the exasperating hike all over again. I dreamed.

In my dream I am home again in Worcester, a young child, and we have just moved into a new house. It is summertime, the sun is shining. We turn off the main road and drive around to the rear of the house. The back porch is piled high with unemptied boxes and bags of garbage. The red roof of our one neighbor's residence is visible at the base of a rolling meadow behind us. I feel ill and run indoors, where I stumble amid the crates and unsettled furniture before reaching the bathroom. I open my mouth, reach in and feel a loose string at the top of my throat. I tug at it, and after a moment's resistance it begins to pull through me. I can feel it tearing at my esophagus, pulling through my insides, and when I look at the ever-expanding length tangling on the floor before me, it is bloody, little bits of scarred maroon flesh stuck to the twine like the cord wrapped around a rolled rib roast of beef. One particularly soft, sizable, brownish lump looks like a piece of my liver. I am disgusted, but also frustrated, desperate to reach the end of the line. When I finally do, my throat aching, my insides burning from the friction of the line pulling through me, just as I heave a sigh of relief, feel hopeful of recovery, I notice another little string tickling the top of my soft palate.

I awoke in frustrated horror, uncertain at first whether I had had a nightmare, then repulsed by the content of my dream. It was morning already and I felt thoroughly exhausted by my night's rest. The same omnipresent dull winter light filled the room. I stood and the lake stared hard at me through the window, its flinty gray surface daring me to pity myself. The sun was nowhere visible, its existence only hinted at by a slightly brighter aura backlighting the cloud cover in the eastern portion of the sky. I clutched my nightshirt around my throat and padded down the chilly hallway to the bathroom. When I returned I found Melinda settled comfortably in my place beside Jane and Michael.

"Let Tommy in bed." Michael shooed Jane up from the crevice and urged Melinda to slide over so the four of us could squeeze in.

"Don't bother," I said, and began gathering my clothes.

"I'm starving." Jane yawned, and all three hopped out of

bed, as if disappointed I had refused to join them but determined not to leave me alone. Melinda found the blue corduroy suit thrown over the back of a chair and gasped her delight.

"I love it!" She stepped into the pants, oblivious to the gigantic rip up the back, the lacy fringe of her pink nightie poking through the vent. I held the jacket for her and she slid her slender brown arms into the sleeves. The suit fit her perfectly; from behind, with her short hair, she could easily have been a teenage boy awkwardly fitted into his first suit of clothes. Only the flash of her smooth bare skin at the throat and neck undermined the illusion of her masculinity; she strutted about the room, flapping the lapels with her thumbs like an overweening peacock. Jane pinched her in the buttocks and chased her down the hallway into the main house.

"Looks like our one-night stand is over." Michael affected brightness in his voice, but lurking beneath was melancholy and regret.

"I know. There's nothing worse than the morning after, is there? It's a reason not to fall in love. Wouldn't life be perfect if we could fall asleep in a stranger's strong arms and wake up miraculously alone in our own bed." The impermanence of love hovered all about us, filling the air with its sad, solitary presence.

"You're dreaming of a world without goodbyes." We were dressing now, and I trembled at the import of Michael's words as I pulled on my pants; memories of long nights with Dennis filled my mind, him asleep beside me while I fantasized about escape. I wondered how I would manage to make it through the day, through the long ride back to Hyde Park, through the long series of goodbyes Michael described. He looked at me.

"Are you all right? You're shaking." He put a hand on my shoulder; only then did I realize how much I was trembling.

"Am I?" My sock flapped wildly at the end of my foot; I had not managed to pull it on all the way. Michael kneeled before me and worked the bunched fabric over my knobby ankle, shook me out of myself, my self-absorption and worry.

"Come on. A jelly doughnut will make you feel better." Jane passed us in the hall as we headed downstairs. She was still in her pajamas, and the dog followed at her heels.

"Looks like you made a new friend." Michael giggled, pointing to the dog.

"You know what I always say." She looked at me, knowing Michael of course did know what she always said: "Beggars can't be choosers." She flitted past us, beckoning the dog after her.

Downstairs Mark was putting on a pot of coffee; several boxes of doughnuts lay open on the counter beside a tall stack of fancy paper napkins. People wandered in and out of the kitchen, refilling coffee cups or depositing them in the sink before heading back out into the nether reaches of the house. A car started up in the driveway, the grind of the engine bursting through the cold air before receding into the imperceptible distance. Already we were parting, moving onto our separate paths like a collection of random particles rapidly dispersing from the force of our brief collision. I didn't even know who half these people were. We sat at the table and talked.

"Did you guys sleep okay?" Mark asked.

"Considering the vintage 1973 mattress, I'd say we managed all right." Michael arched his back, pretending to suffer an attack of lumbago from the lumpy burlap sack. "My poor back." He let out a big, fake groan.

"I slept like a lamb," I falsely reassured Mark. I looked past him at the lake filling the generous expanse of the kitchen windows. I could barely distinguish between the two gray sheets, which was water and which sky, one backdrop gently folded so seamlessly into the other somewhere in the vague horizon.

"That's because you are a lamb." Michael pinched me.

"Baa, baa," Mark bleated.

"No," Michael said, "you're just a regular black sheep like the rest of us." Mark continued to bleat happily away.

Melinda clomped down the back steps and into the kitchen, Chris and their coterie of women friends in tow, each one successively grabbing a doughnut and filing through the front hallway and out the door. We were alone now. Mark loaded the dishwasher, tied the last bag of garbage, and sponged down the long, sparkling countertops while we waited for Jane to finally descend. Michael and Mark began calling up the stairs for her to hurry down, which Jane managed only with reluctance to do. Her hair was wet and wrapped tightly in a towel; she had taken a bath in Mark's parents' glamorous marble tub.

"My goodness," she admonished us, "can't a girl soak for a few minutes in peace and quiet?" She was beautiful in her terry-cloth turban, her scalp completely buried in the bleached twist of the fabric, the skin of her temples and forehead pulled tight in the torque, her eyebrows wispy accents *grave* and *aigu* on the grandly expressive declarative sentence of her smooth, pale countenance. Only when she grinned, revealing her girlish, gap-toothed smile, was the spell of her porcelain perfection broken, only then did she become human, of a piece with the rest of us; but for a powerful few seconds I saw through her, to another person and another universe, her secret self at the center of a whole other world, a world I wondered whether I would ever have the gift of visiting, of sharing with her for even one second more than the space she had with such perfect selflessness just revealed to me.

"Let's go." Mark gingerly unwrapped the towel from Jane's
head, and I watched like a student in a surgical amphitheater
as the heavy bandages are removed from an intensely studied
patient, the first recipient of a long-awaited brain transplant
technology, gasping as the crisp cotton cloths are unfurled to
reveal a complete human being, the audience rising in an
uncontrollable burst of spontaneous applause, Mark the mad
genius who made this miracle of science possible. Jane shook
her wet hair loose. Mark tossed the towel into a hamper in
the adjoining laundry room, and we exited through the side
door to the garage. Mark warmed up the car while Michael
and Jane and I briefly walked around to the back of the house,
beyond the pool, to the sandy cliff descending to the lake.
The icy grass crunched beneath us, and the wind pulled our
words out of our mouths before we could speak, lifting them
inaudibly into the higher atmosphere. Jane clutched my
sleeve, shivering. The wild stillness of the morning was interrupted by Mark's rudely honking and honking, and we ran
in the razor-edged cold to the warmth of the car. Mark drove
us up the drive through the barren trees swaying in the wind
and the house disappeared in the unfocused haze of their
silvery trunks. We were well onto the main road, the radio
politely filling the car with the space left by our silence, when
the city, so recently a memory, became a shimmering reality
again in the linear distance of the wide ribbon of Lake Shore
Drive unfurling generously before us. Our slumber party was
now history, an invisible link that bound us together, and I
was once again standing alone before the forbidding entry to
Blackstone Hall, into which with a twinge of forlorn guilt I
forced my way.

When I emerged again it was dark. The short day had
passed, the evening had arrived, with no word or sign from
Michael and Jane. I had eaten almost nothing since the jelly

doughnut from the morning, just an apple and some crackers that I kept in a little cupboard in my room, and I was overcome with the sensation of my own hunger. I seemed to have forgotten to eat, as if my hunger were like a letter I had stamped and placed in my pocket before leaving the house one morning, only to carry it with me all day and return it to my desk when I emptied my pockets upon arriving home, amused and disconcerted at my absentmindedness. The thought of food brought an accompanying sensation of loneliness; my room seemed dangerously cramped, and my stomach swirled in dyspeptic, arrhythmic motion.

I walked to Ribs 'n' Bibs at the corner of Fifty-third and Blackstone. The plastic barnyard interior was full of the odor of hickory and sweet, dark barbecue; a smoky haze emanated from the charcoal pits tended by two black men, one enormous, the other contrastingly skinny, behind a long blue Formica counter. I ordered a sandwich and fries with sauce and waited at one of the three picnic tables covered in dirty red-and-white checked vinyl tablecloths. A young couple sat at the table ahead of me, the man dousing a cheeseburger with hot sauce from a little glass bottle, the woman clutching a soda, filling the space with a slurping sound as she searched the bottom of the empty can for stray drops of carbonated liquid. The man put down his burger and licked his greasy fingertips, agitated.

"Cut that shit out," he said. "I'm trying to eat my dinner." She said nothing in return, merely took one more long, probing slurp before rising and tossing the can into an orange bin. My sandwich came up; I paid for my meal and began to eat. The couple left and I was alone again, but my hunger was gone, and I now felt only bored, angry at the cold, hating the endless winter, not wanting to face the miserable walk back to my room. I was just around the corner from Jane's apartment, and as I zipped up my coat, staring through the glass

door at the changing traffic lights on the corner, I thought
about walking over and ringing her bell. They had made a
point of surprising me; this evening I would surprise them
instead.

I turned onto Dorchester, into the courtyard of Jane's building, and as I hesitated, unsure for a moment on which side
Jane's entry lay, I was startled by the sight of Chris coming
straight toward me from a doorway that I had just determined
was not Jane's. She spotted me immediately.

"You're a bit on the early side, aren't you?"

"What are you doing here?" Had she been visiting Jane
or some other friend who lived in the same building?

"Do I need an excuse to be in my own apartment?"

"Oh, I had no idea you and Jane were living together."

"We're not. That's her building over there." She pointed
to the entry directly opposite the courtyard from her own.
"We're neighbors. I was just going to go score a little dope
before heading over. Why don't you come with me?"

I followed Chris back across Fifty-third and onto Blackstone, to a gritty, run-down building in the middle of the
block, one I must have passed dozens of times before without
ever noticing. She pressed a nameless bell and we waited for
the buzz to let us in. Two flights up, at the end of a damp,
poorly lit hallway, we stopped before the oddest contraption
of a gate guarding an apartment door. Two heavy padlocks,
top and bottom, imprisoned whoever lived here in his or her
privacy. The gate was heavy and rusted and did not look as
if it was ever opened. We stood there, Chris signing me not
to speak, not knocking or signaling in any other way that we
were waiting or expecting anything, until we could hear several dead bolts being drawn and the yellowing door creaked
open just enough for me to make out a single bloodshot eye
peering at us over a link of chain. Chris spoke at the eye.

"What have you got for me today, Jimmy?" Only her lips

moved, the rest of her body taut, expectant, perfectly motionless.

"Special. Six a bag." The voice was high, crackly, unexpectedly feminine.

"Give me three."

The voice turned away, revealing in the darkened space of the crack in the doorway the dim light of the apartment within, and I could barely spy the man's retreat into the inner recesses; one of his hands swung freely, and in the other a heavy revolver knocked against his waist. I slid back against the wall, hoping I had not been seen. Chris meanwhile fumbled in her pocket, searching for exact change. She was short.

"Damn. Have you got two dollars, Tommy?"

"Sure." I handed her the money, which she quickly counted out, and the man returned. Chris handed him the eighteen dollars and he passed three wallet-sized manila envelopes to her through the rusted gate, then pushed the door closed, quickly sliding the bolts back into place.

"A little bit of local color," Chris observed back on the street. We returned to Jane's building and ascended the stairs; the echo of familiar voices rose over loud music from within her apartment. Strangely enough, she was having a party, and I hesitated on the threshold, wondering if I should even be there, surprised when my intention had been to surprise.

About twenty people milled around the long hallway, the straggling beginnings of a party, the awkwardly early first arrivals whose necessarily ambivalent presence is fraught with anxiety at the uncertainty of what will follow, whether they will be joined by the happy crowd or left stranded in the awful dilemma of having to engineer their escape. Emerging from the bathroom as I walked the long hallway was a handsome man whom I recognized from the Coffee Shop. He was young and trim, neither short nor tall, with thoughtful brown eyes, and he thoroughly avoided my gaze.

The apartment remained essentially unfurnished, as I had first seen it, only in the dining room there was a beige sofa, a summer-porch-style piece of furniture with knobby rattan feet and bumpy brown cushions on a hard plywood support, and a boomerang coffee table, its white surface flecked with opal moonstones and silver sparkles. Michael was not present.

I found Jane on the back porch pumping an aluminum keg of beer which had been foolishly rolled up the back stairs. She pushed manfully on the pneumatic black handle in the middle of the bulging top of the canister, and a yeasty, lemon flow of pure foam shot out the end of the long plastic tube she held in her other hand. People shrieked, pretended to flee in a panic at the now sputtering head of spoiled beer. I held a plastic cup under the hose, only then gaining Jane's attention; she smiled and worked hard to fix me a drink, pretending such absorption in the troubled apparatus of the pump that she could not yet speak. When my cup was finally full, the foam mostly poured off and reduced to a respectable percentage, she filled one for herself, relaxed her grip on the black knob, and walked me back into the apartment.

"Cheers." We bumped glasses. She lowered her head to drink, coyly raising her eyes to me at the same time.

"Why the party?" I had been caught off balance—the last thing I expected to find was a full-scale party, one to which I had clearly not been invited.

"Melinda's leaving."

"I thought she just got here."

"That was over three months ago. This is Melinda we're talking about." Jane sounded exasperated, as though irritated there were things between us which still needed explaining.

"Well, why is she leaving?" I had a thousand other questions; this was not the most pressing of them.

"Why don't you ask her. You think I know everything?"

"As a matter of fact, yes, I do think you know everything."

The kitchen was beginning to fill; a short line had formed at the back door waiting to get at the beer. "Where's Michael?" Another question. Jane just shrugged and pointed into the dining room, then turned away to greet an unexpected arrival. Our conversation was over.

I gulped the rest of my drink and rushed to fetch another. Twenty-four hours before, I had felt at the center of this world, and now something seemed terribly wrong. On the sofa in the dining room I found Mark with a group of his friends. I joined them, listened as they prattled on, occasionally accepting sips from a bottle of tequila. I was well on my way to becoming recklessly drunk, impelling myself forward, and soon began talking. The people around me laughed at what I said, smiled with pleasure at my wild gesticulation, focused on me and anticipated my next words. I have no idea what I talked about, or how long I sat there drinking the alcohol as it was passed to me, but I was apparently very amusing, enough so that the handsome young man, who now presented a vision of un-precedented beauty to my drunken eyes, was casually leaning against the wall near my end of the sofa, watching me, laugh-ing as I told a joke, flashing an unreal smile at me, his lips slightly moist, suggestively parted. He was eyeing me, and I was so excited at the prospect of his companionship that I lost all satisfaction in the attention being paid to me, wished it would cease so that I might have this boy all to myself; but my audience would not be disappointed, now I had so com-pletely grabbed hold of them. In my drunken boldness I ejected Mark from the seat next to me, moved into his place, and very loudly urged the beautiful young man to sit next to me, which he did, whereupon I continued with whatever was the nonsensical tale I had interrupted.

I began to tire of my lunatic ranting and raving and chose instead to strike up a conversation with my new friend, now I had so effectively drawn him within my sphere of influence.

His name was Matthew, he was from Pittsburgh, and without any further ado I asked him to see me safely back to Blackstone Hall; he graciously accepted my invitation. We rose to leave, he leading the way, I trailing behind, grabbing hold of his sleeve. I stopped him at the back door, where I found Jane framed in the narrow pantry. Matthew waited on the porch while I stood before her and sloppily kissed her, leaned into her ear and whispered, "I love you," then kissed her again more carefully.

She also leaned forward, put her arms over my shoulders, and whispered to me, "You behave yourself tonight." She kissed me once more on the cheek. I turned and hurried out the door, Matthew the stranger looking at me with blank lust. He was beautiful, but now that we were rushing together to the street, alone and expectant, I thought of Jane, of our embrace, of our sniping and subsequent tender words. Matthew was simply there for me to hold on to—his presence did not seem to have meaning in itself, only as a representation of something else. He attributed my quiet to the aftereffects of my drunkenness and very gently took the reins of what little conversation we had. I stopped him at the corner of Fifty-sixth and Dorchester, pushing him hard into the brick indentation of a darkened doorway, and aggressively attacked him with a volley of high-intensity kisses, one long, slow pressing surrounded by a storm of fiery napalm contact, hoping to obliterate myself in the force of our connection. He held his own ground firmly, bravely assuming the gauntlet I had thrown down and hurtling it back at me. I pulled myself away and we plodded the few blocks more to my room, where he faithfully got me into my bed. I was already half asleep when he crawled in beside me and wrapped his arms around me, his body warm and downy and perfectly resistant, the strange faint smell of coffee on his breath. In another moment I had melted into sleep.

"Wake up, Thomas. Thomas." Matthew murmured my
name over and over, his lips moving against the back of my
neck, the sound free-falling into the center of my brain, the
puffing of his voice tickling my earlobe, his lips tugging at
the rubbery folds of cartilage, his warm tongue tracing spirals
around the inside of my ear, the warmth spreading in waves
from his mouth at the side of my head throughout my body,
my eyes closed, Matthew grown enormous, his presence filling
the entire space of the room, his salty smell caught in my
nostrils and the top of my throat, myself reduced to a grateful
speck of dust that he was about to inhale, a quickly evaporating puddle, water vapor spreading into the atmosphere of
his presence. However he touched me, his elbow pushed tight
against my side, his big toe scratching the bottom of my foot,
his stomach rising and falling against the back of my rib cage,
the stubble of his cheek grazing my shoulder, he was flawless.
There was no awkwardness, no uncertainty, no strangeness
or doubt in even the most minuscule aspect of our encounter,
and always his voice, his breath, his lips and tongue opening
a hole in my skull.

I was left with no space to think, to feel anything but the
heat of his contact; even my body was lost, all sensation
willfully reduced to an awareness of his countering presence.
He spun himself in circles around me; there was no interruption, no time or space to think about what was happening,
only the gradually widening circle of physical sensation, of
his physical presence, every last square inch of the surface
of my body so enveloped in his that, with my eyes closed, I
was all consciousness, able to see with my kneecaps, taste
with my palms, listen with my lips, feel with my lungs, smell
with my Adam's apple, my center of consciousness freed from
my brain, free to explore the multiplicity of his presence,
until after a profound postponement, a long, blissful, trance-
like wandering where the boundaries between his body and

mine were effortlessly transgressed, I was brought back to myself, to the hard, factual awareness of his difference by the focused calculation of mutual climax, an electrical charge sparking between us, leaving me wide awake and hungering for one more final, transcendent second of unselfconscious union, but left instead with the hard awareness of his elbow jabbing at my shin, his knee pinching the side of my rib cage, his thighs slippery with sweat and twitching, and a feeling of amazement at what had just occurred between us, of disbelief at my surrender.

Matthew curled up beside me on the mattress, taking hold of my arm and folding it over his chest, demanding I hold him, wiggling his backside against me to ensure a comfortably close fit. I clung to him, this sweaty, exhausted creature sleeping beside me, afraid of this reductive finish I had witnessed and the implications for myself. He was an animal acting with perfect animal selflessness and composure—I strained to detect an ounce of uncertainty or doubt or hesitancy in his behavior but could find nothing; he lay still like a tired dog beside me, ignorant of my nudgings, my pokings, my suffocating attempts to awaken an awareness of myself in his consciousness, until I wearied with trying and slept myself.

In the morning, in the shower, I studied his body, searching for signs of difference, for a clue to the magnetic pull he had exerted, for a scar or revealing trace element of his mysterious aura, but he was all scaly flesh and bristling hair, stubby toenails and glazed-over brown eyes. The fire between us was extinguished by the wet spray on our backs, our coarsely choreographed stumbling in the slippery tub an exercise in clumsy avoidance. How could I express to him the magnitude of what I had experienced, the depth of feeling he had released in me, the deeply strange meaning his presence had invoked? Had he shared any of my experience? Did he unconsciously possess some powerful secret fund which I had tapped, or had the feeling come from within me? Sadly, before I had had the chance to wonder fully what about him was so remarkable, he was gone and I was left alone to dwell on my burdensome sense of inadequacy, convinced that I owed whatever I felt to this powerful stranger and was myself weak and hopelessly dependent.

Monday afternoon I sat in the Coffee Shop, depressed, waiting for company to arrive. Only after two cups of coffee and a thorough scouring of the national *New York Times* did Michael finally appear, fully armed with the news of my upstart behavior at Jane's party and departure in handsome young male company.

"Well?" He asked, sliding into the seat across from me. He rolled his coat up over his fist and shoved it into the corner, then shook his head at me.

"Well what?" I was destined to behave coyly with Michael. It seemed pointless to attempt otherwise.

"You know what I'm talking about. How was it? *Him?*" Michael stressed the masculine pronoun, leaning forward into his pronunciation of the word for added emphasis.

"You mean Matthew?"

"Is there someone else?" Had he any idea of the implications? He was impatient, expectant, hanging on my every word.

"It was okay," I lied, laughing, thinking to myself that never in a million years would I explain to Michael what had been as far as I was now concerned by a hundred thousand times the best sexual experience of my life.

"I thought so." Michael knowingly breathed a sigh of relief. "He's cute, but who ever heard of sleeping with a meteorologist from Pittsburgh?" I couldn't help laughing. The ani-

mal who had shaken me to my deepest roots was a future
weatherman.

"That explains why he kept muttering something about a low front in his sleep." I was happy not to have disappointed Michael, to have preserved his illusions about me and my sex life, my denial of pleasure serving to keep the perceptible balance between us tipped slightly in his knowing favor.

I left to fetch a third cup of coffee, and when I returned, Michael was deeply engrossed in the newspaper; he hardly looked up to acknowledge my return, and continued reading in my presence, pursing his lips slightly in sour disapproval at a particularly scandalous event, knitting his eyebrows in consternation and sorrow at some international disaster. The Coffee Shop was crowded, overflowing with conversation, but Michael and I were alone in our booth, the newspaper now spread out over his half of the table, a black smudge of the cheap ink smeared on the bridge of his nose from his habit of pinching and rubbing the spot with his thumb and the first two fingers of his left hand as he read. Michael looked like a peaceful old man in his quiet concentration, the pale complexion of his face shadowed by the hint of dry stubble on his rather sharp chin, the only color a red ring where the collar of his woolen turtleneck scratched his thin neck. The dryness of the winter was in the air, dusty and perfumed with juvenile exhalations of tobacco, in the sea of chapped lips and itching, flaky hands surrounding us. I rubbed my own hands together, picked at the scabrous white knuckles, followed with my eyes the winding narrow grooves in my palms.

Michael remained present but inaccessible. I withdrew a textbook from my bag and desultorily studied its pages, tracing over whole paragraphs with a green Hi-Liter, often slipping in my laziness and marking the back side of my thumb instead. I creased the book open at one particularly gruesome depiction of a cell formation, stringy red splotches swimming in a sickly blue geodesic organic space, and laid my head down against the page, as if listening for the heartbeat of the responsible organism. I closed my eyes and listened to the snippets of conversation floating around me, a woman behind me describing in detail the unwelcome advances of a professor, a group at a table nearby talking through a set of physics problems, from another direction a heated literary debate, and returned from my aural wandering to Michael turning a page of the paper and slapping the fuzzy crease open, erupting in an odd little squeak from the action before settling back down into concentrated perusal.

I opened my eyes. Michael was scratching away at the crossword puzzle, one elbow propped on the table, the corresponding hand tucked in the vent of his beige cardigan sweater, his body hunched forward, his pen rapidly filling in the blank grid of boxes, until there were no empty spaces left and he triumphantly folded the last section of the paper and piled it in the stack he had neatly made against the wall in a corner of the table. I remained slumped forward, my head like an anatomy exhibit in an extravagantly real textbook, sprung to life from the page. I yawned.

"Help," I weakly muttered, rolling my eyes upward.

"I know," Michael answered, my cry not needing any explanation.

"What a miserable day. Does it ever end?" I felt like complaining, bemoaning the general condition of my soul.

"I remember my first Chicago winter," Michael said fondly. "Didn't we warn you about the month of February?" He tapped a bony finger on the top of my head, tap tap tap. I didn't move. Michael wiggled the book out from under me, forcing me to sit up straight. "That's better."

"Thanks." I rubbed my eyes and stretched my arms out over the table.

"So tell me about Matthew. What was he like? Did he do this to you?" Michael wagged a finger at me, paternal and slightly sadistic in his questioning. "No, wait a minute. Do I really want to know?"

"I don't think so. There's not much to tell."

"You know, Tommy, there's always something to tell. If the truth is boring, then you have an obligation to use your imagination." Michael was full of such advice. Never be dull, never disappoint, never admit defeat; everything with a purpose.

"Would you believe me if I told you it was the best sex I ever had?"

"As if there was such a thing." He laughingly dismissed my question. I knew he wouldn't believe me, would assume the opposite of whatever I said, having taught me himself the self-deprecating code in which he and Jane spoke. "Was it that bad?"

"Horrible." I shook my head in emphasis of this ironic truth, ending the conversation.

"Will you walk me home, please?" Michael smoothed his sweater over his shoulders and returned the pen he had been twirling in one hand back to the front pocket of his cracked leather briefcase. I felt flattered by his strange politeness.

"You mean I finally get to see where you live?" Not since our fiasco at Kimbark Village had Michael even admitted to having a home. We stood and pulled on our coats; Michael waved an arm above the thinning crowd at the exit in the distance.

"Please," he repeated, and pushed me gently forward, his hand glued to the padded shoulder of my overcoat. We walked through the courtyard and stood in the cold blue light on Fifty-seventh Street across from the library. Michael led the way north to Fifty-sixth Street and east to Dorchester, stopping before an enormous, dark house hidden behind a high wooden fence just short of the corner where I had so recently been engaged with Matthew. He led me through a gate in the fence to the back porch, up two winding flights of red-carpeted stairs, to a daintily furnished little landing. A bright red doormat shouted WELCOME in curvy blue letters.

Michael opened the apartment door and snapped on a hall light, its too-bright bulb painfully illuminating the cramped attic. We stood in a narrow rectangular hallway; a kitchen sloped away to the right, a living room packed with books and papers sloped to the left, and a bedroom was tucked between two eaves of the roof straight ahead. The ceiling was low at its highest point and rapidly descended into the corners of the rooms. Everywhere I turned there was the danger of a grazed shoulder, a bump on the head, or a swollen black eye. Michael took my coat and threw it with his atop a dresser in the hallway, then offered to put on water for tea. I squeezed into a chair by the kitchen window, bowing my head to fit in the narrowing space, while he filled a kettle with water and bent over the gas stove, squinting into the space under the kettle where the burner and the jet were joined but a flame had failed to rise.

"Damn. The pilot light's out." Michael cursed the stove and rummaged through a drawer in search of a match while the sickly sweet smell of free gas filled the room. He found a box of wooden matches and struck one nervously against the flinty side, only managing on the third try to produce the necessary, hissing flame; then he lit the stove, gingerly holding the stick between his thumb and forefinger, pulling it back frantically the instant the gas caught fire, waving the match madly to kill it. He laid it in the sink under a stream of cold water, as if its smoking remnants were inherently dangerous and demanded careful, mandatory precautions to neutralize them. I had never seen Michael so thin and nervous and clumsy, so frighteningly careful. He struck me as older,

not just older than myself, but older than his ac
older than real time can possibly make one, brittle
nerable and wise, like a survivor from an ancient,
world.

The kettle whistled. Michael filled my cup and maneuve
his way into a seat across the table wedged between us. Abov
the skeleton of a tree in the yard I could discern the faint
outline of the concrete apartment tower centered in the nearby
block of Fifty-fifth Street, and I could hear the traffic of that
busier, bisecting thoroughfare. In the powerful vapor lamps
of the distant boulevard a light snow made its diagonal descent, refracting the yellow light into a diaphanous green
haze. Michael had turned up the heat when we entered, and
the kitchen window broke out into a cold sweat, which slowly
grew to obscure my view into the yard and beyond. We sipped
our tea and Michael spoke.

"Have you ever been in love?" Michael slurped his tea
and arched his brows only a little; he spoke the words in a
lilting crescendo, shaping them into a widening horn of sound,
the first three a tight, rapid unfurling which slowed into a
wide, slow, brassy walk through the next two, and ended with
a clarion emphasis on the final word.

"If you mean psychotically obsessed with some jerk who
treated me like a piece of garbage, then the answer is yes."
I thought of the summer just passed and a best friend lost,
of the months of achingly unfulfilled desire, the perpetual
embarrassment and humiliation of being unable to contain
myself, to free myself from a self-defeating belief in my utter
dependence on this other person.

"Bitter?" Michael chomped down hard on the word as if
he was all too familiar with its lingering taste.

"And yourself?" Surely Michael, older, more experienced,
more worldly, was therefore full of sweet and sour anecdotes.

"Me? Never."

believe you." Was he simply teasing me, or at-
, some larger point?

ink it's only possible to really fall in love once. From
on we're basically doomed to just keep repeating the
ne mistake." He shut his eyes, steeped them in the last
wisps of steam rising from his cup.

"It doesn't exactly sound promising."

"I'm not sure. I thought I was in love once. I met him in
Minneapolis, at a conference, and stayed for eight months.
He was a real socialist, that particular, homegrown kind they
raise in Minnesota. Our love was going to start a revolution.
One day I slipped on an icy sidewalk and broke my leg. I
was in the hospital for over a week, and when I returned
home he was gone, fled to some godawful Communist ashram
in California. Can't you just see them all, meditating in their
Mao suits?" Michael cackled at the picture he painted, then
summed up his feelings in a final phrase: "What an asshole."

"I see your point. I don't know if I've ever been in love
either. I've been delusional, but now I think about it, that
doesn't count." This struck me as an optimistic and liberating
realization; by a simple trick of semantics I could discount
my failures as simply not having been the real thing, freeing
me to recognize and accept the glorious truth if and when it
should ever surface.

"Remember our motto 'Love without lust; lust without love.'
These are words we can live by." Michael sounded tired, not
wholly up to the challenge of our constructed postmodernist
identities. "After all, we are the original Pomo-Homos." He
stood and rinsed our cups, the water thumping against the
stainless steel of the sink.

"Perhaps that's what I'm afraid of." I stood also and looked
at my watch. I was hungry and tired and disoriented by the
wild hissing of the radiators in Michael's apartment. "I'm
going to go get my dinner."

"Look at the snow." Michael rubbed the window clean with a dish towel. A thick layer of frost already coated the limbs of the tree and the surrounding rooftops, the lamps in the distance only hazy spots of light in the dense cross-hatching of the falling snow. "Your shoes—" he pointed. "You'll catch a cold walking out in this weather."

"It's okay. I'll run." Michael helped me into my coat and followed me down the winding stair, freezing now from the blizzard's gale. The back porch was already buried in heavy slush, the path to the gate in the fence indiscernible, my shoes soaked through with my first steps on the ground. I waved a faint goodbye to Michael, who hovered in the doorway, hunched over against the cold. I raced into the wind, the cuffs of my pants damp and dragging me down, my toes twitching in icy pain before becoming numb with frostbite, my coat and hat covered by the time I reached Blackstone Hall with the same heavy, wet coating that hung on the trees and the gutters and the rooftops and every square inch of available surface. The snow continued to fall with increasing intensity throughout the night and all the next day, completely burying the city and bringing all life to a total standstill. When the storm finally ended and the relatively bright winter sun shone on Wednesday morning, the city had become a white cocoon of muffled silence, the snow absorbing all sound so that I could hear nothing, not the sound of my own voice, not even the most piercing cries of pain and shock and pleasure which normally filled the life of the city.

The gray sky finally parted. I was standing at the bus stop on Lake Park Avenue, a light drizzle falling, the wind off the lake damp, my shirt clinging to my back in the cool humidity, when it finally happened. I had grown so accustomed to the unceasing winter, to ice in April, to the dry heat and static electricity, I stopped waiting for the thaw; like my own death I could only hope that when the time came, I would recognize and accept its arrival. This particular Thursday did not begin differently from any in the long series of others that had so far marked the many months of my life in Chicago, my continuing education, my celebration of another birthday, my affair with Dennis. The bus was late, a crowd gathered under the brown plastic CTA shelter, the sky continued to release heavy droplets of rain, when the clouds began to part and the neighborhood glistened in the emerging sunlight. I remembered my mother always telling me as a child when the sun shone and it rained that the devil was beating his wife; I wondered what she had done this day to deserve his wrath.

My spring reverie was broken by a honking horn. Michael pulled up to the curb in a clean little sedan; he looked ridiculous behind the wheel, like an enormous infant pretending to drive. Michael belonged in the library, deep in a pile of crumbling manuscripts, not out on the street, driving, adding to the obscene volume of urban life. He leaned across the passenger seat and rolled down the window.

"Where did you get the car?" I stood on the curb and asked him.

"A professor friend of mine." He twisted his shoulder as he continued unrolling the window, accidentally turning on the windshield wipers. "Want a lift?" The wipers noisily scraped the glass; Michael looked at them frustratedly as I eased into the seat beside him. "Damn. How did I do that?" The bus pulled up behind us, its enormous headlights filling the rear windshield completely. Michael turned to me and asked, "Where do I take you?" He made no comment when I told him, simply put the car into gear and turned onto Lake Shore Drive.

A wall of blue clouds in the eastern sky over the lake reflected the now brightly shining western sun in a magnificent rainbow; shimmering ribbons of violet seemed to spring from the smokestacks in Gary and land somewhere on the uncharted Wisconsin shore. The skyline in the distance picked up highlights from the spectrum and glimmered like the Emerald City of Oz. Michael hummed his appreciation of the scene; I pressed my cheek to the cold glass of the window, afraid to blink and miss a second of the perfectly refracted light. The traffic slowed, Michael swerved with the curve of the highway, and I looked over at a fat Mercedes speeding past us, only to turn back again and find the rainbow had dissolved in the mist, the illusion vanished in the split second I had so feared missing. Michael spoke.

"Big date tonight?" He gripped the wheel tightly, hunched forward, intently watching the heavy traffic flow around us.

"Just the usual." I figured as far as Dennis and Michael were concerned, my little secret had now been found out. "The sex is good."

"I should hope so." Michael was testy, a little self-righteous. "Why else bother?" We turned off the drive, passed the Art Institute, then moved north on Michigan Avenue. We passed the Tribune Tower and I offered to get out at the corner, but Michael insisted on driving me around the block; I had intended to keep at least the location of my affair secret from him, but he was determined to see me to the door, his prurient interest piqued. We stopped in front of the Hotel Madison.

"Satisfied?" I missed walking, turning the corner, the privacy of those few minutes alone in the bustling city before Dennis and I inevitably undressed.

"Are you?" Michael couldn't resist remarking. I blushed, blamed myself for making a linguistic blunder, and popped open the door. He squinted at the neon and called after me, "Behave yourself." Jane's words exactly, I thought as I walked through the shabby lobby.

Dennis had left the door unlocked; I let myself in and he didn't rise from his seat by the window. I sat on the edge of the bed.

"Did you see the rainbow?" He looked at me, the expression in his eyes more tired than usual, and shook his head.

"No." He came and sat next to me on the bed, ran a hand over my forehead and through my hair, kissed the back of my neck, then knelt before me and untied my shoes. He pulled off my socks, neatly packing each one into its shoe, wrapped his arms around my waist, and pressed his cheek against my crotch. He rubbed his nose along the inside of my thigh and with his shoulder gently nudged my legs farther apart. I breathed deeply, settled into the familiar room, allowed the outside world to recede farther and farther into the distance. I could feel his teeth pressing through my pants. He stopped and looked up at me.

"Who was your friend?" I blinked. Why had he stopped?
"What?"

"Your friend. The one who dropped you off?"

"Oh." Dennis had been watching, had seen me with Mi-

chael. "Just a friend. Nobody important." I stared at the top
of his head and held a hand to the side above an ear.

"Just wondering," he muttered before pushing me back flat
on the bed, nimbly biting my thigh again, fumbling my belt
buckle undone. I closed my eyes and vanished, became a
corpse.

After, when Dennis leaned back heavily against the headboard and switched on a lamp, the room seemed excruciatingly small. There was barely space to turn around, to think,
to breathe. Although the windows had acquired one more
layer of winter's dirt and grime, and the brown chair had
sagged a little deeper, essentially nothing had changed; but
Dennis's rented room was a prison and I had never noticed
it until now, and Dennis was its prisoner. In every impersonal
corner, where I had before seen blank anonymity I now saw
scribbled Dennis's name. This room which I had so long
thought of as nowhere, as the place for sex, was Dennis's
room. He was everywhere, in the yellowing lampshade, the
steel sunflower of the showerhead, the paper-thin closet door,
the stalactite plaster ceiling. Dennis had chosen this place,
named it, inhabited it; he owned it.

The night was still early and Dennis rose to dress himself.
He stood in his socks and underwear, buttoning his red-and-
white workshirt, and said, "Can I buy you a drink?"

I winced. Only moments before he had been a naked man,
my equal in bed, nobody. Now he looked like a tired, lonely
train conductor. I wanted to blink my eyes and find him gone,
naked again, nobody again, anything but to see him standing
there, another person, wanting to be my friend.

"My treat," he repeated his offer.

"Sure." I used the bathroom, and when I emerged he was
making the bed, tucking tight hospital corners, snapping the
top sheet back over the blankets, fluffing the pillows against
the headboard. He had laid my clothes out on the back of

the easy chair, the pants neatly folded along the creases, the shirt unbuttoned and the collar smoothed down, shoes and socks patiently waiting in their proper place. I felt embarrassed by this attention to detail. I wondered had he done this before, been doing this all the months I had known him, and I had only just now noticed? I had no idea.

"Ready?" Dennis helped me into my coat.

"Ready." I zipped up, but we didn't move. Instead, Dennis stood before me, looked at me with his worn-out eyes, put his arms around me and squeezed. He kissed me, his lips on mine, his tongue fighting its way into my mouth, his breath wheezing slightly in his nostrils. I waited for him to finish. We walked north, barely talking, only occasionally referring to the evening's mildness, the undeniable signs of green in Lincoln Park. We continued walking, afraid to stop, nothing holding us together but the inertia of our motion, until we had neared Belmont and the strip of bars on Broadway and Clark Street. Dennis haphazardly chose one, invisible behind black glass, the music barely making it to the busy sidewalk.

The bar was narrow and dark, opening to a small dance floor in back. Dennis found a seat for me, ordered two beers, and stood beside me, one hand resting on my knee, the other on the bar. He knocked his bottle against mine, tossed his head back, and drew a long draft; I followed suit. Dennis opened his mouth and said something, but the music was just loud enough to prevent me from hearing. I nodded my head, pretending to know what he was talking about, and he squeezed my knee for emphasis. He rocked back and forth slightly to the beat, keeping time with the motion of his chin, following with a turn of his head whenever a man pushed through the narrow aisle behind us.

I ordered another round. The bar became fuller as we drank, warmer, the variety of men astonishing. One tipped a White Sox cap at Dennis in recognition as he passed, and we both laughed.

"You've been here before," I shouted in his ear.

"How'd you guess?" Dennis was pink from the liquor, his expression muddled and happy, his brow just a little sweaty in the growing heat. He emptied my not quite finished beer and with a wave of his hand secured a fresh one for me. His drunken body swayed to the music, his hips bumping against the leather cushion of my bar stool. I tapped a shoe on the chrome footrest.

"Let's dance." Dennis pulled me off the stool, latched on to my wrist and led me through to the dance floor. Our shirts glowed purple in the trendy ultraviolet light; we were swimming in a sea of black. Dennis held on to my arm, his knees knocking against each other, the music pulsing through us, freeing us to move together without reason or excuse beyond its own repetitious beat. I followed Dennis, reflected his motions, kept countertime to his rhythm. It was easier than thinking, this dancing with him. His person was less suffocating, less unforgivable in the intoxicated atmosphere of the bar. I wasn't dancing with just Dennis; I was dancing with a hundred or more Dennises, men who coupled regularly in unremarkable rented rooms. I was one of them.

We drank while we danced, the liquor fueling our engines, until the room began to spin madly, Dennis the only stable object in the entire universe, and I clung to him, kissing him wildly. Dennis twirled with me, unable to release my lips from his, his hands painfully hot on my back. Finally, I began to feel sick.

We slowed down and eased toward the entry, Dennis supporting me with one strong arm until we were standing alone on the sidewalk in the fresh night air, the street buckling and heaving, the traffic swerving dangerously close. I tried to kiss

Dennis again, but he stopped me, pointing to a group of teenagers turning the corner across the street. I grabbed at his pants and attempted to reach a hand inside, but he stopped me hard and waved inexplicably. A taxi pulled to the curb and I climbed in. Dennis attempted to crawl in after, but I turned and angrily demanded he leave me in peace. In a sickening instant he was gone, the city whirled past me, and I was headed home.

I swam, miserable, through the next day's hangover. The temperature had shot to a record high, the foliage had turned overnight from pale to forest green, and the classrooms were suffocatingly hot, the campus streaked with swinging pale pink and bare white limbs emerging from winter's hibernation. I crawled back to my room after lunch and collapsed, sick and exhausted; I missed the winter, the cold, the departed gray sky. This fulsome warmth did not suit my mood at all; I hid indoors and hopelessly wished it away.

Saturday morning I lay in bed, my shades tightly drawn against the obnoxious sunlight, flipping through Michelet's *History of the French Revolution*, making notes for a term paper, when I was startled by a knock on the door. I wrapped myself tightly in my bathrobe, expecting Jane or Michael to greet me sarcastically, hoping to haul me off to another "See Your Food" adventure. I pinched my nose, and in a high, mincing voice teasingly complained, "Go away, I'm in the shower."

"Oh, sorry," a voice on the other side answered. I let go of my nose and raced to open the door. Dennis stood in the hallway, admiring his reflection in the glass window of the elevator door, standing his short hair on end in perfect formation with one hand, the other looped in his pants pocket. I pulled him into my room and slammed the door shut, as if he were an escaped convict, his picture posted on the front page of every newspaper in town, and both our lives were being endangered by his presence. I felt deeply ashamed, implicated in some terrible crime.

"Hey" was all Dennis managed to say before sitting at my desk. He tilted his head to read the titles stacked there, tapped a ballpoint pen against the edge.

"Dennis. What are you doing here?" I was dazed; the last person in the world I ever expected to have here in my room was Dennis, casually destroying the compartmentalized life I had constructed.

"I wanted to see you." He stood up, began undressing.

"Jesus. How did you find me?"

"What do you think, Thomas. I'm not retarded." He unzipped his fly and pushed me onto the bed. "I missed you." He was enormous, hunched over me, pinning me against the wall with his greater weight. I was afraid, not of his hurting me, but of his wanting me, of his expecting me to participate in whatever was about to happen.

"Stop." I twisted beneath him. He was hot, insistent, breathing down my neck, sweating.

"Let me fuck you." He bit my ear; I closed my eyes, amazed at his energy, taken by the force of his desire to possess me. He was slow and methodical, reining in his urgency just enough to continually modulate and prolong his climax, until finally, in a convulsive frenzy, gritting his teeth and shaking his head like a wet dog, he hit the blank wall of nothingness at the end and, shivering, pulled me into his lap, held me so hard that in my own excitement I felt like crying, we had become so stupid and blind, so completely useless to each other.

"Wow." Dennis heaved with satisfaction. He carried me into the bathroom, ran the shower, shampooed my hair and vigorously massaged my scalp, wrapped me in a towel and briskly rubbed me dry, as if I were a frail child, and I quietly submitted to his doting, until he had returned me back to the bed and lay still on top of me.

I reached above my head and pulled the white tasseled ring on the shade, sent it spinning loudly; the room flooded with light. Dennis was dead weight, gritty red flesh, and I squeezed out from under him. He did not move, but followed me with his eyes and surveyed the room.

"I'm hungry." I began to dress, wondering what to do with Dennis, terrified of being seen with him.

"No," he moaned, rolling over on his back. "Let's do it again." All these months I had gone to Dennis's room at the Hotel Madison with only one purpose in mind, and now he was taking his revenge. I had been so surprised by his presence, so overwhelmed by the sex that immediately followed, I had never received a satisfactory explanation for his being in Chicago on a Saturday morning.

"What are you doing here? I mean in Chicago?" I asked him again. He played with himself, lewdly hoping to arouse me.

"I took a few days off." He looked at himself, almost erect, and attempted with a shake of his head to get me to look in the same direction. I ignored him and finished dressing. He was stiff now and beating himself hard, no longer caring whether I participated this time, intent on coming once more. I thumbed through a notebook and waited for him to finish. When he was dressed we ran down the stairs and I rushed ahead onto the street, pretending not to even notice whether he was with me, was following me to the Greek diner on the corner.

We sat in a booth by the window and I slumped over the table—all my cherished dreams of anonymity were tearing to shreds and I was helpless to do anything in my defense, paralyzed by the fear of being recognized with Dennis, as if

the sex between us were written in capital letters on our brows,
and too embarrassed by my shame at his company to attempt
escape. We ate in silence; I watched the people stroll by on
the sunny sidewalk, amazed they didn't care that Dennis was
here, in Hyde Park, eating breakfast with me after coming
twice in Blackstone 506. Dennis did not offer to help pay
the tab when we finished, simply muttered "Thanks" and
squeezed my shoulder from behind. At last, back on the
sidewalk, I made my excuses.

"Well, I guess I'll see you next Thursday." I held out a
hand to shake.

"That's it?" Dennis looked angry. "What's the matter?"

"Nothing's the matter. I have to study, I'm busy." I felt
exasperated by his persistence. "I want to be alone." I looked
at my watch, across the street in both directions, sweating
nervously.

"What, afraid someone'll see you with your fuckbuddy—
that's what we are, right?"

"You said it, not me." I was dizzy, confused; how had our
eminently simple and convenient arrangement devolved into
this humiliating street scene? "Please, just leave me alone."

"I'm sorry." Dennis sounded genuinely contrite. "I missed
you. I was curious, wanted to see where you live, what it's
like." We began walking toward the lake. "I should have
called you, asked first."

We passed under Lake Shore Drive to the Point, crowded
with sunbathers, picnickers, and Frisbee-tossing students.
We sat together on the rocks, admiring the distant skyline,
enjoying an uneasy truce, not talking, not asking anything of
one another beyond acceptance of the other's presence.

At last Dennis stood and said, "I'll go home now. You'll
come next week?"

"I always do." I started to stand up also, but he stopped
me.

"Don't bother," he said. "It's okay. I'll see you later." And without looking back he walked across the busy lawn and disappeared.

Long after Dennis had vanished I remained on the rocks, glad he was gone, the sunshine more bearable now that I was alone, and reflected on the implications of his visit. I kept reminding myself he was harmless, had no power over me, could not hurt me, but was not fully able to convince myself of these truths. The atmosphere of the Point, the sidewalks where Dennis had walked, the booth we had sat in, the elevator and stairs and my room in Blackstone Hall, all had been irrevocably transformed, sullied by his visit, the clean separation I had fought to maintain hopelessly muddied and blurred. Dennis was a loose cannon, out of control, capable of anything; I was filled with fear of his potentially recurring, unpredictable presence; I wished he was dead.

I returned to my room and napped restlessly in the soothing afternoon shade, tossing with disturbed memories of his visit, his demanding presence closing in on me, suffocating me with his inferior needs. A knock on the door. I burrowed into my pillow, horrified, praying for an escape from the repetition of the past. The knock again. Was I dreaming, or was someone really at the door? A final knock, real, definite, impatient.

"Just a minute." I jumped, nervous, rushed at the door.

"Thomas. Did I wake you?"

"Jane, Jane, Jane." I said her name three times, an incantation to ward off evil spirits. In her presence my room was again transformed, the evil spirits banished, her soothing, erotic attraction filling the space as fully as Dennis's rushing energy had only a few hours earlier. I held her two hands and kissed her on the cheek.

"You look awful. Is something the matter?" She picked up a towel Dennis had left lying on the bathroom threshold and hung it on the back of the door.

"No. I just feel awful." She opened the medicine cabinet
and without my asking handed me three aspirin.

"Good. I mean, here, a few of these never hurt." She filled
a dirty coffee mug with water and passed it along. She opened
the window and turned up the radio; a mellow woman's voice
filled the room, singing of rain, melancholy, sadly welcoming
the rain. "I love this song." Jane was rifling through my desk
now. "It's so vaginal, don't you think?"

"I think you're vaginal." She was dressed for summer, in
white shorts and a pink T-shirt, her legs long and smooth,
slightly knock-kneed. Her hair clung to the sides of her head,
held in place by two thick tortoiseshell barrettes.

"You don't say." She sat down, splayed her legs, rocked
them on her heels in white tennis shoes. "We're going to the
dunes." Jane's plural was inclusive, imperative, did not admit
the possibility of rejection or denial.

"What dunes?" We were at least a thousand miles from
the nearest ocean.

"The Michigan dunes, dummy." She crossed her arms,
exasperated. "You New Englanders are so narrow-minded
sometimes. Didn't you ever notice that pool of water just over
yonder, the one they call Lake Michigan? It has dunes,
too."

"You don't say. When are we leaving?"

"This afternoon. We would have been there by now, but
you weren't home this morning." Jane waited while I packed
a bag, and we walked over to Michael's. He had thrown open
all the windows in his apartment: the wind dashed through
from the four corners of the planet, papers sliding off every
available horizontal surface. Michael was vacuuming.

"Spring cleaning." He looked up when we entered. The
kitchen gleamed; Michael had taken the stove apart and put
it back together again, every knob and rack perfectly free of
grease and grime. A plastic pitcher of iced tea brewed on the

windowsill. Jane poured three glasses and we all stood in the hallway drinking.

"Summertime," Michael proposed a toast.

"The dunes," Jane suggested as a follow-up. They waited for me to finish the round.

"Escape from Hyde Park." Satisfied, we clinked glasses. Jane closed the windows, Michael wound the cord around the vacuum cleaner and stowed it away, I lifted his little suitcase, and we descended to the back porch, piled into the car parked on the street by the gate in the fence. We pulled around to the back alley by Jane's apartment and waited for her to run in and fetch her bag before heading south to the Chicago Skyway.

The lakeshore was a solid wall of industry: breweries, factories, and electrical plants gave way at the Indiana border to the awesome, sulfurous sprawl of the steel mills. The idea of nature, of sand and water, in such a landscape seemed preposterous.

"Just where exactly are these dunes again?" I shouted from the back seat, unable to hide my disbelief.

"Doubting Thomas." Michael beamed beatifically. "Have faith, and you will be pleasantly surprised." We flowed through a clover-leaf interchange on the other side of Gary and moved north, the signs proudly proclaiming our arrival in Michigan. We had long since left the lake somewhere in the west, and the road stretched straight ahead of us, the land on either side forested and hilly in comparison with the unalleviated flatness of Chicagoland. We exited, following a local route through a series of modest intersections, each corner predictably occupied by a convenience store, gas station, fast-food outlet, and liquor warehouse, to a narrower side road, the woods thick on both sides, ranch homes and trailers hiding within, through a pretty village, a wide main street lined with shops, a barber pole, a soda fountain, a five-

and-dime, and finally down a long dirt lane to a yellow-
shingled wooden cabin, the trees stunted and red in the deficient soil, the land behind the house rippling waves of scrub
and grass and sand, the lake just hinted at by a barely perceptible falling off in the distance.

We entered through a screened-in side porch. The house
was small, only four rooms, and musty. Michael moved
through the rooms, throwing open the windows, while Jane
boiled water and rinsed glasses for tea in the kitchen. We
sat on the porch, the sun mellowing in the sky, a cool breeze
picking up, sipping hot tea on a hot evening. An airplane
streaked across the sky in the distance over the lake. Jane
spoke.

"I miss the dunes. We used to come here all the time when
I was a little girl." She rhapsodized, lovingly scanned the
horizon.

"I thought I'd die if I had to spend another minute in that
hellhole on Blackstone Avenue." I vented my relief at being
somewhere new, unfamiliar.

"Spoken like a true Hyde Parker." Michael nodded his
approval of my sentiment.

"We all flee eventually." Jane rolled her eyes, amused.
"It's our irrational instinct for self-preservation kicking in."

"I think it's perfectly logical," Michael contradicted her.
" 'Run for your life,' that's my motto."

"I don't understand."

"Yes, you do." Jane laughed at me, confident she knew
me better than I did myself at that moment.

"It's just another way of being a Pomo-Homo. You remember what that's all about, don't you, Thomas?"

"Yes." I admitted Michael's point. We sat in silence, the
weight of our words settling around us. The evening was
rapidly encroaching; I was anxious to see the lake before dark
and proposed a walk in the peaceful dusk.

At the edge of the scruffy back lawn we followed a dirt trail through a rippled stretch of thorny bushes and grass, a hemline of dense trees on either side, to a sandy bluff over-looking a wide, empty beach and the deserted lake. The trail worked its way down to the water, but we stayed put on the bluff, enjoying the view from its modest height. In the glinting sunset the curve at the bottom of the lake holding Gary and Chicago was invisible, wiped out by the diffuse, gauzy light. We could have been standing at the edge of the Pacific Ocean, the horizon seemed so completely wide open, so limitless. The sand absorbed the sound of our footsteps pacing the hill, sucking the sound into the depths of the earth. The quiet was eerie; these dunes were a strange place, a sacred place, hidden in the middle of the country, not the self-conscious coast, not the overreaching mountains, but a more modest, earthbound, secret environment. From this spot the lake, usually an awkward and inexplicable presence, was like an eye in the middle of the great continent, a floating mirror in the vanity of the face of the earth in which the sky studied its reflection. I was awed by its subtle, natural wonder.

We ate dinner at a diner in town. I was exhausted and bored; I hardly talked and paid little attention to Jane and Michael's chatter. Now that the day was drawing to a close I remembered how it had begun, with Dennis's knock on my door, and I wondered where he was now. Was he angry at me? Did he hate me? I couldn't decide whether I hated him, whether I ever wanted to see him again. I felt so strange, divided in this place with Michael and Jane, like two people leading two separate lives, in two places at the same time, unsure which place I would rather be, not wanting to be anywhere at all.

I sat next to Jane in the booth, Michael across from us, and she punctuated her conversation by every now and then putting a hand on my knee or shoulder, leaning closer to me

for emphasis of a particular word or phrase even as she kept
a steady gaze on Michael, as if my physical presence was the
backboard off which she fired the volleys of shots in her verbal
one-on-one with him. I did not have to follow their conversation much or participate; I was an intrinsic part of the
electricity flowing between them, transmitting the current
back and forth. I was happy in this role, happy to do nothing
in particular, to just be there, to be their silent reflection.

Back at the house we negotiated sleeping arrangements.
There was only one bed and I offered to sleep on the sofa,
but Michael insisted otherwise.

"You take the bed with Jane." He flung himself onto the
sofa as he spoke, draped one leg over its back, folded his
hands behind his head. "I don't mind, really."

"I'll be gentle with you, I promise." Jane looked kittenish.
I was afraid she would be.

"Don't do anything I wouldn't, Tommy," Michael warned.

"That's generous," I answered, remembering how strictly
he adhered to a "try anything once" philosophy. I was confused by Michael's surrendering his place in the bed. I was
convinced of his desire for me, and while relieved at not
having to share the bed with him, I was also worried by his
so easily relinquishing that privilege. I suspected some ul-
terior motive was at work in these machinations but had no
idea what it could be. When Jane and I had climbed into the
bed and sat reading, Michael, unable to restrain himself, did
come in and insist on kissing us each good night. Me he
pecked politely on the cheek, then tucked the covers around
my bare shoulders. Jane he kissed more brazenly on the lips,
at the same time slipping a hand down the front of her nightgown. I watched them, and suspected I would never understand their relationship.

Jane extinguished the lights and the room was dark, darker
than my room in Blackstone Hall or Dennis's room at the

Hotel Madison, where the residual urban light never quite left us. Here the windows were black glass letting on to blacker darkness, the night thick all around, more insistent and real and inescapable. I lay still, with my eyes open, afraid of this unfamiliar darkness. Jane burrowed next to me under the covers, her legs warm and smooth against my own, her back turned, arched against my side.

"Jane." I poked a finger between her shoulder blades. I doubted I would ever sleep again, I felt so afraid of the darkness, but even as I tapped her again, this time on the shoulder, my vision began to adjust to the blackness, the formless room began to assume a vaguely comprehensible shape, and when Jane turned to face me, her features were visible, faint valleys of purple shadow, and I felt less alone, less afraid, happy to be with her. We kissed, slowly, wetly, our bodies barely touching, the bed full of her physical warmth, and in another moment we were sleeping, Jane crouched next to me on the bed; I held my arms around her, grasped her blindly, clinging to her in my frail sleep like a tired rock climber who rests near the top of his personal cliff before finally pulling himself over the ledge to the safety of morning, a new day, its rejuvenating, hopeful light.

When I awoke Michael was sitting next to me on the bed in his short pajamas, a mug of coffee cupped in his palms, his legs bare below the knees. Jane returned from the kitchen with two more steaming mugs, handed me one, and climbed back into the bed, sandwiching me between them. Michael knocked on the wooden nightstand and opened his eyes wide.

"Good morning, Thomas," Michael shouted into my ear, impatient with my sleepiness, as if he had been sitting there all morning like a child anxious to play, waiting for me to finally open my eyes, suspecting that I was only feigning sleep to avoid my responsibilities toward him.

"What do we do today?" I yawned. They both looked at me, amused at my obvious idiocy.

"We go to the beach." Jane had a faint coffee mustache on her upper lip; she licked it clean with a sweep of her tongue.

"People don't actually swim in the lake, do they?" With the steel mills almost visible in the distance, I didn't find the prospect of a dip in Lake Michigan very inviting. "Isn't the water filthy?"

"You'll survive," Michael answered, his voice weary and prophetic. While I washed and dressed, Michael fixed breakfast, and afterward we headed off through the dunes to the beach. There was not a cloud in the sky and the sand burned underfoot. The lake when it finally came into view was a sheet of white sails, the beach a patchwork quilt of families and couples and groups of friends spread across its arcing breadth. The secret power and beauty of the place, which had been so obvious in the desolation of the previous night's sunset, was only a memory; now it was just another crowded beach on the first really hot weekend of the year.

We cautiously descended the bluff, Michael first with a bundle of beach blankets and towels, Jane next with an absurd quantity of sunscreens and baby oils and lotions, myself last with a paper bag full of sodas and fruit and potato chips. Michael chose a spot only a few yards up the shore and spread the two blankets out over the rough sand, and before he had smoothed out the wrinkled edges Jane sat down and pulled a two-liter plastic bottle she had filled with tap water from her shoulder bag and began stintingly rinsing herself with it.

"Jane." I stood over her. "Are you insane?"

"Why? What's the matter?" She poured capfuls of water over her legs and shoulders, ran a wet hand under her knees.

"I can't believe you brought a bottle of water to Lake Michigan. It's the height of redundancy."

"This is tap water, Thomas." She pointed with her wet hand at the pale, blue-green, pacific ocean before us: "That's lakewater."

"Right," I answered. What her point was I don't know, but I gave up trying to understand when Michael looked at me, arching his eyebrows to signify that I was wasting my time.

We settled into the hot sun, the white noise of the water splashing and children playing a filter which ensured us our privacy in this very public space. I lay on my stomach, eyes closed, the sun burning my back. I squinted at Jane, who lay next to me, also on her stomach; she had slipped the straps of her bra top off her shoulders, and her breasts spread out in the waves of the blanket beneath her. Michael lay hunched over a book, his body propped up on his elbows, a towel hooded over his head for shade. I dozed, occasionally sitting up to serve duty by pouring additional capfuls of water on the hard-to-reach spots of Jane's back, who regularly rotated from front to back and side to side next to me like a human rotisserie, basting herself in the sun's heat, anxious to ensure an even, crispy, golden skin.

My head began to ache from the rising temperature, but Michael and Jane were unfazed and I passed alone through the crowded beach to cool off my toes in the lake. I skirted along its edge, the water biting cold; the muddy sand stuck to my feet and produced a clammy, sucking noise when my toes left the ground. I was tempted to plunge headlong into the depths, but instead wet my hands and raced back to Michael and Jane, baptizing them with the spray from my fingertips. Jane shrieked, rose, chased me in anger back to the water's edge, where we splashed each other like a pair of cowards, equally terrified of the cold water, determined to evade the humiliation of a good dunking while furiously working to douse the other. Michael surprised us from behind and dragged us both down into the water then. Now we were underwater, still grabbing at each other, weaving above and below the surface like a family of cetaceous mammals at play.

"You beast!" Jane turned on Michael, who had accidentally loosened her bra in a moment of rough play. She stood waist level in the water, straightening her top, then lurched at Michael, tugging at his trunks, just managing to expose the bare flesh at the bottom of his spine before he pulled himself free into deeper water, when she set her sights on me and I too fled in panic away from the shore. We crawled to a safe distance from Jane, where we treaded water, daring her to come after us; she remained standing in the shallower depth and refused to walk out any farther once her stomach had sunk below sea level. Instead, she slapped her arms in circles toward us, sending up a flurry of white foam and spray.

"I hate you," she cried, like a little girl in a tantrum. We laughed and approached her, letting her splash us as much as she liked, until she was laughing, bouncing in and out of the water, and we stood in a triangle happily sending up a dome of water, the diffuse spray enclosing us in a rainbow of light.

"Three in one," Michael shouted.

"One in three," I added.

"Love without lust; lust without love," Jane completed our mantra.

We collapsed into the surf, the water washing over us, our bodies speckled with sand. Jane and Michael shook themselves clean, rinsed the sand from their hair and the back of their legs, and pleading exhaustion rose to return to the blankets and the sweltering sun. I stayed put, my body numb and comfortable in the frigid water, and played in the sand. I dug holes and watched fascinated as the water seeped in from below and drowned my handiwork. In the wet sand higher up, safe from the destructive force of the lake, I buried my feet, then wiggled them free, the packed sand cracking and

heaving, opening like a fault in an earthquake; I shook my
toes from their damp grave, rinsed them off, and surveyed
the beach.

A crowd of bathers had formed to the south, at the water's
edge, past the lifeguard's high white lookout, and a woman
was running toward them from the base of the bluff, her limbs
streaking jagged shadows. Others raced after her, the whole
beach seeming oriented, like needles around a magnet, in
her direction as she neared the tightening circle in the distance. I skipped toward the bustling scene, frightened but
excited and full of nervous energy, half hoping to witness the
spectacle of some disaster, half ashamed of my morbid ex-
pectations. A group of teenagers splayed out on folding beach
chairs guzzled beer and squinted with glazed eyes at the sky,
oblivious to the unfolding tragedy; rock music blared from a
radio at their feet. A young woman clutched her knees to her
bosom and watched, her boyfriend asleep next to her. The
beach was full of noise, kids calling from the bluff, transistor
radios blasting, a skywriter overhead advertising a local car
dealership, but the noise was empty, hollow.

I stopped at the edge of the ring which had formed; standing
on tiptoe I could make out the figure of a young girl, ten or
twelve years old, in a bright yellow bikini, lying on her back,
her limp feet just free of the creeping tide, her face obscured
by the back of the lifeguard hunched over her desperately
fighting to breathe life into her water-logged lungs. The mother
crouched on the girl's far side, her features obscured by the
hair falling over her face, her hands digging the sand beside
the girl's flat stomach, her own stomach heaving hard with
nervous life, as if attempting to breathe for both of them. A
Frisbee flew overhead, landed in the water, and a teenage
boy ran after it, unaware until he had rushed into the surf of
the little girl lying dead at the center of the fanned-out crowd,

when he grabbed his Frisbee and stood with it watching in the shallow depths.

The lifeguard continued to thump on the girl's chest, hoping to spark a heartbeat, but the crowd began to sense the futility of his efforts and grew restless. The boy threw his Frisbee back in the air and resumed his game, the lifeless girl's presence like the shadow of a cloud one notices momentarily on a hillside while driving on the highway before returning again to the yellow and white lines stretching ahead. The crowd began to thin and my own gaze also wandered, the reaction of the surrounding people now the event of the moment.

Michael and Jane stood at a higher distance, watching me watch, waiting for me to bring them the bad news. I approached them.

"What happened?" Michael held a cupped hand over his brow.

"Some girl drowned." An ambulance had appeared at the far end of the beach, and the girl was borne away on a stretcher, a trail of stragglers following in her wake like the flapping tail of a Chinese kite.

"Let's get out of here." Michael shook his head disapprovingly, as if the girl's drowning in our presence had been an act of shocking bad taste. Jane remained silent, her burnished features beginning to glow from the sun she had so greedily absorbed, a vacant look in her eyes. "It's bad luck," Michael continued, and grabbing Jane by the hand, he hurried us back to the blankets, admonishing us to gather our things together, nervously snapping the blankets and towels in the air, angering an elderly man nearby when the sand blew in his face.

Briskly we climbed the bluff and followed the trail back to the cabin, not speaking, the breeze from behind pushing us along, whispering in our ears, "Quick, quick, quick," with no purpose specified beyond the release of restless energy our hastening entailed. Within an hour we had reached the Interstate and were headed back to Hyde Park.

The drive was fast and silent, and by the time Michael had parked once more by the gate to his house the whole episode had become like a shared nightmare from which we had woken together, frightened and disoriented, desperate to reclaim our sense of reality, of normalcy, to acknowledge the unreality of what had happened, its meaninglessness to ourselves.

Michael's apartment was hot, baking like an oven in the late-afternoon heat; we threw open the windows and lay down together on his narrow brass bed. A rotary fan hummed on the dresser, and the lazy Sunday traffic was just audible on Fifty-fifth Street, a freight train plowing its way through on the Illinois Central tracks like the roll of distant thunder.

"I hate the dunes," Michael said, breaking our silence, his loud voice a shock in the overexpectant, heavy Sabbatarian pall of the closing day. He lay in the middle of the bed, one hand over his head clutching the brass railing.

"They're beautiful," I countered, remembering the strange mirror of the lake in the sunset.

"Don't be fooled, Tommy. Beauty is nothing but a veil for death and destruction." Michael's voice lowered and cracked, but his face was set like stone in a passive expression, revealing no emotion, instead full of a curious, deeply meaningful absence of feeling.

"It's not true," Jane whispered. She kicked off her shoes and raised her legs in the air, hugged her bare knees to her stomach. "It's such a masculine point of view. You think too much with your dick."

"How do you think I got to be such a genius?" Michael grabbed at his crotch, flattened her legs, and rolled on top of her.

"Careful"—I giggled—"the man's brilliance is formidable."

"You watch out for yourself." Michael turned to me, pulled me under him next to Jane, straddled both of us with his spread legs, mounding the three of us together in the middle of the bed. I let him kiss me, the object of his pent-up desire, allowed the first real sexual spark to almost ignite between us, Jane's hands and Michael's combined in a confusing tangle of hair and lips, the tension building to a dizzy frenzy, until, my lips somehow having found Jane's, I landed with a dull thud on the floor, accidentally pushed from the bed. Laughing in exasperation, Michael exclaimed, "This will never work."

"If at first you don't succeed," Jane suggested.

"Maybe later," I put her off; the spell broken, I was painfully aware of my awkward position in this triangle, unsure exactly what, or for that matter whom, I wanted. "I'm too tired right now for group sex." I lay down again, my back to Michael, and closed my eyes; I prayed for sleep, and Michael and Jane beside me likewise each lay still and quiet. The elm tree in the yard cast a long shadow across the room, embracing us in its shade, urging us to rest, rocking faintly, soothingly, in the breeze until I fell into a floating, trancelike sleep.

When I awoke it was almost dark and I was alone. I found Michael and Jane sitting downstairs on the back porch, sharing a bottle of beer, pouring it into two tall glasses. Jane drank from hers and passed it along, encouraging me to drink up.

"Sleep well?" Jane dotingly asked, a hint of maternal concern in her voice.

"Strange, I felt so tired." I felt groggy and my limbs ached. "You look beautiful."

"Me?" Jane looked at herself; her legs and arms were faintly tinted bronze, but her face was the color of fired clay.

"It's true." Michael was as pale as ever, as if his skin were krypton and magnetically resisted all the transfiguring qualities of its exposure to the sun.

"So what do we do for dinner?" I was starving. "The weekend's not over yet, right?" Whether at the dunes or here in Michael's back yard, Jane had hauled me off to be with them for the weekend, and I had no desire to return to my dreary room, full of memories of Dennis, any sooner than necessary. I was terrified of eventually having to go home, of having to leave the charmed circle of their company, of having in parting to acknowledge the larger farewell that was always somehow present, tangible in our conversation.

Arm in arm we walked in the twilight to Giordano's at Fifty-third and Blackstone, the long string of arc lights on Fifty-fifth Street flickering on as we passed, casting the boulevard in a dusty yellow light. We reached the pizza parlor; I held the door for Michael and Jane and followed them in, only to observe Michael make a beeline for a table near the front window where Matthew the weatherman sat eating alone.

"How's the weather in Pittsburgh?" I could hear Michael ask with a straight face.

"Hot and humid." Matthew looked up, rather homely and unfamiliar-looking, his complexion pasty, eyebrows dark and heavy over black eyes, nose wide and unhealthily red; only his lips, smooth, convex, delicately tucked in at the corners, suggestive of what had seemed to me his limitless erotic potential.

"May we join you?" Michael was clearly in a naughty mood, determined to torment me with the misunderstanding that existed between us of my misdeeds; Matthew meanwhile, as I looked at him, began to grow more familiar, the color seeming to return to his cheeks as I recalled what about him I had

first found so attractive: the sturdy curve of his brown neck,
the pendants of his fleshy earlobes, the compact slope of his
shoulders, followed by the physical memory of the touch of
his oily flesh, his acrid-sweet smell, and I was lost, swimming
in the nostalgia of the selflessness I had found in his company,
wishing Michael and Jane away, longing pathetically, hopelessly, to return to the mysterious place Matthew had unwit-
tingly shown me, fighting hard a losing battle to remind myself
that what I wished for was unreality.

"If you like," Matthew assented, and Michael quickly
pulled me down into the seat next to him, directing Jane to
a place next to Matthew across from us. Michael lost no time
in casually draping a long arm around the back of my chair;
he leaned his shoulder close against my own, clearly defining
for me the object of his game, building on the misperception
that Matthew was nothing to me the idea that his own stature
and meaning were therefore somehow substantially increased,
almost as if he thought he was doing me a favor, protecting
me from my folly. I sat there frustrated and painfully watched
Matthew ignore me while Michael pretended to be my lover.

"Weirdly hot weekend, eh, Matthew?" Jane too had joined
the game, winked at Michael to suggest the possibility of a
double entendre.

"A low front from the South; very unusual before Memorial
Day weekend." Matthew was serious; I realized he could talk
for hours about the weather, and I found nothing funny in
Jane and Michael's questioning.

A waiter brought Matthew's dinner, and refreshed with his
plate before him, he also took up the game.

"You two look mighty cozy." He surveyed Michael and
me, lumping us together in his vision.

"We just returned from a simple weekend in the dunes.
Blissful." Michael made eyes at me.

"Don't believe a word of it." I recognized the futility of my protest even as I uttered it; whatever Matthew had possibly meant to me, he was now forever lost.

"Sounds heavenly, I think." Matthew looked at me puzzled, confused by my denial but unwilling or incapable of seriously doubting Michael.

"Don't you know?" Jane practically snickered, a flicker of cruelty lingering in the shrill top notes of her voice.

"All too well." I rescued Matthew with my words; he was too slow and uncertain, not sure what to make of our banter. I was now thoroughly sick of the game, Matthew grown repulsive to me in the mean light which Jane and Michael relentlessly cast on him, while they had not themselves become any more attractive in proportion; only I was more inextricably tied to them, dependent, needy, vulnerable.

We muddled through the rest of the meal. Matthew excused himself when Michael ordered a third round of beers, and our own conversation descended in Matthew's absence into drunken incoherence: we had finally run out of things to say. Back at Michael's, Jane lost no time in removing her clothes and climbing into his bed, urging us both to join her. I was tipsy and exhausted, ready at last to go home. I grabbed my bag from the front hall and announced my intention of leaving.

"You can't leave now, Thomas. The weekend's not over yet, remember?" Jane spoke in her sleep, the words an unconvincing chant, as much intended to reassure herself as to persuade me to stay.

"Good night." I leaned over and kissed her. She was almost asleep, her clothes heaped on a chair, a pink-and-white sock poking out from the bottom of a pants leg.

"I'll walk you home." Michael turned out the hall light and followed me down the stairs. We passed through the playground at Dorchester and Fifty-seventh Street, stopped to sway on the swings. Michael tucked his legs under the seat,

pulled back hard, then sailed forward, legs fully extended.
He repeated the process until he was swinging fast and furious. The triangle of steel tubing above us jumped from the
force of his weight, and Michael lifted forward out of his seat
for a brief second, as if he could almost fly off into the night,
before reversing direction and swinging back to earth.

"Faster, Thomas, faster," he urged me on; my feet trailed
reluctantly on the ground, my body refusing to adopt an aero-
dynamically efficient technique. I pushed the swing back hard
and pumped my legs with the pull of gravity, climbed higher
and higher, my stomach fluttering, an irrepressible giggle of
lightness tickling my lungs, until I had almost matched Michael's pace and we were swinging in tandem, the half-moon
flickering in the sky like a strobe light between the scissoring
trajectories of our unfurled legs.

In an unsuspecting instant Michael had launched himself;
he was airborne, sailing forward, a shadow in the night blurring past the shaded foliage of an oak tree, landing without
a sound beneath its canopy. I stomped my feet on the ground,
kicking up a swirl of dirt, jerking the swing hard in a full
stop, and ran toward Michael's hunched figure. He was standing when I reached him, brushing the seat of his pants clean.

"God, you scared me." I had stopped breathing from fright.
"Are you okay?"

"Good, good," he answered. Michael continued to scrape
himself free of dirt. "I thought I could touch the moon." We
emerged from beneath the tree and continued the short walk
to Blackstone Hall, Michael shrugging off his dramatic leap,
his expression calm as if nothing had happened, only a wild
light emanating from his eyes indicating that something had
changed within him, as if he had seen a vision or been struck
by lightning. He startled me again when we reached the front
pavement and he offered to see me to my room.

"Are you feeling all right?" I worried that the impact of his fall had possibly addled his brain; perhaps he had suffered a mild concussion and didn't know it.

"Fine." Michael leaned on the elevator button, stabbed at it while we waited for the elevator's descent. At the threshold to my room he whistled. I unlocked the door, switched on the light, and Michael stepped in after me, looking over his shoulder as he did so as if for ghosts, but evidently none was present, because he let the door slam shut and fell into the seat Jane had occupied just over a day before, smiling at me unafraid, just as she had done.

"Hasn't changed much." He looked at himself in the mirror over my bed. "Still as depressing as ever."

"Pretty bad, yes?" Seated at my desk Michael was complete unto himself; he filled the room with nothing more than the volume of his physical presence, which in itself seemed perfectly conserved. He stood to say goodbye, and after he had kissed me dryly on the lips and slipped out, almost as if through the cracks around the door, he was completely gone, not the tiniest iota of a trace of his being left behind, creating in his parting a vacuum which also removed with it all trace of Dennis's or Jane's presence, leaving the room empty and barren, and me frighteningly alone.

"It's just so Victorian." Mark sat cross-legged in the middle of a green campus lawn on the following Wednesday afternoon, sucking in hard the smoke from a joint after making this pronouncement, then passed the sticky yellow cigarette to Chris, who drew an equally long puff of the crackling smoke.

"What, illness?" Melinda, returned to Hyde Park as suddenly as she had disappeared, refused the joint and passed it along to me. I eked out a final draw from the crumpled remains, more paper than marijuana. White clouds floated lazily overhead, cutouts against the shifting background of the blue sky. A stream of foot traffic crisscrossed the lawn, fencing us in, and beyond were the bleached limestone walls of the university, marking the outer limits of our academic prison.

"I agree with Mark." Chris nodded slowly, her eyes bloodshot. "Nobody dies anymore. It's such an old-fashioned thing to do. Especially if you're young."

"No one's having sex anymore, either," I said. "No one I know, anyway."

"That's because men are like dogs." Mark sounded mildly titillated. "When the urge strikes, we'll do it with anything."

"Which about explains the extent of my sex life." I pretended world-weariness and desperation, and winked at Melinda.

"For once Mark and I are in agreement." Melinda spread her legs, stretched them out on the grass. "Sex is like going to the bathroom for most men. They just unzip their fly and do it. Ugh." She looked disgusted, pretended to gag on her index and middle finger.

"Please, spare me the lecture on female sexual superiority. I've heard it before." Mark looked down at his fly.

"I just think penises are so ridiculous." Melinda giggled. "I mean, how can you think straight with one of those things?"

"The question is moot." Chris stretched her arms above her head, flapped her stoned eyelids. "I think we're all pretty satisfied with the segregation of the sexes."

"Yes." Mark snapped his fingers, waved at a figure on the edge of the lawn. Jane emerged from the flowing crowd on the pavement, stepped over a low black metal link chain, and approached.

"Did someone die?" She towered over us, sunglasses

drooped on the bridge of her nose. "What's eating you all?"

"The usual." Melinda lay flat on her back, bits of cut grass in her hair.

"Another miserable Hyde Park summer about to begin." They all groaned together in response to Mark's complaint, like a flock of lazy birds bemoaning their necessary flight north.

"Not me." I had been keeping my summer plans secret.

"Don't tell me." Jane cupped a hand around her chin, an index finger pointed along the ridge of her cheekbone, lips pursed in a false effort of concentration. "Cape Cod? Vermont?" Jane amused herself with her disdain for the Northeast.

"New York City," I said, my voice hoarse, my revelation greeted with a round of gasps and finger wagging.

"Why don't you walk me to Harold's and tell me all about it?" Jane remained standing, waiting for me to take up her offer; she looked rather alone and out of place, hovering sober above our stoned circle. I stood, wobbling uncertain on my feet, the breeze like water flowing over me, and we walked away together.

Jane babbled as we moved away from the campus through the neighborhood, tracing the path she and Michael had first introduced me to so many long, dark months before. I floated by her side, lightheaded, caught in the delicate bubble of her aura, dragged along in the wake of its invisible presence, hearing her words but not understanding them, everything she said sounding odd and incomprehensible, as if her soul was communicating directly with mine, only in a foreign language; I felt so close to her and yet so startled, frightened even by her indivisibility, she seemed so weirdly perfect.

By the time we reached Harold's I was more myself again, more conscious of my silently clinging to her coattails, like a lumbering ship, Jane the tugboat pulling me into harbor. I

wondered at her willingness to drag me along, her seeming
to even enjoy it. She pushed her glasses up over her forehead
and pulled me into the storefront.

"Chicken sandwich?" Jane raised a brow at me, leaned
against the filthy glass, waited for me to nod yes before placing
the order. Her figure burnished strikingly against the glow of
the orange Formica counter and the grease-stained mirrors
in the slanting sunlight. She stood with one knee tucked
behind the other, a small foot lifted almost off the ground,
her palms locked to her sides in the curves where her stomach
turned a shallow S into her narrow hips, the frayed ends of
her hair draping her shoulders. I had never before noticed
how very beautiful she was, how desirable, and felt strangely
privileged to be in her company, as if she had singled me
out for some special distinction, as if the honor of her choice
and the accomplishment it implied were obvious to anyone
who happened to see us together.

We carried the sandwiches around the corner to Jane's
apartment, where we sat on the brown sofa, the soggy paper
plates separating us, and talked between sips of beer.

"So what are you going to do in New York?" Jane sat tilted
atop her bent legs, leaning forward into her chicken.

"My father got me a job for the summer, working for an
architect friend of his." My mouth burned from the hot sauce;
I juggled the bites of french fries, dark meat, and Wonder
bread, washed it all away with the warm beer.

"Oh." Jane moved her plate to the coffee table, sat up
straight, and pulled off her socks, wiggled her toes and
stretched her legs. She looked me in the eye, then lifted a
french fry to her mouth. "What will you do without me all
summer long?"

"I'll manage." I had not considered how I would feel upon
leaving my new life in Hyde Park, but Jane's words, intended
perhaps as sarcasm, admitted a sad truth—that as much as

we had shared together, we were not necessary to each other, as she and Michael were. Would we ever reach that stage? Did I ever want to? This realization made her immediate presence all the more desirable, created within me an urgent need to maximize what few precious minutes I had left to spend alone with her, and heightened the erotic tension that always existed between us.

Jane's apartment was cool, gray, and empty, the din of the city a distant echo in the back alley, a radio audible through the open window of an apartment across the way. A porch door slammed shut, the tinsel chandelier overhead tinkled faintly. I pushed my plate aside, and rapidly descending from the high plateau I had been coasting on, terrified of a false landing, the walls pressing in around me, anxiety and terror pulling me down, threatening to break all my ribs and bash my head and spill my brains in my lap, I moved closer to Jane, clung to her in a panic, her bosom cushioning the blow, rescuing me from the brink of certain death, my arms somehow wrapped around her waist, my cheek pushed hard against her breast. I was shaking, almost in tears, and completely mystified by my behavior, although Jane seemed to take it in stride, as if she had been expecting me to clutch her like this, had secretly anticipated and planned for this moment. She pressed the back of one hand against my brow, a nurse taking my temperature, and rubbed circles in the small of my back with the other.

"Poor Thomas," she cooed in my ear, lifting my face to hers, guiding my lips to meet her own in a fragile, lingering kiss. We fell back on the sofa, the flimsy brown cushion slipping beneath us, Jane beside me, arms wrapped around my cold, trembling body, and continued kissing, the woof thread of our tongues weaving back and forth, my bent knee clamped in the vise of her legs, locking her against me. Jane sat up and pushed me away, laughing.

"What's the matter?" I had no idea what I was doing, what
I was supposed to do next; I was stranded, waiting to follow
her lead.

"Whew," Jane exhaled, blowing out the fire which had
kindled between us. "What was that all about?"

"Don't you know?" I had thought I was ready to trust her
completely; the idea that she was as purposeless and impul-
sive as I was was deeply disturbing. Could I trust anyone?

"I was speaking rhetorically." She pushed the cushion back
into place, sat up straight. "I'm not a virgin, Thomas."

"Evidently." I sat up, recovering my balance; the room
returned to its normal proportions, the walls still plumb, my
feet flat on the hardwood floor. "Overcome by the heat of the
moment, I guess."

"It was worth a try." Jane had already, definitively, decided
against any renewed attempt at lovemaking.

"Should I have tried harder?" The situation was becoming
ridiculous, although I had to fight to see the humor in her
rejecting me.

"We don't need this." Jane thought for a moment. "Let's
just pretend the whole thing never happened."

"What would Michael say?" The thought sprang like a
lurking beast from the back of my mind, effectively damping
any smoldering remnants of desire, all the explanation necessary to justify the halting of our dangerous experiment.

"He already knows." Jane uttered the simple truth of our
triangle, encapsulating the dilemma of Michael's wanting me,
my wanting Jane, and Jane wanting me for Michael.

Jane stood and piled our bones together, rolled them in
the stacked plates and packed them tightly in a paper bag,
our lunch condensed, like the hulk of a burnt-out car in a
junkyard, into a compact brown bundle, our conversation
officially ended with her tossing the crumpled mess underhand into the kitchen garbage can. A glass wall had de-

scended between us; I had my nose and cheek pressed, deformed, against this surface, fighting to break through, to reach Jane in the flesh, and my words were nothing but hot air condensing on the invisible plane which separated us, only helping to further obscure the view. I could scratch my name in the mist, write backward with a fingernail a secret message for her to read, but by the time I might have gotten her to attend to my attempts at communication, the words would have long since evaporated, and she would only look at me exasperated and bored by my inexplicable persistence. I was desperate to escape Jane's presence without somehow contributing even further to the miserable complexity of my failure; only the awareness of my excessive self-consciousness kept me from fleeing in a wordless panic, I felt the need for such immediate relief. Instead, I stood grief-stricken and incoherent by the back porch door, as if waiting beside an empty grave in horrified anticipation to discover who had died, worried most of all that it might have been myself. Jane seemed unaware of my mental suffering.

"Goodbye, Thomas." She held the door open. I stepped through, refusing to believe the miracle of our so easily parting, Jane more a stranger to me now than the day I first met her. Walking through the alley I thought of the weekend just past, the little girl lying drowned on the beach, her helpless mother beside her, the crowd rapidly losing interest in the tragedy, searching for a new diversion. Had I been nothing more than just another face in the crowd?

I exited the alley from the wrong end and accidentally began walking north on Blackstone, only realizing my mistake when I reached the corner of Fifty-second Street, by which time I didn't care, was glad after all to be entering new territory, the unfamiliar neighborhood called Kenwood. The square brick apartment houses continued along Fifty-first Street, but behind them were hidden ambitious brick and timber mansions on surprisingly narrow plots, most separated from each other only by a thick hedge or a low garden wall, their short driveways generally ending in an iron gate at the edge of the weedy sidewalk. There was something sad about these white elephants, the way they turned their handsome faces away from the charred landscape of the surrounding ghetto, looked inward to the sanctuary of their few square blocks and the dignity of having once been the city's most fashionable if short-lived address.

I walked west past the vacant lots on Forty-seventh Street, turned on Ellis, and emerged again into a thicket of massive houses, Gothic, Queen Anne, Romanesque, châteauesque, prairie style, nestling shoulder to shoulder in the quiet shade of the street. One boarded-up gray brick building stood out against the rest, the fine, subtle detail of its brickwork, its square columns and long, flat roofline daring examples of what was once the new architecture. Through the cracked wooden fence I could make out the sweep of the terrace cutting into the overgrown lawn. I imagined this house full of people, full of rich, outrageous, optimistic life, the ballroom readied for dancing, hothouse palms blooming in the central atrium, family and guests lingering over their games before rushing up to dress for dinner. A dirty plaque declared the crumbling monster the brief home of one of the city's most prominent merchants, owner of a long-since-forgotten department store, the family moved on to the higher pursuits of politics and banking. I wondered how so much life could have passed so quickly.

I headed home, down Woodlawn Avenue, past the Sullivan house Michael had pointed out to me, shamefully dirty and neglected but not so lonely-looking as I remembered it now that I was familiar with its grander neighbors just up the street. I felt surrounded by a secret life, witness to the failure of an insane and glorious empire, as if I were alone in the

Persian desert before a weathered, dusty gate to nowhere, the sole relic of an extinct civilization, and not walking through Hyde Park, dodging the traffic on Fifty-third Street, tracing the lonely, familiar route to my room in Blackstone Hall. I imagined Jane alone in her empty apartment with nothing more to say to me. I thought of retracing my steps, of hiding in her courtyard and spying, convinced she was even now somehow betraying me, laughing at me, making fun of my having wanted her, pleased with herself and glad to be rid of me. I thought about Jane between passages while reading in bed that night, and fell asleep with the wretched, absolute conviction that she hated me and never wanted to see me again.

I awoke the next morning thinking of Dennis, missing him, glad that Thursday had arrived so quickly, the humiliation I felt at our last encounter transformed by the intervening days into grateful appreciation of his wanting me. My classes that day were slow torture, lunch a beastly penance for my over-eager desire. I arrived downtown early; the rush-hour traffic on the Drive had just begun to build to its mad climax and the lake was covered with boats, the sailors taking full advantage of the newly long day. I exited the bus across from the Fine Arts building and walked a block over to State Street and Marshall Field's. I wandered through the endless maze of cosmetics counters, past a host of salesgirls spritzing perfume and offering the usual incentives to purchase; I found the Frango mints. I bought a one-pound box, gift-wrapped, and with this bundle tucked under my arm proceeded to my rendezvous at the Hotel Madison. Never before had I brought Dennis anything besides myself. When I bothered to consider the meaning of my purchase I hesitated, worried what message the box of chocolates might convey. Were they simply a peace offering, a declaration of truce after our standoff? Or were they an attempt to add a second layer to our essentially one-dimensional relationship? By the time I had crossed the Chicago River and the neon of the hotel became visible, the chocolates weighed a ton and I was tempted to throw them out as a needless complication of what I still considered a simple arrangement. Instead, I clutched them tighter, the shiny green-and-gold wrapping paper clouded around the edges with the sweat from my palms, and knocked on his door before turning the knob, not waiting for him to signal permission to enter, certain somehow the door was not locked.

Dennis lay asleep on his side, his back turned to me, the windows closed, the room stuffy like the airless trains he inhabited. He did not move when I entered; his diaphragm heaved in slow heavy breaths; his knees were bent, his hands folded together in his crotch. I put a hand on his shoulder, his flesh hot through the thin T-shirt; a dark stain marked the spot where the corner of his parted lips just touched the pillowcase. He grumbled slightly, sucked in his lips, blinked his eyes, and looked up at me, an expression of wonder and pleasure evaporating quickly into a more familiar look of recognition.

"Thomas." He said my name as if remembering it after a long struggle, surprised and pleased by the simple sound of himself speaking the word. I sat down next to him, back straight against the headboard, feet dangling over the edge of the bed, and kicked off my shoes. Dennis wiped his mouth on the pillow, folded it over as a headrest.

"This is for you." I placed the gift-wrapped chocolates in his lap, where he let the box rest before gently lifting and rattling it. He listened to the muffled crinkle of the chocolates, his eyes comically threatening to cross from the effort of concentration.

"What is it?" He held the box flat, rocked it like a seesaw in his open palm, felt the subtle shift in weight.

"Open it and see." I was hungry for a Frango mint, more

agitated with suspense than Dennis, who continued to consider the box, to guess at its contents, and seemed by this postponement of his gratification to enjoy reminding me that I had brought him a gift, had given him something, had affirmed through material purchase my thinking of him, my making a place for him in my mental as well as my sensual life. At last he tore at the striped paper, slipped the dark green box from its prophylactic wrapping, removed the lid, and inhaled the sweet, minty odor of the candy.

"Frango mints?" Dennis had never heard of them. "They smell good."

"Give me one, quick." I grabbed at the box as if my life depended on it, as if I were dying from a quick poison and the minty squares of chocolate were the only known antidote; I popped a whole chocolate into my mouth, chewed it hard, the sweet candy instantly neutralizing the bitter poison in my blood. Dennis gnawed around the edges of a Frango mint, his thumb and index finger smudged with melting chocolate, his front teeth coated with the same.

"Delicious." Dennis slurred the word; he held a chocolate on his tongue, let it slowly melt there, opening his mouth wide to show me. I grabbed three more and greedily chewed them one after another, like a chain smoker who uses each smoldering butt to ignite the next cigarette, careful never to allow the fire to extinguish, the mint flavor rising and falling in crescendos on my taste buds.

"You pig." Dennis pulled the box out of my reach when I grabbed for another handful, desperate to maintain my high. "Get your own," he teased me, setting them down on the night table, reaching his strong free arm around my middle.

"I did," I answered, rolling over on top of him. I slid my legs between his, my arms stretched straight against the bed, as if I were doing push-ups, Dennis beneath me, hands resting on my behind. I looked into his eyes, grayer than I had ever

noticed before; his face was red, the surface of the skin a
complicated, unfamiliar landscape for which no map existed.
I lay on top of him, rising and falling on the force of his
breath, my head resting in the curve of his neck, the lingering
aftertaste of the mints almost gone, and remained there, silent
in his arms, while our shadows faded into the twilight falling
over the room.

The neon flashed. I rose and opened the window, leaned
my head out; beyond the night traffic stopped on Michigan
Avenue I thought I could see the lake, an irregular sliver of
deep blue, a smooth patch completing the jagged urban composition. Dennis had risen, was entering the bathroom when
I pulled my head in; the box of candy remained on the night
table. I stood in the bathroom doorway and watched Dennis
pee, embarrassed by the sight of him drooping over the bowl
in the dead, clinical light, as if waiting my turn in a public
restroom, the sound of water hitting water a rude explosion
echoing off the tiled walls. He caught me watching him and
grinned, glad of my attention, then gave himself an exagger-
ated shake, stretching himself long before tucking away and
flushing.

"You're like an animal." Fascinated, I watched him turn
on the faucet, rinse his elbows in the sink.

"Why? Because I have to piss?" He looked up, his face
wet, hands dripping over the basin.

"It's the way you do it." I met his eyes in the mirror.

"You do it differently?" He faced me now, a towel in his
hands, and I felt ridiculous, like a little boy astounded and
worried by the unfamiliar sight of his naked father.

"With my eyes closed." I put a hand over my eyes, another
at my zipper, and pretended to demonstrate.

"Sounds messy." He rubbed his face in the towel.

"It is." I spied at him through split fingers. He pulled my
hand from my forehead, draped it over his shoulder; inspired,

I jumped onto him, wrapped my legs around his waist, and he carried me into the room, bouncing me on his hips, spinning us toward the bed until, within safe range, he flung me back on the flimsy mattress. I sat up. Dennis stood before me, and I unfastened his pants, slipped in a hand to feel what I had just a moment before deemed repulsive. I held on to him, felt his erection grow in the grip of my fingers, bared the blue-veined, one-eyed creature to the light of the room, returned its monomaniacal stare until Dennis began insistently rocking his hips, impatient for my lips to unseal and the work to proceed, which it finally did.

We spent most of the night in bed, reconstructing in fast-forward a history of all our past relations, the last of the Frango mints disappearing sometime after midnight. I had fallen asleep, for the third time, when Dennis nudged me awake, not, as I expected, with a further itch to scratch, but to complain of a different kind of hunger. He proposed a pre-dawn breakfast, and after groggily dressing, we walked in the pale darkness to a diner on State Street just north of Oak. The restaurant was surprisingly busy, full of young people ending a night on the town, solitary businessmen fortifying themselves for their pursuit of fortune, workers relieved of the night shift. A handful of cheeky, world-weary waitresses, the Atlases of this spinning otherworld, paced through the maze of booths and counters in sensible, rubber-soled shoes, coffee flowing from their ministering pots, full plates settling and empty plates rising from the tabletops in their certain hands, pencils, pulled from bouffant hairdos, hitting notepads as orders were taken and tabs calculated.

I watched Dennis eat his plateful of eggs and potatoes and toast, and only sipped at a cup of coffee myself. I thought of sleep, of returning to the Hotel Madison, of climbing back into bed, Dennis huddled over me, staying there until late the next day, when we would begin all over again. Dennis,

sensing my thoughts, proceeded to shatter my fantasies of
non-stop sex.

"I have to be at work in four hours." This fact seemed to amaze him. "I wish we could just stay in bed for the next three days."

"What for?" As I uttered the word, thinking myself very clever, I had a vague, unsettling memory: wasn't that Jane's joke? Dennis missed the point of my humor, just held my knee under the table as if that were enough in itself to signify the profound depths of his desire.

We paid the check and walked to Michigan Avenue, the sun just risen over the lake, a gauzy spot of undramatic white light in the cloudy sky, the daylight a chemical catalyst causing the osmosis of Chicagoland, the city an empty vessel slowly, almost imperceptibly filling with people from the suburbs commuting toward a state of equilibrium. Dennis did not invite me back to his room; instead, he offered to hail me a cab, but the day now already begun, I deemed the expense a needless luxury. We walked to the corner of Randolph, where he waited with me for the local bus.

"Well." Dennis shrugged, the bus visible, stopped at a traffic light just a few blocks away, our night rapidly coming to an end.

"Thank you, Dennis." Why was I thanking him?

"Goodbye, Thomas." Dennis squeezed me hard and kissed me on the lips. The bus pulled to the curb and he pushed me away, began walking north, not looking back until I had settled into my seat. A black woman at the front of the bus frowned in disapproval at the sight of our parting; Dennis squinted, frustrated, not seeming to see me wave at him. The bus pulled away and I slumped into my seat, sorry I had not taken good, full measure of Dennis standing on the sidewalk, instead half ignoring him, left with a photograph pulled from its developer without fixing and turning fast to black.

I never saw him again. I hadn't consciously intended this to be our final parting; the bus crept forward through the desolate hulk of the South Side, the driver pulling over at Forty-seventh Street and disappearing into a twenty-four-hour grocery, returning a quarter of an hour later with a full brown bag cradled in his arm, a long loaf of white bread poking out the top, while in the seat ahead of me a slender, brown-skinned young man held a compact pistol in his lap and absentmindedly cleaned it, like an old woman with her knitting, soothed by the noise of the cartridge clicking in and out, the feel of chamois cloth slipping over the black metal, twirling around the short barrel, poking through the trigger, and I watched transfixed, barely remembering to jump off the bus at Sixtieth Street by the *Sands of Time* statue, the platter of the Midway glistening with dew, Dennis nothing more than a phantom of my imagination now that I had safely returned to my home universe.

The following Thursday came and went without my rushing north to the Hotel Madison, and only for a faint second, while sitting in a neighborhood bar with Michael and Chris, pouring a second round from a pitcher of beer, did I even think of Dennis, not to miss him, or guiltily remember he was waiting for me, but instead to feel certain, without an ounce of doubt, as if it were broadcast at the top of the news for the whole world to hear, that Dennis was at that same exact moment somewhere else, gone, not waiting for me, not expecting me, not wanting me, as through with me as I felt through with him; had we been living on separate planets we could not have been farther worlds apart, Dennis content to live in his, I existing in uneasy truce in my own.

I have often thought of him since, not to miss him or to regret not knowing him any better, for I knew him as best I could, not to think much about him really at all; rather to ponder the strangeness of not seeing him, of knowing him and then never seeing him again, of passing all the days of my life without a word or a trace, of the absolute finality encapsulated in an ordinary moment on a quiet street corner, only a whisper of the wind off the lake, the hazy gray sky hinting at another prematurely hot summer day, a siren on the Drive like the cry of a baby waking hungry and cold, the traffic lights unfolding in sequence like a royal red carpet down the avenue, no traffic present to stop in respectful attention, only a lonely figure waving in a blur on the pavement, features gray and blank, like the brick and concrete of the empty skyscrapers surrounding, then gone, an extraterrestrial visitor, just passing through, its presence made briefly visible by some unwarranted miracle.

NEW YORK

I had no idea, when I crossed the Williamsburg Bridge for the first time, that I was about to begin a new life. I was sleepwalking, my year in Chicago a dream ended, New York not yet a waking reality, my mere three weeks in the city like the slow dawn of a summer morning, each day begun with a series of false awakenings, the birds chirping outside my window in the little room in the stranger's house where I was staying, urging me to rise, seductively singing of the new day's infinite hope, one strange bird in particular, day after day, at the first break of blue light, throwing himself insistently against the wide pane, terrifying me with the thump of his feathered head repeatedly hitting the glass, then retreating stunned to the rail of the fire escape, where he shook in a frenzy before lifting and swooping at his own reflection again and again, until finally, the mysterious conflation of circumstances which precipitated the bird's self-flagellation dissolving, his matutinal ritual ended and he swooped away through the neighboring garden, leaving me to return to my pillow in a state of dazed concern.

A young architect, perhaps moved to pity by the sight of me hunched over daydreaming in the white plastic cubicle of my work space, invited me to a barbecue for the Fourth of July, and excusing myself as best I could from the invitation my father's college friend and his wife had obligingly extended, I set off for Brooklyn, following the directions my newfound friend had scrupulously written for me in an affected architectural script, blue ink on green-tinted graph paper. I spent at least an hour underground, lost in a fetid tangle of subways, the sick wind blowing through the tunnels like the stultifying harmattan descending from the Sahara, obliterating all vegetation in its dust-laden swirls. I waited for the J train at Canal Street, while an elderly Chinese man brazenly peed on the tracks as it pulled into the station. The subway rolled through the darkness, passed Delancey Street, then raised its head to the New York evening, like a prairie dog scenting the wind for signs of danger before emerging in search of supper, and confident the coast was clear, we climbed onto the bridge.

The sky was streaked with violet rows of clouds, heavenly fallow fields, and through the slanted ironwork of the bridge the Manhattan skyline rose flat and gray and softly rounded at the edges, the stacked tower of the Empire State Building bathed red white and blue, the Brooklyn shore dominated by an enormous sugar factory, D-O-M-I-N-O lit up in huge curving neon against the backdrop of an expanding waste of warehouses. The train remained elevated on the Brooklyn side, where it creaked slowly to a halt at Marcy Avenue, first stop in Brooklyn, my point of departure. I descended to the street and walked west on Broadway, back toward the East River, past an abandoned plaza where two magnificent old bank buildings, the dome of one glowing orange like a Roman basilica, lent an aura of dignity to the otherwise decrepit scene.

I turned north and passed under the bridge at Bedford Avenue, the roadway overhead buckling from the flow of traffic, an eerie thunder signaling the bridge's imminent collapse. The street was overflowing with people. Groups of old men squeezed around card tables playing dominos, surrounded by their friends watching, shirts raised in proud

display over distended beer bellies. Children darted through
the spray of open fire hydrants, cupping their hands over the
valves to wash a bus as it rambled through. Buxom girls in
halter tops swaggered on the corners, taunting boys gathered
swaggering on opposite corners. Skinny men, faces dirty and
heavy-lidded, called out the availability of a dizzying variety
of drugs, one on the corner sweetly whispering "Black Magic"
as I passed, another in the middle of the block barking "Special K," a woman farther along mysteriously, plaintively
crying "Blues, blues." And above it all was the music, me-
rengue and salsa and bossa nova blaring from every open
window, from the bodega at every corner, from the social
clubs and crowds barbecuing on the sidewalk, from the cars
parked two deep on the side of the road, hatchbacks open,
speakers pounding out the deafening sound, no one speaking
a word of English.

I turned again toward the river at Grand Street, the crowds
quickly thinning as I moved away from Bedford Avenue, only
an occasional family gathered on a stoop, a single radio playing for a dozen or more people. I crossed Berry Street. The
neighborhood was transformed into loft buildings and warehouses, silent and barren, and the East River was visible a
few blocks ahead, a violet ribbon separating Manhattan from
the outer reaches of the city. I found my destination, a fea-
tureless industrial building across from a scrap yard, rang a
nameless buzzer, and stood waiting. A trickle of people drifted
past me through the streets toward the water's edge. Tony the
architect appeared in the entry and led me up two flights of
a darkened stairway, through a red steel door, pausing at the
threshold to say, "Welcome to Williamsburg, Thomas."

The loft was long and well lit; an elaborate steel framework
hanging from the tin ceiling ran a complicated display of
fixtures. The floors were painted black, a sloppy trail of white
whimsically laid on top in mockery of an English garden path.

A loose accretion of plywood, plaster, and Sheetrock on rollers sectioned the space, with a painting studio at one end marked by square patches of canvas stapled directly to the walls. A well-equipped kitchen at the other end was full of a dozen or so people wrapping vegetables in aluminum foil, packing Tupperware containers with burgers and hot dogs, preparation for a barbecue on the nearby piers. Tony introduced me.

"Thomas is interning at the office for the summer." Several heads nodded approvingly. "He's from Chicago."

"Worcester, actually," I mumbled, feeling like an idiot, as if anyone cared.

"Second City, Windy City." A tall woman in cut-off jeans and black boots stepped forward, offered me her hand. "Oscar here. Glad to see you, Thomas." Her handshake was firm, her eyes blue, hair dyed black; her whole sturdy frame bespoke strength and self-assurance.

"Oscar?" What had her parents been thinking?

"Barbara, actually. But that's such a sissy name. I prefer something more butch." She laughed, threw her head back, and neighed like a thoroughbred.

"Here you go, Thomas." Tony handed me a tray of marinated zucchini spears, lifted a bag of charcoal, and shouted, "Let's barbecue, folks!" We filed out of the loft, a caravan set to cross the wilderness, crowds of people pouring now through the streets, firecrackers raining from the rooftops. Oscar walked by my side, filling in details about herself and the neighborhood between my polite questions.

"You live nearby?" I was mystified by my surroundings, the noise and drugs and poverty; I doubted whether I belonged here.

"Don't be fooled by appearances." Oscar sensed my hesitancy and doubt. "Williamsburg is actually teeming with white people." We climbed through a hole in a chain-link fence, brown weeds scratching at our ankles, and neared a long network of rotted docks stretched along the shore of the East River. The waterside wasteland was dotted with glowing fires, the river loosely paved with boats gathered for the fireworks. We walked single-file across a flimsy wooden plank to a pitted concrete platform, where Tony began fussing with the barbecue and another man hastily set up bar, handing round jumbo plastic cups full of ice, then a pitcher of some unspecified concoction to follow. Tony soaked the coals in lighter fluid, casually tossed a match at them, and a wave of oohs and aahs rippled through the party as the hissing flame shot to life.

Cherry bombs exploded in the water, the sweet smell of their smoke slowly carried away on the muggy breeze, which seemed to coat my skin with its sticky, invisible presence. A shadow chirruped in the distance, walked the plank, and stood in the light of the diminishing fire by Oscar's side.

"Thomas"—Oscar pointed a big open hand at me, another at the newcomer who had put an arm around her waist— "here's Blythe." She looked at least a foot shorter than Oscar, and squinted at me through her thick black glasses, her cheeks puffed and pale. She wore a cut-off T-shirt, her underarms visibly unshaven, her legs stocky and muscular in the cut-off jeans and high black boots that seemed a prerequisite among this social set.

"Hello." I nodded, felt queasy; the concrete seemed to drift underfoot with the rhythm of the water noisily lapping at its porous sides.

"Cheer up." Blythe pushed her glasses up her nose, pulled a pack of Chesterfield Kings from her shirtfront pocket, and lit a cigarette, gloomily swallowing a cough as she sucked in the smoke, the glow of the ash painting the night air in her trembling fingers.

"I'll try." I laughed, Blythe's anodyne dark humor easing my own painful awkwardness. I bumped my cup against Oscar's and took a long draft of the lemon-salty drink. Tony began laying burgers on the grill, taking orders for degrees of doneness while commissioning me to pass around Chinet plates. A cannon boomed in the distance; its echo seemed to deflect from the wall of skyscrapers across the water back to the Brooklyn side. A puff of smoke floated lazily out in the middle of the river. The first of the fireworks burst into a circle of white light overhead, and a wave of excited applause spread audibly through the throngs pressed all along the waterfront. A figure with a bicycle on the shore carelessly dropped it to the ground and strode over the wooden plank, bounding breathlessly into our midst, limbs swinging in a swirl of unbridled, enthusiastic activity like a Tasmanian devil, a tornado of animal energy, spinning wildly from the force of its inner turmoil, this man coming to a perfect halt by my side at the barbecue, hands raised, ready to receive the plate I offered him, a scoop of potato salad and a handful of pickles following.

Cannons thumped in rapid succession, followed by the muffled whistle of the shooting rockets, a moment of expectant silence preceding each flower's opening, the sky full of the spectacle of strange blossoms, purple, red, green, magnesium white, unfurling in mad, ecstatic urgency, spending themselves in a furious flash of brilliance, their void instantly filled by an even more profuse display. The city was electrified; the whole Manhattan skyline, as if plugged into the glow of the exploding fireworks, radiated a dome of blue light. The Williamsburg Bridge was reflected perfectly in the black water of the East River. A subway stopped in the middle of the span, the crisp silhouette of a lone passenger pressed against a window distinctly visible, the traffic moving across the bridge's outer lane stitched together in the red and white threads of brakelights and headlights.

A final storm of electrical light sliced a hole in the sky,

offering a possible glimpse through to another universe, another life, before an invisible hand pulled the plug and the dull brown night resumed its ordinary urban glow. Thin trails of smoke and ash streaked away in the breeze, the dusty remnants of so much energy rapidly dispersing into the ether. I faced the stranger beside me, followed the trail of his eyes as he lowered his craned neck from the heavens above to the food before him, and raising a hot dog to his open lips gulped down an enormous bite. Oscar slapped him on the back.

"Stuart, where've you been? It seems like ages." Oscar furrowed her brows, squinted at Stuart, as if to suggest a lover's disappointed disapproval. "Not in any trouble, I hope?"

"Working." Stuart chewed away, pushed the pink end of the hot dog into his mouth, licked a drop of mustard from his index finger. "Besides, it's barely been a week since I last saw you."

"Well, it felt like forever." Oscar lowered her eyes and gazed into her cup, then raised them again at Stuart. "You missed Blythe's opening. I can't believe you didn't show up."

"Whoops." Stuart looked vexed, then contrite; or was he just pretending? "I forgot." He shrugged, didn't bother to apologize. I studied his features, eyes green and glinting yellow, ears sticking out the side of his head from short thick black hair, his forehead slightly shiny at the very top. Something in his posture attracted me: his shoulders casually stooped, his figure radiating an aura of languid self-confidence, energy in repose, a coil evenly tensed to spring into action. I could already imagine falling in love with him. Perhaps he read my mind, sensed my quavering presence within his magnetic field, for he turned, as if noticing me for the first time, and brazenly looked me over from head to toe, cocking his head slightly to one side before fixing me with his determined stare.

"So, Oscar, who's your friend? You don't plan on keeping him all to yourself?" Stuart held me with his eyes as he spoke, a look of intense curiosity glimmering through his more steady stance of reasoned interest.

"Of course not." Oscar sighed, shook her head at me in some vague suggestion of warning, sad with the knowledge that I was already hopelessly lost, and made the introductions.

"Thomas." He paused, as if momentarily lost in thought. "I hope you like Brooklyn so far, Thomas." Stuart offered his hand. His fingers were short, brown, thick, and muscular, smudged with paint, nails carefully clipped, cuticles well scrubbed. He nodded his head in rhythm with his handshake, as if in a calculated attempt to bring me under his hypnotic spell, his lips seeming to murmur secret messages directed straight at my spine, where I felt a faint tingle climb its way up and lodge somewhere near the base of my brain, as if I were a bird, tagged by some scientist, who would then have to live the rest of its days in the wilderness with the uncanny recognition that its every move was being followed, its every habit studied, its entire existence involuntarily, irrevocably connected to something greater than itself.

"Yes," I said, a simple affirmative all I could muster; anything else seemed necessarily redundant, even dangerous at this point. The coals had by now reduced to a clean gray ash; Tony stirred them, tossed the glowing remainder into the river, and announced that the party was moving back to his place. Single file we crossed the plank back to the shore. The rotted wood bent ominously underfoot. Stuart retrieved his bicycle and walked between Oscar and Blythe, while I stayed to the side and listened to him offer Blythe his apologies, lightly mocking himself, wheedling his way back into their favor. The streets were full of the crowds receding into the distant neighborhoods. Police cars were parked at every corner. Stray firecrackers and bottle rockets continued to launch unexpectedly from fire escapes and open windows.

We reached Tony's building. Stuart leaned his bike against the brick wall, stretched a hand behind Oscar's back, and grabbed hold of my elbow. I stood beside him, felt the heat of his hand on my arm spread through my body, listened in quiet amazement as he excused us from the assembling party.

"Tom and I are going for a walk." Stuart moved his hand to my shoulder and turned to me, certain of my approval.

"Very well." Oscar shrugged, as if anxious to avoid responsibility for whatever was about to happen. "Don't ever say I didn't warn you."

"Walk slowly." Blythe coughed into her fist. She dropped her smoldering cigarette and smoothed it into the pavement with the thick heel of her boot.

"Yes," I answered, another affirmative the only necessary word. Stuart kept a hand on my shoulder, a pinky riding over the collar of my shirt, just scratching the side of my neck, and balanced his bicycle with his other hand. We turned back toward the river, swam upstream against the still-flowing tide of people, walked in silence until we had reached Wythe Avenue, where Stuart pointed south at the bridge and the high walls of the sugar factory, signaling our turn in that direction. The streets were almost empty here, the music blasting from an occasional car as it passed and the distant thump of a leftover firework solitary reminders of the holiday just celebrated.

We walked in silence to the base of the bridge, the dirty black stone of the Brooklyn pier an enormous, gaping cavern. The concave underside of the roadway curved above us in flattened perspective, the two bell-shaped towers of the bridge squat and compressed; the stringwork of the suspension floated between them like a Cubist guitar, picked apart and put together again all wrong. A prostitute emerged from the shadows, walked beside a slow-moving delivery truck, until a mustachioed figure leaned over, clicked open the passenger door, and the truck gathered speed, turned the corner, and disappeared into the darkness.

"Watch out for the Williamsburg whores; they're nasty." Stuart scratched his sideburn, pulled his ear. We emerged from under the bridge. Stuart raised a hand to my chin, pulled me gently toward him, our vision perfectly level, his lower incisors flashing between slightly parted lips, radiating their own organic light. His lips barely pressed against my own, hovered there like a butterfly delicately sipping nectar, fluttering airily before retreating sated. "Are you up for a big walk?"

"Yes," I answered for the third time.

"Good." Stuart nodded, satisfied. We turned at Broadway and stopped before a green storefront, the windows papered over, where he opened the door and without switching on the lights pushed in his bicycle. We resumed our walk, turning south at Bedford Avenue. The vacant lots, burnt-out buildings, and bodegas transformed at Division Avenue into rows of tidy Jewish storefronts, hand-painted Hebrew lettering on all the signs and in all the windows, metal grates stretched across every possible means of access, an air conditioner in every other of the heavily curtained windows in the apartments above. We passed over the Brooklyn-Queens Expressway, where traffic was backed up even in the middle of the night, and continued along quiet tree-lined streets, every old school and church building clearly converted to the uses of religious education, a Hasidic resident caught now and again scurrying through the neighborhood, his long black gabardine coat, absurd in the oppressively hot city night, trailing behind. Stuart bombarded me with questions.

"Did you have a boyfriend in Chicago?" His voice rose in a suspicious tone.

"Sort of." How could I explain Dennis?

"What do you mean 'sort of'? You don't remember?"

"I mean it was no big deal."

"So he's history?"

"Ask me about something else."

"Okay." He considered for a moment. "Who's your favorite painter? Not including me, that is." We had finally reached the two topics he cared about most, and I was embarrassed to admit my ignorance on both counts.

"You're the only one I know." I watched him scratch the back of his neck. I found him exceedingly beautiful, felt lucky to be in his company. His green eyes darted over me like pinpricks; my stomach felt jittery and tight. The shadow of his beard, the rounded knobs of his bare ankles defined a whole universe of being, an undiscovered planet, and I was a satellite drifting through space, falling into his irresistible gravitational pull, about to settle into predictable orbit.

"I'm glad. I wish that could always be true." I sensed a touch of megalomania in his voice, was lulled by his low murmuring, and imagined a fatal softness at bottom, an unspeakable vulnerability seeming to cushion his words, translate them into a whole other language, a profession of love I never before imagined possible. I puzzled over his character, charmed and mystified. Stuart was older than me and possessed a fund of secret ambition. I had a typically puritanical notion of the artist as hedonist, childishly gratifying his every egoistic whim, oozing animal power and reckless sexual energy, yet Stuart was cool, gathered, intensely in control, a seasoned captain confidently steering the ship of his intellect.

"You make no sense." Perhaps that's what I liked so much about him.

"You're beautiful." No one had ever before said such a thing to me; I stared at him in disbelief, searched his features for a sign of dissembling, untruthfulness. I thought I found something in the vacant flickering of his eyes, a touch of masterly manipulation, but I gave up the search when he pulled me against him, rested his chin on my shoulder, and squeezed me hard, like a child pathetically embracing a missed parent returned from a long journey, only the barest trace of sexual excitation present in his clasping me. Dennis had never held me this way; nor had Michael ever even approached the altar of self-sacrifice and surrender Stuart seemed to climb so effortlessly. I felt on the verge of a great discovery.

"This way." Stuart turned us around, and we walked north up Lee Avenue to the empty plaza where the subway descended from the bridge, then west along Broadway, retracing my steps from earlier in the evening. At Driggs Avenue Stuart led me up a dimly lit promenade, a concrete walkway ascending beneath the train tracks onto the bridge, the roadways inbound and outbound level on either side. We emerged from under the tracks, the DOMINO sign seeming almost within arm's reach. The rusted tangle of the suspension bridge was a vortex impelling us forward; trucks rumbled under us, the bridge swaying from their weight; an empty subway rolled by, blasting its horn as it passed. Stuart seemed unafraid of our dangerous isolation and proceeded instead to the center of the span, where we leaned against the meager railing, the water flowing in the distance beneath us, the tangle of the Lower East Side crouched on the nearby Manhattan shore, the BQE a distant ribbon of traffic on the Brooklyn side.

Stuart folded an arm around my waist, another over my shoulder, averted his eyes from my own before closing them; our lips met, this new embrace uninsistently, sweetly erotic, all the hard angles and rough edges I expected missing, replaced by an infinite variety of well-planed, sometimes wet surfaces. The lights on the Empire State Building switched off; only the slender tower at the very top was still streaked with white. A helicopter chopped its way through the night

air, lowered itself like an overworked insect at the Thirty-
fourth Street heliport. A barge full of garbage floated by; its
single headlight cut a yellow triangle through the black surface of the water. Stuart whispered in my ear, gestured at the
Manhattan skyline, the bridge sloping away toward the magnificent island, before together we turned and hand in hand
descended to the Brooklyn shore.

I offered no explanation to my father's confused friend three
weeks later when I packed my bags and moved out. Stuart
waited for me on the front stoop. He grabbed my black suitcase when I emerged and pulled me down the block of brown-
stones like a terrorist excitedly executing a hijacking he had
spent years planning. He hailed a taxi at Central Park West
and tossed my things into the open trunk. I looked back,
thought I saw a figure standing in the open doorway I had
just fled suspiciously watching us, and felt thoroughly sick
to my stomach as I stepped into the cab. Was I making a
horrible mistake?

"You're all mine now." Stuart pressed close against me in
the back seat, curled an arm between my legs and under my
knee, rubbed a bare leg against my own. The Museum of
Natural History floated by the open window, the sidewalk
overflowing with people.

"What are we doing?" I looked at him, horrified, imagined
leaping from the taxi at the next red light.

"Relax." Stuart shook my leg. "Don't you trust me?"

"I don't know." I felt embarrassed by Stuart's confidence;
how could he be so sure?

"I know." Stuart smiled, leaned over, and laid his head
in my lap, staring up at me like some needy house pet shame-
lessly demanding attention, not minding the driver's sneaking
a look at us in the rearview mirror.

"Did you say Williamsburg Bridge?" I nodded, watched

the driver look us over, then, deeming our affair uninterest-ing, turn up the Sinatra on the radio, humming along with the Voice.

I sat bolt upright, stroking Stuart's cheek and hair, my blood pressure slowly dropping, my stomach settling as I rhythmically petted him, my panic passing into a more man-ageable, vague discomfort by the time we turned onto De-lancey Street and wended our way through the Sunday-afternoon traffic onto the bridge.

Broadway was empty; the irritating echo of some awful punk-rock group practicing in a nearby loft filled the street as the taxi made a wide turn and headed back for the bridge, leaving us stranded alone on the hot pavement. We carried my bags into the green storefront and piled them in the stream-ing light by the window full of Stuart's canvases.

Stuart pulled off his shirt, wiped his brow, and fetched a glass of seltzer while I surveyed my new home, the familiar space changed in my eyes, foreign and a little foreboding now that I officially lived here. Beyond the studio in the front window was a living area; a wooden table with two chairs and a sagging green love seat pushed against one wall faced a sloppily installed kitchen on the other, and a tangle of plumb-ing and electrical conduits ran through the flaking tin ceiling above. A door at the back led to the bedroom lit with a leaky skylight, beyond which a heavily barred window and rusted metal door let onto a dirty, overgrown garden, the bathroom attached at the very end as an afterthought, like an outhouse. How could I not have noticed before how cramped and dirty and dark this place was? The aura of romantic pioneering I had imagined was gone, replaced by a sinking awareness of the dingy reality. Stuart read the look on my face.

"It's not so bad, Thomas. A couple of gallons of white paint, some plaster, we'll have this place fixed up in no time." He stood beside me and illustrated our future home improve-

ments with broad, extended brushstrokes, waved his tan arms
excitedly as the picture in his mind came into view, the hairs
rising in profile on his chest like a ridge of trees blanketing
a range of low mountains on the horizon. I ran a hand over
them, Stuart barely taking notice. He handed me the seltzer.
"Use your imagination, Thomas."

"I am." I touched him again, traced the curve of his breast-
bone with my index finger, landed my palm securely on his
hip.

"We'll start tomorrow. Oscar and Blythe will help."

"Tomorrow," I repeated. I ran the back of my slightly wet
fingers against the side of Stuart's neck, the surrounding dirt
and disarray unimportant in comparison to the immediacy of
his presence, his desirability; his vision of the future was
assurance enough for the moment, his warm body a kind of
hedge against all bets. My nose itched, tingled with his tart
scent.

"Did you know?" Stuart dropped onto the love seat.

"Know what?" I leaned over him, dizzy, as if he were lying
at the bottom of a deep ravine and I was plummeting toward
him, shocked to find myself still alive after the fall, marveling
I hadn't crushed him to death with my crashing weight. He
raised his arms over my head and opened his mouth, but no
word of answer emerged. Instead, he kissed my neck and
ears and nose and forehead, spoke to me in a wordless language, his every touch composing a seamless, perfectly gram-
matical sentence, a remarkably continuous thought, his
tongue punctuating the whole, marking the necessary pauses
and occasional longer stops. He slipped a hand in the back
of my pants, unbuttoning the front with the other, and worked
his way out of his own clothes as he worked me out of mine.
The flooding perfume of his body, his radiant, almost scorching warmth was overpowering, intoxicating, grown more so
through familiarity, like a drug one thinks of as medication

or recreation and discovers has become a necessity, his body seeming to transmit to my own, as if in a Stone Age tribal ritual, some vital essence without which I would not survive. The idea that I had lived almost my whole life without knowing this person seemed fantastic, impossible, he had so quickly become so essential, the floodgates now thrown wide open just as compelling when they should later be reduced to only the slightest trickle, just one tiny drop of his essence enough to unleash the physical chain of memory, start the ceaseless craving to which I had become hopelessly addicted.

When I awoke several hours later I was naked and alone in the bed, the skylight above almost dark, the door closed, music mingling with the sound of hushed voices in the next room. I lay still and listened, like a child sent to bed early who wistfully attends to the comforting noise of his parents' nearby entertainment, struggling to identify a familiar laugh or cough, the words themselves unintelligible, only the vague murmuring of generic language. I felt strangely tired, overwhelmingly exhausted, as if I had just woken unsatisfied from a hundred years of sleep and could think only of returning, of never waking at all. The door creaked open, the room flooded with light, and Stuart tiptoed through to the bathroom, surprised when he emerged to find me awake. He said nothing, only smiled cryptically before sneaking back out and closing the door behind him. I rose in a lazy trance and dressed, washed my hands and face, the figure brushing his teeth in the bathroom mirror a stranger, the lost child in a fairy tale who finds safe harbor with too-kind strangers and worries what his hated real relations are at that moment thinking.

"Finally." Oscar leaned against the kitchen sink. Blythe sat with Stuart at the table. "We *thought* you were hiding in there."

"Why didn't you wake me?" I stood in the doorway and squinted at Stuart, feeling somehow betrayed.

"Because you were sleeping." I was stumped by Stuart's peculiar logic.

"Something to drink?" Oscar reached into the refrigerator and handed me a beer; the paper label soaked with condensation came off in her hand.

"Thank you." I sat on the love seat.

"Just a little housewarming; it seemed the neighborly thing to do." Blythe drummed her tar-stained fingernails on the table, agonizing over whether to smoke her last cigarette. She finally gave in and lit up.

"Stuart was telling us about your plans to fix the apartment." Oscar rolled her eyes at a gaping hole in the wall above the sink.

"Tom's domesticating me." Stuart scratched his upper lip. "I'm practically housetrained already."

"You were hardly the dirty-painter type to begin with"— Blythe looked across at Oscar—"unlike some guys we know."

"Tell me about it." Oscar laughed. She finished her beer and popped the top off another.

"So far it's been pretty easy." I meant to say I had no idea what I was doing.

"Your work looks great, Stuart. Very impressive." Blythe pointed over her shoulder at the canvases piled up front.

"Definitely," Oscar concurred. "Although some are a little too Matisse-y."

"Matisse-y?" Stuart sounded displeased; I sensed trouble ahead.

"Yeah, you know, Matisse-y. That's an adjective: like Matisse." Oscar and Stuart glared at each other, on the verge of drunken argument.

"Why don't you just tell me you think they're garbage."

Stuart spoke softly, sarcastically. "You know, not everyone can be a conceptual artist. I know you find the idea ridiculous, but some of us still believe in painting."

"What can I say, Stuart, we live in different centuries." Oscar attempted to turn the discussion philosophical.

"Painting is so romantic, so sentimental, so self-important," Blythe continued.

"So dirty." Oscar wrung her hands in disgust.

"I know, I know. According to you all, it's nothing but an expression of man's unique ability to piss while standing." I followed Stuart's words, fought hard to believe in his romanticism. "You say postmodern, I say late romantic. Same old argument."

"What about you, Thomas?" Blythe aimed her thick lenses at me.

"What do you mean? What about me?" I was unused to talking with these people, still struggling to situate their ideas.

"What century are you living in?" Oscar drunkenly spit out the words.

"Same as me, obviously," Stuart said, reaching a hand out and brushing my knee.

"Let's not assume," Oscar said, cocking her head, waiting impatiently for my answer.

"Actually"—I paused, deliberated before taking the plunge, prayed my words would not fall flat—"I'm a Pomo-Homo. At least I used to be."

"I knew there was something special about you." Blythe laughed, stood, and turned up the radio. "I love Dionne Warwick."

"Goddess," Oscar agreed. "Postmodernist homosexual; I love it." Oscar played with the words, pleased at how comfortably they fit the framework of her regular vocabulary.

"What does that mean?" Stuart was less impressed.

"I'm not sure I know anymore." I tried to explain: "Some-

thing to do with inscrutable literary theory, my inability to
ever know your true intentions."

"That definitely makes you one of us." Blythe sounded
satisfied.

"What," Stuart joked, "a lesbian conceptual artist?"

"I don't think so." I leaned forward and kissed the back
of Stuart's neck.

"Very funny." Oscar shook with fake laughter. "Come on,
let's go for a drive." She opened the refrigerator door, removed
the remaining bottles of beer, and passed them around. Stuart
came and sat next to me on the love seat; he whispered in
my ear. His voice tickled, his arm was slippery around my
waist, and I giggled, felt lightheaded and surprisingly
carefree.

"No secrets." Oscar wagged a finger at us.

"It's hardly a secret, Oscar." Blythe twirled her thumbs
together and cracked her knuckles, her fingers awkwardly
unoccupied without a cigarette. "Drink up, guys. I need my
nicotine."

Oscar finished her beer. She grabbed Blythe around the
waist and they shuffled toward the front door, where they
leaned against the wall, Blythe invisible in Oscar's tall
shadow. Stuart stood, pulled me up after him, gathered the
empty bottles together in a brown paper bag, and switched
off the radio before leading us all outside. The evening was
hot and sticky. The bridge hummed with traffic, rubber on
metal buzzing like a plague of locusts always approaching,
never arriving, stuck in a permanent middle distance. We
piled into the front seat of a blue pickup truck, Oscar riding
high at the wheel. She turned us around and we drove into
the Brooklyn night.

We waited at the corner of Marcy Avenue for Blythe to buy
cigarettes. A curiously mixed crowd descended the double
set of stairs from the station overhead; conspicuously young

Hasidic women, their hair strangely static and disheveled, were surrounded by large numbers of children all dressed in matching outfits; a group of young women, their skin varying shades of brown, each holding a baby in her arms, some with a toddler or two in tow, skipped down the steps, crying out to each other in Spanish; young men singly and in pairs maneuvered their way to the sidewalk, dispersing into the convenience stores arrayed on each corner; older men, faces grizzled with white stubble, and older women weighed down with plastic bags full of discount Sunday shopping, stuck close to the iron railing; a spattering of identifiable artists completed the picture in their jeans and black shoes, knapsacks or leather bags slung across their shoulders.

Blythe bounced off the curb and landed next to me on the narrow seat. She slammed the door shut, propped a foot on the dashboard, an elbow out the open window; the light turned green and we headed down Broadway. The side streets were full of traffic, cars honking, figures leaning out windows and dangling on fire escapes, children playing everywhere. At Myrtle Avenue we emerged from beneath the elevated tracks onto a boulevard; steeples rose on either side behind sizable brick houses, most only the hollow remnants of a once-bustling middle-class prosperity, and the square shadows of tower after tower of public housing formed a wall against the backdrop of the heavy sky. Before us rose a black mound, uninhabited, wooded. We swerved onto a shady roadway, swept along the base of this hill, and climbed its side, Brooklyn unfolding to our right; the trailing lights of the Verrazano-Narrows Bridge hung like a string of pearls around the neck of New York Harbor. A procession of jets circled noisily in their holding pattern over the borough.

We passed under a stone gate onto a steep, winding path; the dense forest on either side quickly cleared into a vast gray slope closely paved with granite. Thin strips of grass ran in a tight grid between the evenly spaced monuments, a sizable stone crypt usually marking the ends of each row, clusters of black obelisks and silvery pyramids the more ostentatious signs of grief. We continued past endless fields of inconsolable loss, wending our way through hairpin turns, unexpected dips and rises, until we arrived at a high, clear prominence. A rotary circled the top like the rings at the bottom of an inverted glass bowl, and a thick flagpole was planted in the center above an enormous concrete base, Queens spilling north to the Long Island Sound, Brooklyn reaching south to the Atlantic Ocean.

Oscar parked along the edge of the closely cropped, artificial-looking turf. The silence was shocking when she cut off the motor; we were at the heart of a vast necropolis, an appropriately crowded vacuum solemnly, patiently absorbing the life of the huge surrounding city. Stuart pinched me, pushed me out after Blythe, slid across the hot vinyl, and followed. Oscar ran circles around the flagpole while the three of us sat on the grass and surveyed the view, her heavy soles clomping on the pavement like a horse's hooves, her panting similarly equine.

"The city's like a dream from up here." I had already become callously familiar with the striving Manhattan skyline, but this broader, sprawling intersection of rivers and harbors and oceans was an enigma, more like a great living organism than I had imagined, the lights flowing along the tangled network of highways like blood cells viewed through a microscope scrambling blindly to their predetermined tasks.

"More like a nightmare." Blythe's ghoulish features lit up briefly in the explosion of a match hurtling off flint. Stuart stretched an arm around my waist.

"Beautiful," he sighed. Was he referring to me or the view?

Oscar trotted up, ran in place. "You know," she panted, "they say there are more dead people buried in Queens than living."

"That's because they don't usually bury living people," Blythe wearily corrected her.

"You know what I mean." Oscar dropped to the ground.

"I prefer not to think about it," Blythe gloomily answered.

"Blythe suffers from an unreasonable fear of dying." Stuart spoke with surprising lightness.

"I don't think it's unreasonable." Blythe rose and shook her legs. I shuddered, felt afraid in Stuart's arms, his touch no longer comforting, instead unpleasantly warm and sticky.

"Are you all right? You feel cold." He held me tighter, shook me gently.

"I feel funny." I stopped, my hands and feet numb, panic rising, stuck in my throat, the city below us impossibly far away, the nearby car my only means of escape, escape seeming at that moment both urgent and futile. Stuart crouched on the ground and pulled me under him, wrapped himself about me like a blanket of human flesh, and together we rolled down the hillside, sky and earth tumbling around us, spinning an intricate streaked web, breaking apart when we slowed to a halt, the stones spread out like stubby black fingers poking through the dirt in all directions. Stuart crawled on top of me, pinned my shoulders down flat with his elbows, ground his hips against my own, cupped his open lips over my mouth, smothering me, suffocating me, sucking the breath of life from my lungs. I heaved, pushed him off me, and screamed, possessed with absolute terror, convinced I was about to die. Stuart knelt beside me, stunned, while Oscar and Blythe, taking my scream for a macabre joke, hollered back from the hilltop, their voices falling from high-pitched, full-throttled horror to low, teasing laughter. Like a wave hitting shore the terror washed over me, broke, and subsided,

leaving in its wake a shimmering stillness, Stuart the glistening, welcoming wet sand in which I buried my face and
hid from the darkness.

"What are they doing?" Oscar sounded irritated, as if she
suspected we were playing some prank; her words struck me
as garbled, disembodied, her approaching footsteps a delicate
tremor of the earth.

"Oscar, Oscar," Blythe called after her, angry, hinting at
caution, unable to stop her, instead trotting up to us, a shadow
in Oscar's shadow. Stuart and I lay locked together on the
ground, hearts pounding, rocking in a violent embrace; his
fists squeezed so hard at the small of my back I felt my kidneys
would burst. His rib cage seemed to fold into my own like
the metal grate of a turnstile, while our thighs pinched painfully tight and our lips joined in a cannibal kiss. Oscar and
Blythe stood still, watching us like a pair of innocent by-
standers at the scene of a crime, too shocked by what they
see to avert their gaze, compelled by the shame of their
fascination to bear witness.

Stuart relaxed his hold on me. I breathed deeply. Air
miraculously filled my lungs, spilling over to inflate my arms
and legs, causing me to float gently to the surface. I felt my
diaphragm slowly contracting and saw the world returning,
the blackness thinning, a carpet of twinkling lights unfurling
ahead of me. The cushion of air deflated and the ground was
hard beneath me, the grass damp and slimy on my elbows
and knees when I sat up. Stuart stood beside me shaking his
limbs loose. He reached a hand out and pulled me up, smiling
faintly self-satisfied in the gloom as if newly possessed of
some secret knowledge he had been searching for, a newfound
power hidden within himself exposed like a fissure in the
earth by a sudden earthquake of building emotions. He shuddered, flapped his arms, and jogged off alone up the hill.

"What was that all about?" Oscar finally broke the silence.

"Good question." I watched Stuart disappear over the top of the slope and wondered where he was going.

"You're all shook up," Oscar said, "white as a sheet."

"Did you see a ghost?" Blythe asked, her voice hopeful and curious.

"No, I wish. Just a glimpse of my own cowardice." I was thoroughly myself again, anxious to return to the city, to the world of the living. "Let's go home." We hiked back to the car. Stuart was nowhere in sight when we reached the summit. Oscar hollered for him, cupped her hands around her mouth and yodeled, waited in the ensuing silence for an answer before shouting again, this one echoed by Stuart's muffled, distant reply.

"He does this sometimes," she said, wearily familiar with his habits, "just wanders off without a word of explanation. You'll get used to it." We settled into the truck and slowly drove through the cemetery, finally catching up with Stuart by the gate we had entered, where he stood stretching, a spirit-gymnast performing his nocturnal calisthenics. Oscar honked the horn and called out to him, "Need a ride?"

"Thanks." He poked his head in the window and looked us over, like a hitchhiker forming a snap judgment, before running around the front and squeezing in beside me and Blythe.

We endured the long ride home in silence, Oscar cursing now and then at a fellow obnoxious driver. The Williamsburg Bridge loomed ahead of us, distant and inaccessible; pieces of the towers hovered disembodied over tenement rooftops and warehouses, until we were clear on Broadway and the full expanse, glimmering metallic gray, flooded with light, arched in a single effortless motion over the East River, daring us to cross its easy length, leaving me to feel somehow stuck on the Brooklyn side, disappointed. Oscar barely stopped long enough for Stuart and me to safely jump out, as if we

were skydivers being pushed reluctantly from a plane at ten
thousand feet, the truck hurtling forward almost before we
had both hit the pavement. No one bothered to say goodbye.

Stuart unlocked the front door. He pushed it open, pocketed his keys, stepped back on the sidewalk, and raised a
hand as if to lay it on my shoulder before returning it to his
side without having touched me.

"I'm going for a walk." I looked at him and shook my head,
frightened by the distance in his eyes and the sinking awareness that I was not invited. "Alone," he answered my pleading
expression before turning his back and marching up Broadway. I watched paralyzed as his shadowy figure disappeared
around the corner at Bedford Avenue, wondering should I
cry, tears in his absence seeming pointless, and instead began
to hate myself for whatever I had done to deserve this. I was
seized with shame and hurried inside, as if the sky and the
moon and the stars along with every brick in the surrounding
buildings could see the sting of rejection on my wounded
face, were laughing meanly at me for having expected anything, for having wanted to be held, tenderly kissed, carried
across the threshold and sweetly laid to rest, for having imagined low words whispered in my ear, tickling my brain, a
wave of a warm giggle spreading through my whole body. I
was forced instead to hide alone under the dirty sheets with
only my pathetic sense of the inevitable to console me.

I lay shivering in bed for what seemed like hours, clinging
frailly to the edge of sleep, until a flash of lightning lit the
room, followed almost immediately by the crack of nearby
thunder, the first drops of rain to hit the skylight ominous
and foreboding, like pebbles warning of an avalanche. A
violent, sheeting downpour ensued, a great flood of water
coursing over the steel-reinforced glass, gushing noisily
through the gutters, the whole world dissolving in the wetness,
my bed a lifeboat floating out to sea on the rising tide, the

rhythmic hammering of the rain singing me to sleep with a bright promise of peaceful far shores, Stuart naked, drowning helpless in the streets until I happen to float past him, throw him a life jacket, and fish him out with an oar, his clothes swirling past the prow, his hair soaking wet dripping on my eyes and nose when I kiss him, his body damp and slippery in my arms when I hold him. I thank God we are together, safe in our tight little ship, a pair of brave sailors weathering the storm, land visible on the horizon, the rising sun breaking apart the clouds with its ultraviolet rays, our boat pleasantly bobbing on the settling ocean, riding the incoming tide to the safety of shore and a deeply forgiving release into the certainty of sleep in each other's devoted arms.

We lived the rest of the summer in a happy confusion of joint compound, plaster, water sealant, latex primer, semi-gloss and glossy paint, deck enamel, brushes, rollers, drop cloths, spatulas, coveralls, and the sundry other accoutrements of home improvement. By the end of August the walls had been patched and smoothed and painted, the floors scrubbed and enameled, a collection of new furniture gathered from a nearby garbage heap and cleverly refurbished, everything coated with a layer of white paint, as if that substance was a magic elixir, the alchemist's secret ingredient for turning lead into gold, no problem resistant to solution by its potent effect.

Always Stuart and I were together, constantly deranging each other's work with eruptions of affection, the shaky stepladder, a dirty drop cloth, the platform of the front window, the cast-iron tub stations in the unfolding drama of our passion. Beneath the busy surface of our domesticity, however, compelling me to rush home whenever I should happen to be out on an errand or inevitably pull Stuart into the bed for a few delaying moments before he was due somewhere in the city, was nervous anticipation of the approaching Labor Day weekend and our first trial by separation. Stuart was going home, without me, and I faced the prospect of his disappearance with muffled panic. I collected our minutes together with a desperate inability to envision the future, as if the evasive present moment was all we had, maddeningly insufficient and unsatisfying. The day of his departure arrived with cruel speed, and the imagined length of his absence was already an intolerable eternity of mental suffering.

I sat at the kitchen table on a Friday morning, unable to eat my breakfast, the bowl of cereal before me a bitter reminder of my solitary physical being, the vulgar necessity of material nourishment. I watched through the bedroom door as Stuart frantically paced in his underwear, packing a hard-bodied dark green suitcase full with dirty laundry and books.

"What are you doing?" I shouted. Stuart didn't answer, just continued to run in a concentrated figure eight under the skylight. I crouched in the doorway, watched him hurl a book from the shelf across the room into the open suitcase. "Are you really going to read *Modern Painters* between now and Tuesday?"

"Shhh." He scowled at me. "I can't think." He sat on the bed, crossed his legs, hummed softly to himself.

"Stuart," I whispered, afraid to disturb him, unable to keep away. I crawled toward him, sat on the floor by his feet, wrapped an arm around his leg, and repeated, "Stuart." He shook his head, almost startled, and looked down at me.

"Don't look so sad, Thomas." I couldn't tell which dominated in his voice, compassion or irritation. "I'll be back before you know it."

"I know"; but I didn't believe it. I was certain this was the end and he was making a terrible fool of me. His leg twitched. I squeezed a hand between his thighs, pressed a cheek against his bare stomach, felt his hot skin burn the features off my face. He grabbed me by the shoulders, lifted me, pulled me on top of him, rolled me over on the bed and straddled my hips, leaned over and kissed my neck.

"Will you miss me?" I detected a sadistic note in his voice, a lingering suggestion of malignant intent.

"I miss you already. I can't help it." I felt as if I had just confessed a crime, been tricked into an undeniable admission of guilt.

"This should give you something to think about while I'm gone." He nibbled my ear, wiggled out of his briefs, slid forward, and dangled himself over my face, poking my eyes out with two swift thrusts, deafening me with a pair of taps to the side of the head, reducing me to a senseless, stiffening reflex, beating me into willing, grateful oblivion. The fateful suitcase still lay open at the foot of the bed when Stuart withdrew. He released me, sat up grinning, and with a seeming question in his eyes wiped a sticky finger across my lips and down my chin, followed by the witty rejoinder of his grainy tongue, a reminder that no quantity of ecstatic coupling could account in my mind for the immeasurable loss I was about to experience.

The alarm clock sounded inexplicably, the buzzer announcing the end of our game. I lay still on the bed, shadows of traffic on the bridge flitting across the skylight, and listened to the blunted sound of water thumping flesh. Stuart sang to himself in the shower. He emerged naked, glistening, refreshed, danced a jig around the room, twirling a towel over his back, pulling it between his legs. He threw each article of his clothing spinning in the air before slithering into it, until he was fully dressed, the suitcase closed, the show over, not a wrinkle of worry or concern distorting his handsome forehead. I found his attitude unbelievable, could explain his good mood only as a form of personal contempt for myself, a deliberate attempt to maximize my misery.

He phoned a car service, checked his watch as he laid down the receiver, and came and sat by me on the bed. "They'll be here in five minutes." Need he adopt such a gleeful, mocking tone? He held my hand, turned my averted cheek toward him, looked me hard in the eye. "Don't cry." He almost laughed, checked himself, instead hugged me tight, rubbed his smooth fists along my aching tender spine. I hid in his silent embrace, ashamed of my sadness, waiting for him to miraculously announce he was staying, couldn't bear to leave me; I was shaken from my fantasy by a honking horn. Stuart slowly released me, kissed me, a happy glint of emotion perceptible in the corners of his eyes. In another instant he was gone, and the room was black and empty, dangerously quiet. The obnoxious echo of the still-dripping shower boomed painfully against my eardrums, companion to the tortured trickle of my own tears.

I spent the rest of the day pacing the apartment, wondering how I would manage without him, unaware how effectively my worry filled the time. The minutes passed so painfully slowly I felt like a condemned man anxious at last to die, the anticipation of fear so much greater than the fear itself, the four days looming ahead of me an insurmountable barrier to my future, an imaginary vessel full to the brim with unreasoning, relentless anxiety of anxiety.

The daylight I simply ignored. The outside world ceased to exist, and the thought of attempting to escape my prison never entered my head. Had there been iron bars on the windows and an armed guard posted at the front door I could not have imagined myself more stuck, more utterly consigned to serve sentence in solitary confinement. When at last I heard a hand tapping against the front window I shook with paranoia, vandals the only possible source of such harassment, or had my lonely mind simply invented the distraction? A louder rapping followed. I crept forward and peeled back a bit of the vellum covering the lower portion of the glass, startled to find Tony, my forgotten architect friend, squinting back at me, smiling in happy recognition, urging me to let him in, unaware I had been locked up for the night, the warden gone with the key and not expected until morning.

Tony pounded once more on the door. "Open up, Thomas, I know you're in there." He seemed to be enjoying the joke. He continued, "Or I'll huff and I'll puff and I'll blow the door down."

"Sorry." I drew the dead bolt, creaked the door open, and let Tony in; an image of myself as one of the three little pigs about to become bacon flashed in my brain. Tony's fangless smile reassured me of my safety.

"Looks great," he commented, observing the thoroughness of our home improvements. I just looked at him sullenly, unable to appreciate his compliments, the perfectly painted walls the hateful companions of my unutterable suffering, nothing exactly to brag about. "Anyway, that's not why I dropped by," he said, put off by my aloofness.

"Come on in and see the rest." I tried to buoy myself, adopt a lighter tone. "What's up?" I waved him in, turned on our newly installed lights, and looked him over, surprised I had never before noticed how handsome he was, tall and thin, with easy brown features, like Gary Cooper in *The Fountainhead*. What was the matter with me? Stuart had barely been gone half a day yet my mind was suddenly awash with dirty thoughts, Tony only half dressed, his body contorted in a variety of sexual poses. I blinked at him, terrified he might be reading my mind, but he only leaned oblivious against the arm of the sofa and tapped a foot on the freshly painted floor admiringly before explaining his mission.

"I ran into Oscar this afternoon. There's an opening at that new gallery over on Bedford Avenue. She asked me to stop by and invite you." He tipped his head slightly before continuing. "She said you were home alone and might want some company."

"Oh, she did." The dirty thoughts were beginning to subside, like steam let off from the heat of my morning with Stuart. "She thinks of everything."

"Oscar never misses a beat," Tony assured me with conviction. "No one has secrets from her. Are you coming?"

"Just a minute." I quickly washed and dressed, the consuming misery of my loneliness reduced, when I finished, to a tight knot in my stomach, a pinpoint of hyperdense matter at the center of my being, weighing me down, draining me of all physical or mental sensation.

The evening was cool and the tangle of lower Manhattan sparkled beneath an orange-blue sky; the city was astoundingly beautiful in Stuart's absence. As always, Bedford Avenue was a sea of people. An especially large crowd huddled groaning and wailing before a sidewalk altar, dozens of candles burning on a low bench covered in black velvet, flowers piled three feet high against a brick wall spray-painted with a black tombstone, a great white cross, and the message "RIP Luis—We love you." I noted the dates carved into the tombstone, calculated the span of Luis's brief life, and wondered how his fifteen short years had ended. Several women crouched in tears before the sputtering flames, muttering in prayer, while husbands, brothers, and sons meandered mournful and dazed along the curb. Their heartfelt grieving was nothing more than a sideshow to the drug-driven continual party of this infamous stretch of road, the dealers at every corner defiantly selling their wares, people patiently waiting in line for entrance to the crack house on South Second Street as if it were an exclusive nightclub, entrance a selective mark of distinction.

Tony and I waded through the worst of it, pressing forward with studied nonchalance, studiously avoiding eye contact with the most aggressive pushers, their punishing, piercing gaze in the wink of a lash capable of burning a hole at the center of one's soul, baring in the fraction of an instant a more intense view of human deprivation and suffering and conceivable ill will than is imaginable in an ordinary lifetime. We emerged on the other side as if from a biblical scene, our preservation under such circumstances seeming somehow miraculous, no less so considering its almost daily occurrence.

Past Metropolitan Avenue the neighborhood became almost completely Polish, strangely separate and quiet despite only two blocks' distance from the most virulent urban squalor. The men and women walking the streets in their gray shoes and synthetic fibers seemed to have just turned a corner in Warsaw or Crakow and been magically transported to Brooklyn. Above the door of each little shop a handwritten cardboard sign inevitably proclaimed MOWIMY MY POLSKI, and the windows displayed the same meager merchandise I imagined had driven these people to flee the consumer hell of their East Bloc homeland in the first place, while the tidy yet ramshackle decay of the empty side streets struck me as somehow equally reminiscent of the charming deficiencies of their inhabitants' birthplace.

A crowd milled about on the sidewalk at North First Street, the artists of Williamsburg proclaiming their Bohemian presence to their Eastern European neighbors. Music spilled from a crowded, brightly lit storefront. A barrel full of ice and beer blocked the entry. No one seemed aware of the Surgeon General's repeated stark claims concerning the hazards of smoking; a cigarette was present in almost every free hand or dangling from tobacco-hungry lips. I spotted Blythe through a crack in the postered window swirling a bottle in her hand as she nodded mechanically at some stranger's conversation.

Tony chatted happily beside me without introducing me to

his friends, leaving me free to interject my presence at an appropriate juncture in their easy talk or wander off in search of other amusement. I squeezed into the gallery and inspected the assemblage pinned to the walls: murky color photographs of incomprehensible subjects were surrounded by news clippings, bumper stickers, and high-school-yearbook snapshots. Scotch tape scarred every surface. I moved bewildered around the edge of the room, amazed that these people didn't care that Stuart was missing, had gone, had left me to suffer alone, that my worry didn't cast a pall over this gathering, seemed in fact to go completely unnoticed. Blythe cornered me, then complimented me. Her kind words struck me as disrespectful, insulting in their failure to appreciate the desolate condition of my soul.

"Thomas, you look cute tonight. Did you get a haircut or something?" She nudged me; was my despondency somehow becoming?

"Really?" I shrugged and glimpsed my reflection in the darkening window, limbs and features all in their proper place, hair standing stiffly at attention atop my head. I didn't think it possible that stranger in the mirror could ever look cute.

"Don't take it personally," Blythe joked.

"It's probably the weather, heightens the color in my cheeks." I listened to my self-deprecating words, puzzled by Blythe's flattery. "Interesting show." This was more question than opinion, and I waited for Blythe to explain what I should think.

"You should've seen the last one." I couldn't tell if she meant it was good or bad.

"Why?" I asked, Blythe not seeming to mind my inept question.

"Pathetic," she answered, and for an instant I thought she was referring to me. I felt useless, my presence a slobbering imposition on her valuable time, before I returned to myself and the realization that she was describing the previous show. The torrent of her vicious criticism ended in an abrupt query: "Did you see Oscar out front?"

She frowned at my negative reply and daintily shot her cigarette with one hand into the near-empty beer bottle she held in the other. She set it down on a shallow ledge in the window; a sizzling wisp of smoke rose through the green glass neck like a drunken genie fumbling to escape; Blythe looked sharply around the room—no sign of Oscar anywhere. I spotted her familiar, muscular frame wrapped around a parking meter along the curb.

"There she is." I pointed, and we pushed our way outside. The sun was almost completely set, the sky dusky blue, ringed yellow at the edges, the slanted debris of the abandoned Brooklyn piers brown streaks against an enormous white chemical storage tank at the end of North First Street.

"Are you surviving without Stuart?" At last someone had noticed. Oscar's words were like a key set to unlock a pack of kenneled emotions, the tears almost welling in the corners of my eyes brought to heel by her concluding, "You look like you're managing fine."

"Tony rescued me, thanks to your advice." I swallowed my tongue and wondered at the evident privacy of my unhappiness.

"I don't see how anyone could ever miss Stuart," Blythe said in her lackadaisical drawl. "I always think of him as a kind of necessary evil."

"But that's why we love him"—Oscar looked at me—"because he's such an asshole."

"Our asshole," Blythe completed Oscar's thought. Were they making fun of me? I could only hobble along and pretend to enjoy the joke.

"That certainly gives me something to feel good about." I considered the ironic potential of this statement, but felt little consolation in the possibility that I loved the wrong man; I was instead suspicious of the manner in which Stuart's friends spoke of him behind his back, as if their mildly insulting banter intended some deeper meaning, a careful suggestion of warning or perhaps a guarded expression of concern for my welfare. Only why should they care?

"You know, Thomas, this is the first time all summer we've had you to ourselves. Stuart's practically kept you locked up in that love nest on Broadway. I think we should celebrate your newfound freedom." Oscar had a plan, and like a hurricane gathering force, myself the panicky calm at the center of the storm, she swept us along in her path. "Let's go to Kasia's for dinner."

The Stuart-bashing continued during our meal in the dirty garden of a crowded Polish restaurant several blocks north on Bedford Avenue, where a diminutive Slavic waitress set before us platefuls of stuffed cabbage and boiled dumplings. Her blond hair was suspiciously mismatched against thick black eyebrows, and a beauty mark on her upper lip made her look like a Communist Bloc Marilyn-impersonator. The restaurant was full of the eclectic neighborhood crowd: three policemen sat under a tree beside us making fun of a dieting fourth as he launched with relish into a heaping plate of steamed vegetables; young artists argued over the merits of their contemporaries' works; Polish laborers, in their work boots and coveralls, still dusty from a hard day's work, sheepishly grinned at the bouncing waitresses, pointing and giggling behind their backs as they pounded the brick patio with their thick-soled shoes.

"So has Stuart been paying his rent?" Oscar launched the next wave of the assault.

"I bet he didn't tell you how he got evicted from his last apartment." Tony fired off a further round.

"No. But you just did." A leaf floated down from the slender tree above us, grazing my mashed potatoes before settling on the table.

"Jesus, Oscar, everyone we know has been evicted at least once." Blythe rose to Stuart's defense. "You may as well get used to the vagaries of the artistic life, Tommy."

"But you admit Stuart is uniquely proficient at living on nothing." Oscar was insistent.

"Yeah, I guess you could say he has a certain flair for the suffering lifestyle."

"That's an understatement," Tony slipped into the argument.

"Not like anyone would ever guess from looking that you guys are artists." I speared a dumpling with my fork, scooped some grilled onions on top with my knife, and waved the whole thing at Oscar before popping it into my mouth. I liked to hear them talk about Stuart, almost preferred they make fun of him, tease and insult him, their irreverence a cushion which kept me afloat, kept me from sinking too deeply into the pit of despair which had opened upon his departure. As long as they kept talking, I didn't much care what they said, was glad to learn something of Stuart's past, as if they offered me a glimpse into his secret life, a view Stuart himself could never present, himself the obstacle to my seeing him clearly.

I looked at my watch and wondered where he was at that exact moment, what he was doing, whether he was thinking of me, missing me, suffering as I suffered, counting the minutes until we would be together again, the intervening time, like Zeno's paradox, seeming somehow insurmountable, each passing second nothing but a painful reminder of all the other seconds which must yet come to pass, the possibility

of his return requiring the invention of a whole new calculus,
a mathematics of love and desire and obsession and anxiety
to describe the sick geometry of feeling where our lives in-
tersected, to explain my own future survival, understanding
like death, inevitable, yet grace somehow always intervening,
four days left, two, one, twelve hours, six, three, one, thirty
minutes, fifteen, ten, five, one, twenty seconds, ten, five,
one-fifth, one-tenth, and on and on and on into an eternity
of darkness. Would it ever end?

I dropped my fork; a black screen descended before my
eyes, a ripple of kneading motion rose from my feet through
my legs and up my spine, my head spinning in blank space
before I slowly came to a halt and the filmy coating of my
vision lifted. Oscar and Blythe and Tony looked at me as if
I had just beamed down from another planet, materialized
from out of nowhere.

"Better inspect that landing gear, Thomas." Blythe skewed
her eyes at me, pursed her lips tightly around her cigarette.

"Where've you been?" Tony and Oscar laughed at my obvious spaciness. I blinked at them and smiled. I watched a
blue-gray cat crawl through a crack between the palings in
the rotting wood fence separating Kasia's back yard from the
laundromat next door, then slither beneath my chair and
saunter boldly into the open kitchen.

"I was thinking of Stuart," I said.

"Well, maybe you shouldn't." Tony scraped a gravy stain
from the corner of his mouth, crumpled his greasy napkin
into a tight ball, and flung it into the pool of sauerkraut juice
on his otherwise empty plate.

No one spoke while the waitress cleared our table. Her
fearsome presence cast a pall over our conversation; the pe-
culiarly hybrid culture of her appearance and dress humbled
us into hushed admiration of her alien life, a meek reminder

that what for us was destined only to be a way station in the larger path of our lives was for others a goal attained, a struggle overcome, an end in itself. My earlier sense of exhaustion began to return, a tired, frightened belief in my own weakness, my utter inability to cope with the necessary separation, to escape the spiraling double helix of longing and sorrow which would keep me pathetically rooted, waiting for Stuart to come home. The solace of company dissolved into an unbearable self-consciousness, a ravenous craving for solitude.

"I think I have to go home now." I pretended to be sick, to have a headache, anything to excuse myself, to escape to the desolation of my cushioned cave on Broadway.

"You're not coming out with us tonight?" Oscar's voice rose in disappointment, as if my gloomy needs took away from her own burning desire to shine.

"Are you sure?" I nodded yes to Blythe's question, unable to explain how deeply my desire to be alone stemmed from an awful uncertainty.

"Maybe we'll see you later this weekend." Tony sounded hopeful. "There's a big party over in the East Village on Monday. Very glamorous."

"I don't think so." Monday, the day before Stuart's return, the end finally in sight; I was beginning to cherish the prospect of a very lonely holiday, four sleepless nights, each a vigil for the receding dawn, daylight holding my hand, comforting me into expectant sleep.

"You want a ride home?" Oscar offered. I accepted, refusal too complicated to bother with. We paid our check and filed out through the restaurant, past a glass display at the front entrance full of cheesecake slices, bowls of Jell-O topped with rosettes of whipped cream, and hefty scoops of rice pudding muddied from sprinkled cinnamon. Tony left us on

the sidewalk. He laid a hand on my shoulder in affectionate
expression of concern as he said goodbye, watched as we
climbed into the truck, and I detected a palpable hint of
erotic reluctance in his departure, a veiled admission of un-
credited insight into my thoughts. Oscar gassed the engine
and spun the truck around North Seventh Street. We barreled
down Driggs Avenue, swerved through the double-parked
cars, Oscar daring a taxi to hit us at the intersection of Grand
Street, leaning hard on her horn, hurling an obscenity out
the window in a cathartic release. Our whole breathless ride
was like a dangerous game, an elaborate joke with unac-
knowledged grave consequences. I held my breath, exhila-
rated by Oscar's reckless driving, my face flush with the
euphoria of extreme danger when the truck screeched to a
halt on Broadway.

"Thanks for the ride," I finally exhaled, jumping from the
truck.

"Don't be a stranger to us, Thomas." Blythe watched while
I fumbled with my keys and let myself in, waved at me slowly
as the door swung shut. Alone at last, I paced the dark
apartment; I felt cold and restless, longed for a solution to
my inner turmoil, escape from the prison of my emotions. I
was a claustrophobic, horrified by the trap of my mind, with
nowhere left to run and hide; everywhere I turned I was faced
with the singular shadow of my phobic state, my missing
Stuart, my panicky doubt of ever seeing him again, my fear
of both of us dying, lonely and forever separate. I bundled
myself in a blanket and lay shivering on the bed, wide awake,
staring determinedly at nothing, no heat or tears rising to
shield me from the frigid blasts of raw terror buffeting my
frail frame.

Hours passed. The brighter lights of the bridge had turned
off. Only the faint glow of the dimly lit roadway was visible

through the skylight when I rose, my brow clammy with sweat, the second hand of my watch atop the dresser on the other side of the room pounding like a battering ram at my eardrums, and pulled one of Stuart's sweaters from a lower drawer. I rubbed the wool against my cheek, Stuart present in its earthy odor, and pulled the sweater over my head, my arms lost in the generous sleeves. I hugged myself in a feeble gesture of consolation before drifting out into the street, only the brightest of stars visible through the reflected illumination of the nocturnal metropolitan sky. I slinked my way up Broadway, my feet not making a sound on the pavement. An empty bus was parked growling by the bank building at Bedford Avenue; the driver dozed in his seat. I ducked under the bridge and contemplated the black promenade rising between the ascending lanes of traffic before sucking in my gut and marching resolutely forward. My heart pounded from the vigorous pace of the climb. Stuart's sweater itched at the back of my neck, stuck to the sweaty rail of my spine. A shadowy figure on a bicycle appeared in the darkness, whizzed past me, a lingering insult echoing in the energetic trail of his passage.

I emerged from beneath the subway tracks into full possession of the great bridge. Less than a year before I had boarded a train and headed west, determined to begin a new life, yet here I was, starting all over again, this gargantuan city twinkling benignly before me, a gigantic sponge generously offering to absorb my misery, like a huge coral reef inviting me to attach myself, become a living link in its awesome structure. I shrank from the challenge and slowly retreated, my whole world contracting as I did so from the stretch of continent I had so recently crisscrossed to the several hundred square feet of imagined domestic bliss which, like the legendary maelstrom, sucked in my past life, effectively disposing of all my personal history, perhaps shredding

it to its subatomic substance, more likely casting it into cosmic
abeyance, leaving me utterly single and naked and present,
a free molecule desperately searching for some meaningful
reaction, a lasting chemical bond, Stuart the absent, imma-
nent, supersaturated solution which alone would absorb me.

What else could I do but pray for his safe return?

F I V E

Dykes on Bikes roared down Fifth Avenue. I watched from the curb at Eighteenth Street the host of bare-chested women in bikers' gear gas their engines, raucously lead the lavender procession of Gay Pride like a trailblazing, futuristic wagon train through Manhattan's great central canyon. Behind them marched the hopeful settlers of the new frontier, bearing a thousand banners, each proclaiming a stake in the new territory, shimmering in the relentless June sun. Interspersed between the regiments of foot troops were islands of glitter, flatbed trucks buried in sequins, the Empress of New York and her court regally waving their blessings to the adoring crowds. And everywhere the familiar, patented and registered, overly muscled brown body soaked in an idealized sweat, every biological gyroscope uncannily synchronized, spinning at a steady two hundred cycles per minute, the perpetual gyrations of ever-striving sex in the navigational balance, disco on parade.

Sometime between Girth and Mirth and Greater Gotham Gaylaxians Stuart had wandered off in bored search of refreshment, while I wilted in the creeping parallelogram of shade cast by the western wall of Fifth Avenue, counting the minutes till his return. The pulsing, flowing crowd slowed, became silent. I listened to the hidden noises of the city: a chorus of air conditioners hummed an exhaustive tune; the subway a block over beneath Broadway grumbled dyspeptically; a shrill awkward laugh pierced the buzz of low whispering all around. I fell farther into the shadow of my chosen retreat, leaned heavily against the cool marble backdrop of my commercial entry for support, until a red baton spun high in the air and the celebration resumed, Stuart still nowhere in sight.

"Thomas." I stared at two pairs of legs stopped before me, one golden and muscular, the other slender and paler, rising above blue canvas tennis shoes. An eerily familiar voice called my name; had something happened to Stuart?

"Thomas Hobart." I looked up and smiled at Michael smiling at me squinting. His white features appeared bleached almost beyond recognition in the hard sunlight, his face a faded ivory palimpsest, only the vague scrawl of his eyebrows and lips visible floating in the convex yellow pool framed by his unchanged black hair.

"Hello, Michael." He stepped into my circle of shade and became himself, leaned and kissed me three times: left cheek, right cheek, left cheek. I felt strangely at ease, as if there were nothing unusual in our meeting, as if it was the most ordinary occasion in the world, as if he had always expected I would never return to Chicago without offering a word of explanation to anyone. There was not an ounce of reproach or regret detectable in our affectionate ensuing banter, replaced instead by an intelligent faith in the human interest of our lives as they work themselves out, a highly reasoned acceptance of coincidence as not just probable but inevitable.

"So"—Michael nudged me—"where is he?" One simple educated guess and our game of explication was reduced to a ritual, more important for the formal relations it described than the content prescribed in advance.

"What makes you think there's a man involved?"

"Tell me you're not in love," Michael challenged. He

twitched his nose, scratched between his eyebrows with an index finger.

"He's around here somewhere." I shrugged, Stuart's whereabouts never easy to explain or justify. Michael's nameless companion had remained standing beyond the edge of our darkness. I nodded at him and asked, "What's your explanation?"

"Tommy"—Michael waved a hand at me, then drew his friend forward—"Lucas." Lucas grinned, embarrassed and shy; his teeth were spotted brown, the water wherever he came from evidently not fluoridated. He was taller than Michael and wider, his brown eyes swept by long, delicate lashes. His soft, messy hair sprouted like chicory from his square scalp. He stood just behind Michael and slightly to one side; together they created a curiously chiaroscuro effect, Lucas the edges of depth surrounding Michael's highlighted presence.

"What are you doing in New York?"

Michael looked at Lucas before answering my question, as if seeking and gaining permission to speak for both of them.

"I'm teaching for the summer. I only left Hyde Park three weeks ago, but apparently that's all it takes in New York." He paused, threw an arm around Lucas's waist, and kissed him. "Lucas is my most promising student."

"So it seems." Lucas was radiant, absolutely glowing in the lamp of Michael's affection.

"I learn fast." Lucas smiled. He pulled Michael closer beside him, heightening the illusion of depth.

"You must always remember," Michael said, "Tommy is one of the original Pomo-Homos. We had a famous one-night stand." Lucas shook his head, obviously familiar with the story of our slumber party. "For a brief moment in time we were practically the same person, witness to a great historical event."

"It's true." The past returned to me. "The world's only one-night stand of a political movement." I recited our catch-phrase, all the while reflecting how miserably I had failed to meet its standards, had foolishly fallen in love. But perhaps that had been the point of my brief union with Michael and Jane, to reinforce my unalleviated sense of inadequacy: "Love without lust; lust without love."

"Hi, hi, hi." Stuart strode up between us, spun a little circle of greeting before staring at Michael and Lucas, barely able to contain his surprise at my knowing someone unfamiliar to himself.

"Michael just moved to New York from Chicago," I summarized. "This is his friend Lucas."

"Oh." Stuart held the sound, coddled it meaningfully with his rounded lips. "You must know Tom from before." He laid special emphasis on the final word and dismissively wagged a painterly finger in the air, his motion thick with the suggestion that he had rescued me from a life I was desperate to forget, his presence by my side the irrefutable evidence of how completely I had disowned whatever had preceded our life together. He seemed unnecessarily cool, not so much distrustful or suspicious of Michael as simply anxious to maintain a kind of distance.

"Lucas and I were just headed home for some iced tea. Why don't you join us? It's right around the corner." Stuart looked at me, doubtful, seeking escape, but I held my ground, certain Michael's politeness would prove a force equal to Stuart's leanings in the other direction. We walked down Fifth Avenue and turned west on Fifteenth Street. I skipped between Michael and Lucas, sampled their bantering commentary on the seemingly endless parade. Stuart trailed behind us, drifting in and out of focus, inserting himself into the conversation just often enough to reinforce the unsettling effect of his unpredictable attention span.

We ascended the stoop of a brownstone in the middle of the block beyond Sixth Avenue and climbed the tight curving staircase of a once substantial private home, a multitude of doorways ranged across the width of each landing, sagging tired on rusted hinges. Michael stopped two flights up; he fumbled with his keys, giggled before turning the lock, flung the door open, and sarcastically cautioned us: "One at a time, please."

We crowded into a dark studio apartment. The rotting wood floor sloped at a sharp angle from a double bed on one side of the room to a kitchenette opposite. Frilly red curtains, their bottoms brown from the dust-laden breeze passing through the open windows, only added to the maroon gloom of the shade cast by the high, windowless brick wall opposite. The refrigerator door was covered with antique postcards, and a collection of women's hats hung on the wall above the bed. I sat at the foot of the bed next to Lucas. Stuart asked permission to use the bathroom. His failure to close the door properly behind him, and the consequent resounding echo of foamy water, damped Michael's attempt to begin conversation, and the roar of the flushing toilet was not followed by any aural evidence of hand washing. Stuart reemerged and squinted at the bright bulb hanging from a mauve tasseled shade in the middle of the room. He disingenuously asked Michael, "You live here?"

"It's disgusting," I caught myself thinking out loud, too late.

"It's a sublet." Michael set four glasses on the narrow kitchen counter and filled them from a glass pitcher. "Only a woman could truly inhabit such an airless, yeast-infected room."

"Ouch," I said, surprised by his venomous words. A look of irrefutable appreciation, however, drifted across Stuart's face.

"That's the truth." Lucas nodded, amused by Michael's misogynistic put-down of his sublessor.

"Here, sit down." Michael pulled a folding chair from the closet. He set it open across from me and offered it to Stuart, who had remained awkwardly standing, not bothering to assume the only other available seat in the room, beside Lucas at the head of the bed, into which Michael slid after handing round the glasses.

"Cheers." I raised my glass.

"To New York and new beginnings," Michael proposed.

"To Pride," followed Lucas.

"To Tom." Stuart drew his chair closer. He laid a hand on my knee and held my hand in his and kissed it before throwing his head back and drinking his iced tea in one swift gulp, never releasing his firm hold on me; his warm, sweaty fingers twined tightly around my own.

"Feels like mating season," I joked.

"It's certainly a labor of love in this heat." Michael didn't sound as if he minded the exertion.

"I sort of like really hot sweaty sex," Lucas said loudly. "All slippery and wet."

"Please, you're making me blush." Michael feigned modesty, his complexion rosy from remembered pleasures.

"As if that were possible," I said, remembering his "try anything once" philosophy.

"You should see," Lucas continued in his randy vein, his enthusiasm for Michael's sex like a faucet screwed all the way open, the water growing hotter and hotter as it gushes, the room finally dripping condensation from the accumulated vapor. Lucas had till now remained mostly silent, and his talking changed my developing picture of him and Michael, my initial impression of their perceived difference replaced as I watched by an overwhelming sense of their interconnectedness. Michael seemed to absorb Lucas's color, to radiate an unfamiliar glow of robust health, a physical aura of calm and relaxation, while I imagined Lucas was somehow more composed than his normal self, and I interpreted his recounting their energetic couplings as a kind of gentle improvisation on Michael's penchant for self-deprecation, the hard edge of irony replaced by a soothing, refreshing sincerity.

"You should come out with us tonight." Lucas had worked himself into a frenzy of excitement; he twisted to the strains of imagined dance music.

"I don't think so," Stuart answered. Michael looked at me, tilted his head with the mildest curiosity, and I felt my spine stiffen.

"Stuart hates crowds." I felt I was melting under the heat of Michael's gaze, the faint frown of concern on his face more painful to witness than the most vigorous and outspoken signs of alarm or disapproval, the possibility of his worrying about me, caring for my happiness, an excruciating burden I did not think I could bear. My greatest fear was that Michael might make some bold attempt to abuse his executive privilege and force an entry into my heart. Stuart let go of my hand and stood up.

"We'll do dinner some other night." Gingerly Stuart moved to draw attention away from himself, to declare his lack of interest in whatever meaning Michael's sidelong looks held for me.

"Right." Lucas seemed genuinely to look forward to the occasion.

"You think you can escape so easily?" Michael asked, a hint of his old familiar wistful self present in his voice. "When do I see you again?"

"Actually"—I had not yet bothered to mention to him— "we're fellow academics. I transferred last winter."

"Very good, then. I'll take you to lunch." We made no

specific date, but Michael issued his invitation with a certain confidence.

"Goodbye." Stuart turned for the door, impatiently fingered the knob. Lucas and he shook hands, Lucas eagerly flapping his arm up and down, Stuart limply allowing his own to be pumped. Lucas then squeezed me in his arms, sighing over my shoulder with the heartfelt resignation of an old friend before kissing me on the cheek. Michael opened the door and kissed me goodbye on the lips while Stuart, with his back turned, waited at the top of the landing. He grumbled, "Let's go, Tom."

Halfway down the first flight of stairs I stole a look back. Michael stood in the doorway monitoring our descent, Lucas behind him, arms clasped loosely around his waist, cheek pressed tenderly against one shoulder. I met Michael's eyes; I read a tingling passage of regret in their comforting sparkle, the physical glow of his comfortable happiness with Lucas heightened by this glimpse of the old sadness. He was changed, only I couldn't exactly say how, whether for better or worse, seemingly both. I blinked, and out of the corner of my eye as I looked up I could see Lucas lift Michael off the ground and twirl him in his strong arms back into the room, the giggle of their voices carried along by the breeze of the slamming door. I stumbled, steadied myself on the banister, and limply followed Stuart back to the street.

We remained silent during the subway ride home, conversation impossible on the burrowing L train. The East River was a great weight pressing from above, a formidable darkness, and the lights of the Bedford Avenue station flickering at the Brooklyn end of the tunnel brought a grateful sense of relief; I clung to them as irrational insurance of my survival. Stuart bounded out of the station and stood ready at the corner to offer me a diet soda when I emerged into the light.

"So that was your friend in Chicago?" Stuart barely suppressed a sneer, and we began the long walk down Bedford Avenue. I watched him turn his head to smile at me, admired the sharp lines of folding flesh along his neck. His jealousy surprised me, I felt so permanently aware of his physical charm, the liquid spell he cast over me, the superiority of his athletic frame.

"Just a friend," I answered. Memories of Dennis flitted through my mind, secrets I had hidden from Stuart and was determined once again not to share. "Nothing special."

"He likes you." We waited for the light at Metropolitan Avenue, prepared to plunge into the squalor of the south side. "A lot."

"What does that mean?"

"He's obviously in love with you." Stuart spoke sweetly, admiringly. His words reached like tentacles inside my brain, massaged my mental weak spots. "I don't blame him."

"You must have been hallucinating." I shivered slightly, recoiled.

"You could see it in his eyes, the way he looked at you." Stuart sensed my discomfort, and certain he had found a sore spot, he dug in, picked at my embarrassment as if it were a dry scab, scraping away the hard red flecks to reveal the remnants of a moist pink wound beneath.

"Anyway, I don't know what difference it makes. Lord knows, I'd never sleep with him." We passed beneath the bridge, and I imagined my words trailing off unheard into the echo of the rebounding roadway overhead.

"That's good," Stuart said, turning the corner onto Broadway. "Because he's sick."

"What are you talking about?" Stuart seemed to have crossed a line, overstepped the bounds of decency. I mistook his accusation for the overreaching effect of what had seemed to be his initial jealousy, a suggestion of neurosis or some other character disorder, a calculated deflation of Michael's purported affection for me as it might reflect my own desirability.

"I mean what I say." We had arrived home. "The man is sick."

"I still don't understand. How do you know he's sick? What's the matter with him?"

"You *are* dense sometimes, Thomas." Stuart rapped a knuckle on the top of my skull. "Let's see, gay man, approximately thirty years old." Stuart pretended to think for a minute. "What could possibly be the matter?" He pulled off his shirt, ignored my staring at him in disbelief, grabbed me by the shoulder, and said, "Come on, let's take a shower."

I followed him speechless into the back of the apartment, unable to answer his charges. Stuart ran the water while I undressed. I stood before him as he sat on the edge of the tub, felt his fingers trace the shaded curves of my numb body, the water coursing over the clear curtain, pounding down at us from above, yet somehow we remained dry. Stuart turned around and I stared at myself in the mirror of reflective dew slowly building on his arched back, his hands pressed against the bottom of the tub, face lost in the shining slippery vinyl. I looked down at his damp thighs splayed against the cold ceramic, barely aware of my own actions, his smooth haunch like some animal I had never before seen, and tore forward inside him in a blank convulsion, only a sharp tingling in my feet returning me to the heat of Stuart's panting beneath me, laughing, the shower curtain torn from its hooks, the bathroom flooding with water.

"Wow." Stuart slowed the flow of water with one hand, reached another behind, and pressed me against him. "That was incredible. Did you see stars?"

"I think I'm going to throw up." I slumped to the floor, faint and sick to my stomach. I heard a ringing in my ears. Stuart fixed the curtain, slid his arms under my shoulders, and lifted me into the shower. "Pretty good, huh?" My queasiness began to pass, replaced by a pleasant surprise at the persistence of our passion. I washed Stuart's hair, kneaded his scalp with my quaking fingers. He hummed a satisfied response, rinsed himself, and left me alone in the shower. Our talk about Michael remained unfinished.

My neck and back burned in the hot water. Was I blind? What had Stuart seen to make him so sure? Michael had looked beautiful to me, relaxed and healthy and happy in love, not nearly as pale or thin or ghostly as I recalled. Was his improved complexion simply a trick of the New York summer sun? No one could be remembered from the Chicago winter as radiant and tan. But Michael had struck me as more than just physically relaxed, and Stuart's intimations of ill health made me doubt my much greater impression of his calmness. Had he always been sick? The possibility of persistent illness would require the unthinkable revision of every aspect of our past relations. Perhaps the ease I felt in his presence was simply the result of our each so obviously being attached to someone else, a kind of resolution to the unfired erotic charge which had always existed between us; only now I was left to contemplate a whole new dimension in the complicated choreography of our crossed paths.

Still, I wondered. I briefly suspected Stuart of playing some trick on me, but dismissed my paranoid doubts of him; he was too certain. Stuart knew, had guessed Michael's secret. And the more I considered, the more I figured Michael knew of Stuart's knowledge. I turned off the water, feeling utterly confused, unable to fully believe Stuart, his observation however planted like a bad seed in a fertile patch of my imagination, where it was bound to grow unchecked.

I climbed into bed, exhausted, and found a warm patch in the sun still streaming through the skylight. Stuart stood in his underwear in the kitchen, rinsing a paintbrush. I looked at him and he smiled back at me, waved a wordless distant greeting before returning to his work. I pulled the sheet over my head and listened to the faint reassuring scratch of bristle on canvas, like squirrels scampering through the gutters on a rainy day, as I drifted into my habitual afternoon sleep.

I awoke to find Stuart beside me in the bed. He lay on his side with one hand curled in a loose fist before his parted lips, thumb flexed loose as if he had fallen asleep sucking it. I patted him on the rear end and whispered in his ear, "Stuart-monster, wake up."

He scrunched up his nose in mild irritation and rolled over. His exposed cheek was red and wrinkled from the crumpled sheet; he looked like an enormous baby, one of those cartoon-character professionals who leap from their bassinets at the end of a hard day's work to chomp on a cigar and belt down a swig of whiskey. I laid a hand on his hip, rocked him gently. "Stuart," I murmured, "wake up, Stuart."

He jerked his elbow, jabbing me in the ribs. "Ouch." I sat up straight. He pulled the sheet over his shoulders, seemingly pleased to be left alone, and the irritated curl in his lip unfolded as if he had been asleep the whole time, his sweet dreams successfully defended from my pesky presence beside him. I searched his face for signs of wakefulness and caught him slyly smiling as I rose from the bed. He stretched himself out across its width like a conquering hero settling into satisfied possession of his expanded dominion. I retreated to the kitchen, where I reclined defeated on the little sofa in the twilight and awaited Stuart's rising, myself the vanquished sovereign who humbly hopes to retain some portion of his former dignity in whatever diminished capacity may be offered him.

Stuart followed soon after me. He sat at the kitchen table and yawned. "I'm starving. Shall I take you out for dinner?" His offer surprised me; I felt like a yo-yo angrily flung away into space, only to be hurled in again and cradled in his strong palm, the tightly wound string pinched in a slip knot around his right index finger defining the outer limits of my sleepwalking.

"Mexican?" He repeated his offer.

"Sure." I shrugged, wary of his generosity.

In a moment he was dressed and we were walking north through the neighborhood, up Wythe Avenue past the sugar factory. The last pink rays of the sunset lined the edge of the cloudy sky like a painted ribbon on a blue china tea cup, and a cool breeze off the East River hinted at lowering temperatures and the possibility of rain. Floodlights bathed the park at North Twelfth Street in a fluorescent glow; a drunken crowd barbecued, cheered the local softball teams, dozens of middle-aged Puerto Rican men squeezed into tight-fitting blue- or red-striped white spandex uniforms. Across the river Michael and Lucas and tens of thousands of others continued to celebrate, and I imagined I could hear their whooping and hollering as Stuart and I drifted farther north through the deserted industrial edges of Greenpoint, wandered like a pair of sole survivors along the fringes of the city until we reached our restaurant, a favored hole in the wall only a few blocks short of the Newtown Creek, which separates Brooklyn from Queens.

We assumed our regular table at the front of the nearly empty room. Our friend the natty waiter approached. He bent his lithe, slender figure forward in a deeply appreciative bow before greeting us with exquisite politeness. "Good evening, gentlemen. How do you do tonight?" He hovered over the table, anxiously waiting for us to respectfully return his salutations, his tense smile slowly relaxing as we did so. At last, our orders complete, he turned to the kitchen, but stopped short and knowingly commented, "I am surprised to see you here tonight."

"It's like there's some international conspiracy which says we've got to flock to the piers once a year like lemmings or something." Stuart squinted, irritated at the retreating waiter. "Like salmon swimming upstream to their deaths."

"You make it sound so horrible." Stuart tended to cherish his unconventional wisdom. "I think it sounds like fun."

"You wanted to go?" He looked at me exasperated. "Why didn't you say so? We could have gone." I felt as if Stuart was setting a trap for me with his words, and carefully I sought to avoid falling for the bait he so casually laid.

"I didn't really want to go," I said. "I just thought it sounded like it might be fun."

"Well, it's not," Stuart assured me. "It's crowded and smelly and the music sucks. It's basically nothing but a bunch of fan dancers from New Jersey." I had no idea what a fan dancer was, but I hid my curiosity.

The necessary distraction of our meal effectively changed the topic to the reliable savor of the food before us, something on which we could easily agree. We enjoyed the calm satisfaction of predictable pleasures, the subtle certainty of a mole sauce as sublime and reassuring in its way as the sun's daily rising, winter's release into spring, the moon's seduction of the tides, the heartache and turmoil of life buried beneath the accumulated small comforts of blessed habit, this meal indulged in reason enough in itself for our shared existence, the common cause that binds us together and carries us through the discrete succession of days which describes our lives.

By the end of our meal all differences had been set aside and I was left instead with the remarkable impression of Stuart's lasting company. He was there, right there, sitting across from me, looking at me, sleepy and happy, and all I could see was the miraculous durability of our domesticity. How lucky I felt, how grateful to be living this muted life of yoked ambition and desire. I looked at Stuart and saw reflected in his eyes the curious joy I had seen in Michael's, the glimmering sadness and hope of his parting glance like the pale dawning of a cherished dream about to become reality.

Sated, we paid our bill and began the slow walk home.

Once again Tony barbecued on the Brooklyn piers for the Fourth of July, and Stuart and I almost managed to pass the holiday without a single mention of its being the first anniversary of our meeting. I felt keenly aware of the day's significance and sensed a similarly heightened sensitivity in Stuart's own shifting mood on the eve of the date, yet we both shied away from any conventional form of sentimental or romantic display. What did it mean, the passage of this year together? Our lives resembled no familiar model; no ritual I knew existed to memorialize what we shared, nor did any prescription seem to exist for our future. I felt only a heightened responsibility, a frightening obligation to savor Stuart's company, and a dread of living in the world without him.

Oscar at last broke the superstitious spell which held Stuart and me in silence. In her fearless, unsuspecting manner she slapped me on the shoulder, pointed at Tony hunched over the glowing charcoal, and asked, "Do you still blame the man for all your troubles? It was his fateful invitation, after all, which brought you here."

"On the contrary," I said, convinced in retrospect of the inevitability of the past year and the foolishness of not gratefully accepting one's fate, "I owe Tony everything."

"What do you owe Tony?" Stuart typically tuned in late, peeved by the suggestion of my indebtedness to anyone else.

"We might never have met if it wasn't for him."

"We'll send him a thank-you note in the morning," Stuart joked. He drifted for a moment into his own thoughts before continuing: "I guess tonight is kind of our anniversary."

"I guess so." We were neither of us visibly moved, rather grudgingly seemed to agree, as if it were a joint confession.

"You guys are such wimps," said Oscar. "Blythe and I took a bubble bath, ate champagne brunch, then screwed around for hours on our anniversary."

"I was never exactly the candle-burning, flower-bearing romantic to begin with," Stuart defended himself. "Tom and I trust each other, and that's what really counts." I stood beside him as if posing for a picture, Oscar the camera neutrally recording our presence. I had nothing to add to Stuart's summation, my only task to smile and say "Cheese."

Stuart headed home as soon as the fireworks had ended, citing the urgency of his most recent work as excuse. I stayed behind, determined to join the party I had missed the year before. We trudged back to Tony's loft, where he pulled a blender from one of the kitchen cabinets and waved it over his head to the applause of his guests. A bag of ice, a bottle of rum, and several boxes of daiquiri mix were ranged in stations on the kitchen counter. Someone turned on the stereo and the apartment filled with the voice of Doris Day, the blender's grinding motor rudely punctuating her perky lyrics like a guttural reminder of the seamy underside of the domestic life she so cheerily represented. I poured myself a hefty drink.

Oscar leaned against the wall by an open window and I sat on the sill beside her. The eternal partying on Bedford Avenue echoed in the grimy back courtyard like a dim reminder of the illicit pleasures and dangers always lurking just outside the securely locked doors of our safe haven. One false move and I might be sucked into the underworld, disappear in a narcotic nightmare fog, teeter over the precarious cliff edge of my life into irredeemable darkness. What inexplicable force, I wondered, preserved me from my inevitable fall? I finished my drink and Oscar fetched me a second.

"Karen Carpenter was such a genius." Oscar handed me a full glass and launched into a reverential appraisal, shouting across the room for someone to turn the music even louder. "A real ironist. Somehow she takes the most artificial sentiment and makes it pathetic. But even while she reminds us how pathetic and stupid it is, still she believes it and suffers and makes us believe it."

"Too bad Richard is such an asshole." The ridiculous swelling music carried me along a tide of irresistible pulpy feeling. "I think he killed her."

"He was jealous," Oscar said. "He knew she had all the talent and he hated her for it." She hung her head in quiet regret. "What a tragic waste."

The music changed and I stumbled up to the kitchen counter. Tony rose from behind the open refrigerator door. "Looking for something, Thomas?"

"More please." I held out my glass to him, loosened my grip. Tony caught the glass in his open palm, rescuing it from shattering contact with the tile floor. The blender roared and he returned me a full frothy portion of the icy, sweet concoction. His cool wet fingertips lingered on my wrist as if searching for my pulse before his duties as host returned him to the needs of his clamoring guests. I wandered into the nether reaches of the loft, sank before the blast of a rotary fan onto a stiff futon, where I sat with my eyes closed, sipping my drink and meditating on the continually campy music.

I opened my eyes and a tall figure approached, took my unfinished drink from my hand, and sat down beside me;

Tony had followed me into this darkened private corner. He laid a hand on my thigh and with his other smoothed the back of my neck. I leaned toward him. His fingers gently dug into my flesh, pressed the cavity between my shoulder blades, urging me to collapse against him like a toy dancer on a pedestal when the bottom is raised. I felt the heat of his breath in my ear, a moist tickle on my earlobe. My spine melted and I buckled over into his arms. He caught me and held me, cradled my neck in his elbow as he rubbed my loose sides and lowered me flat. He kissed my forehead, my temples and cheeks, reached an ever-probing hand around my waist, another behind my head, combing my hair with his fingers as he pressed his lips against mine before turning his cheek and whispering, "You're too good."

The music stopped. The buzz of the party became visceral, voices rough and unfiltered in the space between songs, dishes clinking, feet stomping, doors opening and closing, hundreds of odd, unharmonized noises clattering for individual attention before the resumption of song cast them together in a coherent whole. The room spun slightly and I stood in a panic. What was I doing? Tony held my wrist, unaware of the horror I felt. The breeze from the fan grazed my legs, blew Tony's hair over his forehead.

"It's okay, Thomas," he said, tugging me down toward him. "Stuart won't care."

"I have to go," I said, pulling myself free, the knot of fear in my stomach dissolving into sickness. I ran for the door and tumbled down the stairs. Grand Street was dark and deserted and the pavement seemed to roll slightly underfoot. My pulse slowed to a calmer pace as I walked, and when I turned the corner down Berry Street I felt almost myself again, only drunker than I had realized. The neighborhood was basically quiet, only a few kids sitting on stoops or leaning out windows. I had crossed South Second Street and considered myself safely through the worst of Williamsburg, when I heard a scattered tinkling, like the sound of pebbles thrown by the handful across concrete. I continued fairly steady on my feet, swaying only a little. A moment later I heard something whiz over my shoulder; a sharp rap on the back of my skull followed, accompanied by a gleeful, mean laugh.

I turned and faced a band of previously unseen teenagers, their ringleader, who had thrown the first stone, pointing an accusatory finger at me and disparagingly tossing off for the benefit of his friends: "Stupid white faggot. Go back to Manhattan." His voice trailed off into Spanish. I froze, felt the strange heat of the wound to the back of my head, stared at the boy staring at me, and thought he looked kind of cute.

"*Maricón!*" they shouted in unison, and began walking toward me. I staggered back, turned again, and ran in drunken abandon toward the bridge, unaware whether they made any effort to follow me, my throat dry by the time I reached Broadway, my legs throbbing with white streaks of pain, my heart racing so fast its doubling pulse pounded a deafening beat in my ears. I felt in my pockets for my keys, but my fingers were shaky and numb and only became entangled in the sticky fabric of my shorts. I kicked the door. I intended to shout Stuart's name, cry for help, but when I opened my mouth only a hoarse whisper emerged.

"Tom?" Stuart called from the other side. I fought to answer him but choked on the words. I felt tears welling in my eyes, struggling to reach the surface. Stuart cautiously opened the door and I collapsed sobbing and curled myself around his sturdy legs. He crouched beside me, loosely holding me by the shoulders. I looked up into his eyes, but he did not look back at me; instead, his gaze was fixed above me at the canvas he had left to answer the door. "You're drunk," he said. "I have to go back to work."

I remained huddled on the floor and watched panic-stricken his turning away from me. Not until I weakly stood and soberly approached his easel did he notice the blood-matted hair at the back of my scalp. He laid down his brush, touched a hand to my head, and muttered, "Jesus, Tom, what happened?" I was unable to speak. I wanted to cry, but my tears had inexplicably dried up, as if by some strange process of transmigration, so that when Stuart looked at me, frightened now, tears were trickling over his flushed cheeks. I shook my head at the blinding studio light, the fear I felt finally passing into an exhaustion of relief, and blacked out.

When I came to, I was sitting in the empty tub, my head swaddled in a towel damp from my blood and sweat. Stuart sat on the toilet impatiently waiting for me to recover my senses. "God, you scared me." He sounded annoyed at the disturbance. "I thought you'd been shot or something."

"Some neighborhood kids." I found my voice again. "They chased me down Berry, threw rocks at me."

"That's all?" Stuart dismissed the incident. "Stupid bananas!" He washed his hands, as if cleansing himself of the disturbance, leaned over the tub, and absentmindedly kissed me, seeming completely uninterested in the danger I had just escaped, glad I had recovered enough for him to return to his work with an easy conscience.

My head still ached over a week later when I finally crossed paths with Michael in the library. I had stood in the center of the busy atrium lobby distractedly trying to decide where to begin some necessary research when I felt a tugging on my shirt-sleeve. "There's a faculty dining room on the twelfth floor," he said, pointing to the upper reaches of the hollow cube of space. "Can I treat you to lunch?" I gladly accepted and followed him to the express elevator. He seemed to have a light spring in his step, to bound across the marble surface in his black sneakers; even his walk struck me as somehow different than I remembered, not nearly so heavy or constricted as was all our constant scurrying across the cold flagstones of Chicago. He looked quite jaunty in his summer clothes, a worn leather briefcase cradled under his bare tan arm, a Panama hat deftly tilted over his brow; to my vision he presented a regular picture of health.

We emerged from the elevator and stopped to look down over the metal railing of the open stairway. The lobby floor undulated in a tightly woven pattern of black and gray and white. "It's a Palladian design," Michael explained. "Taken from *San Giorgio Maggiore* in Venice." His passion for architecture was undiminished. "The building is Philip Johnson, but I don't find it such a convincing use of space. It's too grandiose a gesture for open stacks—a concept, by the way, which in itself I find offensive. I think the Ford Foundation building on Forty-second Street is more human."

"It's sickening," I said of the view.

"It's intentionally hostile; an old man's slyly misanthropic tweaking of our noses." Michael seemed satisfied with his observations, as if he was letting me in on a cynical joke that I didn't wholly grasp. "Come, let's eat." We passed through a double-glass door into the dining room, where tweedy professors, hunched and shuffling, waited their turn in line around a crowded buffet. Michael steered me to a table by the window in the rear. The highest peaks of the downtown skyline rose above the apartment block directly opposite, and a yellow-brown cloud of ozone settled over the city, pollution-green highlights flashing ominously in the broken rays of the sun.

"Amazing we actually breathe that stuff," I said, transfixed by the view.

"I find I like New York in the summertime." Michael gestured at the buffet, and we joined the grazing academic herd. He flipped a soggy chicken cutlet onto his plate and heaped a spoonful of chickpea salad on top. "But maybe that's just because I'm in love." I slopped some food on my plate, settled on a mound of wilted romaine lettuce as the most discriminating of my equally unappetizing choices, and we resumed our seats.

"You sound so married." I chewed a lettuce leaf.

"I know." Michael smiled. "I've become disgustingly self-satisfied. Who would have thought?"

"Not me," I grumbled, jealous of Michael's contentment, ashamed of my own restlessness.

"Is this the part where you spill your guts, break down in tears, and compulsively confess everything?" Michael sat up straight and looked at me, concerned, a twinkle of experienced indulgence in his eyes. "Stuart doesn't beat you, does he?"

"I don't know," I caught myself muttering. "Sometimes I wonder."

"Hmmmmmmm," Michael empathetically hummed. "I know. But stay with him anyway."

"How can you be sure?" Did Michael have any idea what I was talking about?

"You can't." He shrugged, as if completely unfazed by this awful uncertainty. "Do you love him?"

"Yes." I nodded, unable to find the consolation I sought in this admission.

"And you think he's handsome and sexy and you like the way you feel when you're standing next to him in a crowded room?" I acceded to all these points. "Then believe me, stay with him."

"There goes my Pomo-Homo identity out the window," I

said, exasperated. I waited for him to rise in defense of our catchphrase.

"Remember, Tommy, the whole point was that it was a one-night stand of a political movement. That's what made it so right." He pushed his plate away and began to outline his new philosophy for me. "Sometimes it's little things that matter most. Maybe he's not perfect, but he's there, and that's pretty good. It's just really nice not to be alone for a change. I tell you, I never thought I'd feel so turned on every time I saw a man carrying a bag of groceries."

"I know what you mean," and I meant it.

"The world is such an unpredictable place. What's wrong with wanting a little stability? Wanting to fend off the darkness, if only for a little while?" Michael framed his questions against the backdrop of a larger canvas. "So you fell in love; you'll get used to it. Besides, who says you have to be happy all the time, can't share hard times and troubles too? Sometimes it's hard to tell the difference between pain and pleasure." Michael was way ahead of me and I struggled to catch up. What was he driving at? Why did I find his words so hard to understand? In conclusion he chuckled to himself: "It'll all be over before you know it anyway."

Were these the words of a dying man? I was hopelessly confused, convinced Michael was not telling me something, but terrified to guess what it might be. I hated to assume anything, but his resignation, and even more his exhorting me to stay with Stuart, were like compost turned into the earth around the budding weed Stuart had sown in my imagination. If Michael was sick, why didn't he tell me? I felt betrayed by the possibility of his secrecy, like a stranger left to trespass guiltily in the cold yard of a once-friendly house where he is no longer welcome. I dared not ask him if he was sick, yet search as I did in his eyes for an indication of

illness, I found nothing, was instead overwhelmed with the
impression that I had never seen him look better.

"Are you all right?" Michael squinted at me, my worry for him deflected back to myself.

"Fine." I felt the bump on my head mildly throbbing. "Only this humidity gives me a headache sometimes. How is Lucas?" Michael leaned forward and rested his elbows on the edge of the table, his chin wedged in the cradle of his joined fists.

"I'll tell you what I like about Lucas." His head bobbed on his folded fingertips as he spoke. "He's nice to me."

"That's a concept."

"You know, there's nothing to compare to basic politeness. It's so unbelievably simple and so depressingly rare. And it makes all the difference." Michael laid his arms together flat on the table. "I've known so many jerks in the past, I still can't believe how considerate Lucas is." His hands returned to his lap. "He's just plain decent."

"I wish I could say the same about Stuart."

"I'm sure he loves you, and that's what matters most." Michael surprised me; he discounted my misgivings without any inquiry, dismissed my intimation of Stuart's churlishness despite his own disquisition to the contrary. Did he perhaps intend to suggest a separate standard, that the rules which governed my life with Stuart were somehow alternate, though necessarily applicable, from those which applied to himself and Lucas? We stood to leave and I felt an odd tension between us, as if we were two objects of utterly opposed density pleasantly surprised to discover that when placed in the balance we had the same mass. I trusted Michael too much not to feel that he was in some sense complimenting me; obliquely he referred to our difference not to discourage or condescend but to convey instead a perception of my worth, and Stuart's appraisal of Michael's feeling for me came immediately to mind. Was this Michael's way of finally saying he loved me?

Back in the lobby my original purpose for having entered the library returned to me, but I ignored the call of the microforms and instead followed Michael out to the park. The day was intensely hot and Washington Square overflowed with summer zanies. We started to cross toward Fifth Avenue but were stopped by two crowds facing each other at the intersection of the paths opening to the fountain at the center. Separating the walls of people were six garbage cans lined in a row, beer cans and broken glass bottles propped along the rims of the ones at either end, while halfway down one of the paths a scrawny man on a skateboard shouted for silence. He waved his arms wildly over his head and bragged about the daredevil feat he was about to perform. Stray pedestrians, unaware of the impending stunt, flitted across the man's path of flight, until his coast suddenly became clear and he launched himself.

"Watch out," he shouted, "here I come." He crouched low on his skateboard. His right leg swept the pavement, propelling him forward, and he aimed directly at the length of the cans. In another instant he was airborne, flying like the star of a demolition derby over his uniquely urban obstacle, knees pressed against his chest, the skateboard held under him with both hands. He cleared the final can and gracefully landed, legs extended, arms raised, wheels spinning noisily. He snapped to a halt, bounced the board up in the air, and, to the bursting applause of the crowd, caught it with one hand.

"Amazing," I murmured. He pulled a kerchief from his pocket, deftly tied it into a pouch, and worked the crowd for donations. I dropped a dollar in the red cloth sack and met his eyes for a second, their unflinching steely distance un-

mitigated by his graciously nodding thank you. I felt frankly
envious of this stranger, of the seemingly raw willpower which
enabled him to perform such a stunt.

"That was nothing," Michael said. We pushed through the
dispersing crowd. "I've seen him do the same thing in
the middle of traffic over on Fourth Avenue. He waits for the
lights to change, then . . ." Michael arced his right hand in
imitation of the man's trajectory and slapped it down hard
against his left palm. I had aimlessly followed Michael out
of the library, reluctant to leave him, but when we stopped
at the corner of Eighth Street the gravitational field which
had dragged me in his direction reversed; I felt strangely
repulsed, compelled to turn away like a comet passing some
cold planet at the outer limit of its elliptical orbit before
hurtling once more toward the sun.

"Thank you for lunch." I almost offered Michael my hand
to shake, but gratefully managed to avoid such an awkward
gesture.

"You're always welcome, Tommy." Michael pecked me on
the cheek. Why was leaving him so difficult? I wanted to
blink and find him gone, race down Eighth Street choking on
the filthy New York air. He started to say something, a final
admonition, but his words were lost in the blasting of a horn
and the cursing of a taxi driver, and in another second my
dream had come true and I was walking alone east on Eighth
Street, mopping my brow with my shirt-sleeve, loving the
heat, and picturing Stuart sweating before his easel in his
underwear. I savored the image; I missed him, couldn't wait
to be with him again.

I walked the Bowery, past the row of restaurant supply
stores below Houston Street, the sidewalk cluttered with fifty-
quart mixers and glass-fronted commercial refrigerators. Delancey Street was clogged with trucks scrambling to cross the
Williamsburg Bridge, and the whole Lower East Side stank

like an open sewer. The black exhaust of the traffic combined with the cloacal urban stench to create a supremely decadent odor of urban decay, a rank assault on the senses, an effluvium so dense I felt it settling on my skin and in my hair, could almost taste it, like a bacterial culture spawning at the top of my windpipe.

I climbed the scorched bridge. The city viewed from the center of the span was a hazy blur; no breeze disturbed the chemical stew of the atmosphere. From the Brooklyn landing I could make out the skylight above our bed, and I imagined Stuart and me asleep together in the middle of the night, blissfully unaware of the massive engineered world towering over us. I was safe in Brooklyn and Stuart was there, waiting for me. What more could I possibly want?

I had my wisdom teeth removed at the beginning of August, and spent four groggy days bundled sweating on the sofa in the kitchen bleeding through the raw caverns in my gums. I lay still, sipping orange juice or diet Coke through a straw, and studied Stuart's mysterious work habits through my codeine haze. Like a kinetic lexicographer I compiled a dictionary of Stuart's body language, catalogued the ways he scratched himself to indicate various degrees of frustration or excitement, a mild tug on his ear usually preceding some minor adjustment, an aggressive scraping of the side of his neck indicative of a serious setback, the quick time-outs to adjust the positionings in his crotch generally followed by a flurry of activity. He was beautiful to watch, mesmerizing.

When my bleeding finally stopped, Stuart suggested a celebration. "Now that you can eat, why don't we have a dinner party?"

"You mean *entertain*?" Stuart had traditionally been wary

of our ever receiving company, arguing the inviolability of
his work space.

"We never do." Stuart had already begun planning the guest list and menu. "We could invite Blythe and Oscar, some other neighborhood people, Tony, even your friend from Chicago if you want."

"Michael," I reminded him.

"So you want to?" I nodded yes, and Stuart hopped from foot to foot with excitement; I had never seen him so happy.

"You're in a good mood." I remained seated on the sofa watching him, wary of Stuart's good spirits. He came and stood over me, reached out his arms, and raised me standing beside him. He placed a hand on my hip, another behind my shoulder, and we swayed together in a slow dance to the music playing in his head. I felt dizzy on my feet from my days of reclining, pleasantly weak in his warm, sturdy arms. He kissed me on the neck and behind my ear, pulled back, and looked me in the eye.

"Tom Tom Tom." I was on the verge of tears. "You're so handsome. Do you know that?" Another word and I would have burst out sobbing; I kissed him instead, anything to avoid his speaking kindly to me.

We phoned the invitations that same night. Michael listened in disapproving silence as I gave instructions on how to get to Williamsburg; when I'd finished, he jokingly asked, "Why on earth do you live there?" I just held the receiver steady and didn't respond. "Never mind," he continued. "It was a stupid question. See you Saturday."

Stuart grabbed the phone out of my hand and dialed Oscar's number. I could hear her squawking on the other end of the line when he told her we were having a party. "Because Tom can eat again," he evidently answered her questioning our purpose. "Because we're in love." He laughed.

"You call Tony." Stuart attempted to pass me the phone.

"Actually . . ." I feigned a sudden urgent need, locked myself in the bathroom, and thoroughly flossed my teeth and brushed my gums, as if my scraping away at the tender pink flesh could somehow loosen the paranoid guilt of my memory, dissolve it into a rinsable solution.

The Saturday of our dinner quickly arrived and proved depressingly hot. Stuart and I followed each other through the farmer's market in Union Square, selecting tomatoes and corn and lettuces and peaches. The temperature seemed to rise higher and higher in the few short hours we remained out of doors, until by the middle of the afternoon, our shopping complete, when we rounded the corner on Broadway, almost home, the mercury topped 100 for the first time that summer, and our entertainment seemed likely to become a horrible fiasco.

"What do we do?" I stuffed the wilting vegetables into the overfrosted refrigerator and slumped sick to my stomach over the kitchen sink, pathetically attempting to cool myself in the brown water spewing weakly from the faucet. Every fire hydrant in Brooklyn must have been open, reducing the water pressure to a dismal low.

"Let's not panic, Tom." Stuart had propped the front door open, hoping to move some air through the apartment, but instead, the fumes from the traffic on the bridge only seeped their insidious way into our bedroom. A stray dog, familiar from the neighborhood, poked his scarred snout in the entry and I shooed him away and closed the door.

"Nothing helps." I touched Stuart's wet arm; his skin felt disgusting, hot and slimy. I tried washing my hands again.

"We have no choice." Stuart proposed a methodology to get us through the long afternoon and evening ahead. "We pretend like nothing is the matter, get everyone really drunk, and sweat like pigs."

We bravely forged ahead with our plans. Stuart washed the salad and husked the corn; I boiled the hot fudge sauce for dessert; Stuart set up bar; I prettied the table. The apartment meanwhile continued to heat up, our slightest activity seeming only to contribute to the moisture in the atmosphere, the ceiling and walls merely the more solid defining limits of the viscous substance of the humidity. The radiant energy of eight more human bodies in such a cauldron was a daunting prospect; to prepare for the inevitable disaster we strategically positioned all our available fans in hopes of ventilating the room enough to keep the party from suffocating.

Stuart was still washing up when the first knock came on the door. I checked my reflection in the mirror, forehead already beaded with sweat only moments out of the shower, and prayed for an unwarranted success before escorting our first arrivals across the threshold. I opened the door and Michael thrust a bouquet of wilting flowers at me.

"Welcome." I motioned Michael and Lucas in, held the flowers to my nose, and pretended to enjoy their dying odor.

"It's unnatural," Lucas said, imitating with a tilt of his head the effect of the heat on the drooping blossoms. "Even the flowers can't stand it."

Michael scanned the apartment like a coyote surveying the desert horizon for prey. "So this is the new bohemia," he said in his best grown-up voice, like a confused parent struggling to make a positive statement.

"That's being generous." Stuart emerged at his most charming, warmly kissed Michael and Lucas each on both cheeks. "You must want something to drink. Vodka, maybe?"

"We are parched. Who on earth ever heard of the J train?"

Michael flapped his hands before his face in a futile gesture against the heat. Lucas wrapped an arm from behind around Michael's stomach and spoke over his shoulder.

"We'll stick to soda, thank you." Michael frowned and Lucas squeezed him tight, then released him. "Remember, dear, got to be careful in your condition."

What condition? I swallowed my question. Always these hints floating in the air, never a positive assertion; we seemed to be playing by the old Chicago rules: assume what you will but ask nothing, and don't expect the truth for truth's sake. Someone banged on the door and Stuart ran to open it.

Tony stumbled in, complaining loudly about the heat and ignoring his date as if he were some stranger who had followed him home on the street. "You would decide to have a party on the hottest day of the year. I need a drink quick."

"He's cute," Michael whispered in my ear.

Tony approached and I made the introductions. "Tony is an architect." Stuart handed out the drinks and we sat around the makeshift table. I took a first sip and nearly gagged on the overpowering alcohol content. "Lord, that's strong." Stuart just winked at me, lifted his glass, and encouraged everyone to drink up before a troubled look crossed his face and he remembered to turn on the music.

"Stuart has a weak spot for Sinatra. Anything with a Nelson Riddle orchestration, actually." Another bang on the door, my turn now to answer.

"You're going to need this." Blythe handed me a bag of ice. An unfamiliar couple stood behind her.

"Feels wonderful." I welcomed her brother and his fiancée from out of town. "Where's Oscar?"

"We had a fight," Blythe said. "She'll be here soon."

"Not serious, I hope." Stuart mixed their drinks.

"The usual domestic squabble. A baby fight, really. Nothing broken." Blythe sounded as though she almost regretted the lack of lost property.

"Tommy and I never fight." Stuart grinned.

"Liar." Lucas called his bluff.

"The best thing about fighting is the sex afterward." I was already feeling the heat of my first drink and wondering how on earth I would manage to get dinner on the table.

"Lucas and I need no excuses," Michael said.

"Send me a postcard a year from now and tell me about it." Stuart headed for the door; Oscar had arrived. He guided her to the table, then, urging silence, raised a small white envelope over his head.

"My friends"—he wiped his brow—"may I present to you the cause of our celebration." He flipped the envelope upside down and my wisdom teeth rattled like a double set of dice over the table.

"How perfectly disgusting." Michael gaped. Oscar was doubled over with laughter, loving Stuart's little joke, while Blythe explained away the incident to her relations. Tony picked up my teeth and held them in his open palm, examining them as he would the precious discovery of a tedious paleontological dig, his eyes scrunched up as if he were reconstructing in his mind the magnificent creature to which they had once belonged.

"They're beautiful," Tony sighed. He passed one to Oscar, who scratched at it with her thumbnail, then sniffed it.

"Recognize the scent?" Stuart made fun of her. He collected my teeth, folded down the top of the envelope, and stowed them away in his front pants pocket. The room was excruciatingly hot, but the fans blew a steady breeze across the table and the music grew ever louder as Stuart cleverly refilled drinks; by the time I set the salad on the table, everyone was thoroughly smashed, dipping their hands in a bowl of ice as it passed down the line, moistening their lips with their frosted fingers. The heat, Stuart and I happily discovered, turned out to be strangely intoxicating, a fatal excuse for all sorts of otherwise unaccountable behavior. Our guests remained glued to their seats in a kind of fatalistic passivity, a surrender to the force of nature, a social inertia, allowance for anything, while Stuart and I circled the table, serving and clearing through the storm of chitchat, until we had made it clear to dessert and the real party seemed set to begin.

I wandered from my place and caught Lucas drinking warm vodka straight from the bottle between spoonfuls of his hot fudge sundae, more a lukewarm soup of chocolate and vanilla swirls than the desired palate-teasing hot-cold contrast I had intended; not that anyone complained, or even noticed. I pried the bottle loose from his candy-sticky palm and helped myself to a swig of the neutral spirits, then dropped into his comfortable lap.

"I thought you weren't drinking?" I slid sideways over his spread legs and grabbed the back of his chair for support.

"I wasn't." Lucas bounced me on his knee. "Michael was right about you."

"Michael's right about everything." I admired Lucas's flushed complexion, his mellow brown eyes and tousled hair; even his crooked smile seemed more than intelligible. "What did he say?"

"Only how good you are." His words sounded awfully familiar.

"Strange, Michael says the same thing about you."

"Michael's better than all of us put together. He's the smartest, kindest person I ever met." Lucas poked a finger in my cheek. "Too bad you don't have any more wisdom teeth." He tried to pop his finger in my mouth, but I stopped him. I was slipping away from him, crashing toward the floor;

he splayed his legs and I disappeared under the table.
"Whoops." His distant laugh echoed as if from the top of a great canyon. I emerged kneeling on the other side, eye level with Blythe's crotch. She petted the top of my head and handed down the bottle of liquor.

"You and Stuart should get married." She tapped her foot against my thigh. "You're such a good couple." I wasn't quite sure what she meant; nor did the idea of marriage appeal to me.

"Is it so obvious?" I phrased my question as an expression of embarrassment, happy with the impression Stuart and I seemed to be creating.

"Are you kidding? You two are like the fucking *Tom and Stuart Show*. You guys should be in syndication." Blythe closed her eyes and slid an ice cube across the lids. I hobbled to the head of the table and crowded into Stuart's seat, careful not to interrupt his heated discussion with Michael.

"It's a sin, it's a sin, it's a sin." Michael was solemnly nodding his head, the only sober person in the room.

"That is so ridiculous." Stuart was equally emphatic. "If I want to kill myself, why shouldn't I?"

"Because you'll go to a dark dark place and stay there a very long long time." Michael sounded quite sure of himself.

"How do you know?" Stuart challenged.

"I don't," Michael answered perversely, as if to suggest the question was silly and his answer obscenely obvious.

"It's one big dirt nap." Stuart laughed. "That's what I say; and when it's over it's over. I don't understand how anyone can believe anything else."

"There is no explanation for it, that's the whole point," Michael practically pleaded. Stuart dismissed his argument with a shiver. "Why something over nothing?"

"All I know is, I couldn't live without the possibility of ending it all." I had never heard Stuart utter such completely morbid thoughts; how had Michael managed to unearth this articulate darkness?

"That's pure foolishness." Michael was unfazed by Stuart's histrionics. "Someday you'll have children and blush at the memory of thinking such a thought."

"I could never have kids. The thought of being responsible for something that has to face its own death horrifies me." Stuart was horrifying me; he was practically gushing the most hideous kind of self-indulgent morbidity, with Michael at the pump handle furiously working to keep up a steady flow.

"That's real uplifting." Oscar joined the conversation.

"I understand what you're saying," Michael said. "I just think your attitude is a luxury of youth. I'm not much older than you, but I can't afford to think like that anymore." Michael settled into his most secure sage persona. "It's easy to think about how horrible life is when you're young. Personally, at least, I've lost the taste for the struggle."

"Does this mean we'll never raise a family together?" I stroked Stuart's hair; he looked especially pretty in his distress, and I felt my place by his side especially proper.

"Cancel that turkey-baster baby." Oscar referred to a long-cherished plan she and Blythe harbored as their best hope for reproduction short of the idealized parthenogenesis.

"Tom comes from good strong New England stock. I'm sure his genes would be an admirable addition to the pool." Stuart shook loose from his night visions, twisted his neck and shoulders, and relaxed in his chair like a brooding hen nervously rising from her full nest to fluff her feathers, her down settling light and airy back into place. "He has good strong

teeth." Stuart peeled my lips open with his thumb and forefinger to display my orthodontically correct smile. He let go
and I sucked on his thumb, tasteless but highly suggestive.
"What's left of them, anyway."

"At least he's not an unreliable egomaniac." Oscar dropped
the words without a hint of irony. She looked at Michael as
she spoke. Was she weighing the potential advantage of my
genetic material in comparison to Stuart's, or did she instead
imply an apology or excuse for Stuart's sudden invalidism?

"He's worse." Tony had moved to our end of the table.
"He's a painter."

"I think Tommy is just about the sanest person I know."
Michael settled on the first interpretation. "And Stuart quite
obviously his perfect complement." Or had he?

"Ready?" Lucas stood behind Michael, resting his hands
on his shoulders. Everyone was standing now, milling drunkenly about the room, pushing the chairs against the walls.
Once more Stuart raised the volume of the music, and the
rippling liquid sound pounded the walls in great crashing
waves. The floor creaked from Oscar and Blythe's heavy dancing; Michael and Lucas were locked in a two-step in the
bedroom. I saw the lamp on my dresser flicker on. The yellow
light tripped some long-unused switch in my mind, and I left
Stuart twirling in Tony's arms with memories of Michael's old
tricks flooding my imagination as I swerved through the traffic
of sound toward the bathroom. Michael was fast at work
when I emerged a moment later, rifling through Stuart's night
table.

"What do you think?" I asked. He held Stuart's fabled
copy of *Modern Painters* up to the light, studied the penciled
notes on the inside front cover.

"I think he's charming and handsome." He laid the book
down. "I think you're very lucky."

"You are shameless sometimes." Lucas stood Michael up. "Come on, it's way past our bedtime." I followed them to the front door.

"Leaving so soon?" Stuart held his palm up in genuine distress.

"It's after two in the morning." Michael rolled his eyes and pretended amazement at the hour.

"I can't think of a better way to have spent the hottest day of the year. Thank you both," Lucas said in his easy, gracious manner.

"Someone take me home." Michael's voice betrayed his secret exhaustion.

"I'll get you a cab," Stuart offered. He turned to me: "Be back in a minute." Lucas and Michael and I hugged in a sloppy huddle before they scurried off behind Stuart up Broadway. I waved at them, but they never looked back. I waited till they disappeared under the bridge, then retreated into the apartment. Blythe's brother and his fiancée were clearing the table, with no help from anyone else. I turned up the lights and lowered the music. The fans I had barely noticed most of the night rattled loudly, their only effect to recirculate the foul air I now found oppressive and sickening.

"The party's over," Tony sang in his best Judy Garland imitation. His date had passed out on the sofa; Tony kicked him in the shin.

"Good night." I pushed them out the door, anxious to be rid of Tony before Stuart returned. Tony's date wandered into the street, unaware of Tony's halting, pathetic efforts to paw me, a desperate last-minute stab at flirtation. "I said good night." I shoved Tony off me.

"It's just a matter of time, Thomas. You'll see." He started after his friend, who was waiting now across the street. "Ever since the first time I saw you . . ." I caught the drunken incoherent whisper of his words as I slammed the door shut after him. Oscar was rinsing plates in the sink. I sat by Blythe on the sofa and stole a puff on her cigarette. Stuart returned, breathless from jogging down Broadway. He unplugged the fans, the transparent quiet of the music in their echoing wake a soothing release. He swept up the near-empty bottle of vodka and squeezed in between me and Blythe. We each took a final swig. Stuart took my arm in both his hands and began kissing it, his lips unbelievably hot and tingling, moving methodically from my knuckles over my wrist, lingering in the broiling desert of my elbow before ascending the heights of my shoulder and the side of my neck. I was melting, pliant like wax on the verge of turning liquid; if there had been a thermostat in the room I would have turned it higher, I had never felt so hot, so loose, so fully of a piece with Stuart; I wanted to just lie there and bake, rise together like a braided loaf, our pores opening further and further like the expanding springy glutinous dough, until they magically set, the fully developed structure of their crumb tender light and firm, our buttery flesh a tangled crusty nourishing staff of life, our hearts touching.

Blythe cleared her throat and struggled to rise. Stuart ignored her, only expanded into the space she vacated, his hands up the back of my shirt, lips pressed against my belly. I squirmed under his ticklish nibbling, guiltily troubled by his neglect of our lingering guests. "Stuart." I nudged him. He was completely oblivious, gnawing at the top button of my shorts, putting on quite a show.

"Stuart," I said again, this time with more edge in my voice. I clasped his cheeks in my palms and raised his head. His skin was an unhealthy red, streaked with the white impressions of folded denim. His hair was soaking wet.

"Don't mind us," Blythe drawled, and lit another cigarette. Her brother and his future bride stood waiting patiently by the door.

"Where's Oscar?" Stuart asked, as if worried she might have missed his public display of passion.

"Menstruating in your toilet."

"I'll smoke to that." Stuart helped himself to a cigarette, passed it along to me. Oscar appeared in the bedroom doorway.

"We won't disturb you boys any longer," she said. I tried to sit up straight, but Stuart wouldn't let me. "Please, don't bother. You've clearly got your work cut out for you."

"Thank goodness Thomas can eat again," I heard Blythe joking as they let themselves out.

"At last." Stuart dove in where he had left off, his lips and teeth and fingertips a tropical storm of activity raging at my center of gravity. I resisted his seduction, sought a postponement of pleasure.

"Not so fast," I cautioned. He lay perfectly still in my lap, his head rising and falling on my breath. I felt weirdly sated, lost in his surreal nearness, outside myself casually measuring from a vantage point on the ceiling the intersection of our bodies, hypothesizing our prospective nakedness as a rational measure of our life together. Was this the moment I had been waiting for, a necessarily depersonalized spot of unanticipated objectivity? I was not the least bit surprised by my detachment; rather, I welcomed it, recognized in the movie I seemed to be watching in my head some kind of haunting foresight, a suggestive power of the imagination, even at its most vulnerable, perhaps precisely at its most vulnerable, grounding itself like a lightning rod, channeling the most dangerous and powerful of natural currents to a safe discharge in the uncomplaining earth.

Stuart moved again, resumed his low growling and nimble

teething, raised me like a spirit from the dead. Whatever the danger, it had passed, and I submitted with unaccustomed and hungering satisfaction to his caresses, certain I had been awaiting this passage all my life and unspeakably grateful it had finally arrived.

Neither Stuart nor I was home the day the bridge collapsed. I was sitting at the back of an overheated classroom putting the final touches to the final essay question of the final exam that would secure my baccalaureate degree when a section of the track bed fell from the middle of the span into the East River with a graceless thwack and the trains rolled to a nervous halt. By the time I had finished college that early May afternoon, traffic had been diverted north and south and the bridge officially closed. I waited patiently in the dismal light of the Canal Street station for almost an hour, weighted down with the ingredients of a celebratory menu, before a scratchy voice, barely intelligible through the shrill interference of the Transit Authority's aged public-address system, announced the interruption of service. Too tired to much mind the inconvenience, I walked through the tangle of Chinatown toward the bridge, intending to catch the bus to Brooklyn instead. Delancey Street was a disaster, and an impatient crowd of elderly Hasidic women waited at the bus stop completely oblivious to the barricade of sirens and lights cordoning off access to the Brooklyn-bound lanes. I was left no choice but to continue walking.

Already a spirit of shared suffering had developed among the weary commuters who trudged the rusty promenade, strangers saluting each other as they crossed paths in their interborough passage. The day was mild, the afternoon air full of exceptional promise. The towers of the bridge hummed like a tuning fork in the brisk wind, their whistle a tune of unprecedented high spirits and adventure, a Whitman-like song of the great island's uplifting humanity, Manhattan at its most amazing. Most striking was the quiet, the massive failure of the cars and trucks and buses and trains in their assault on the senses. The city seen from the center of the disabled span formed a silent spectacle, as awesomely still and full of natural wonder as I remembered the Michigan dunes from three years before.

I rested midway across the dilapidated walkway and marveled at the variety of persons thrown together even at this unusual extreme. A familiar form rose on the slope I had just climbed, its step springy and suggestive. Stuart approached, removed himself from the current of inconvenience, and stood by my side. I didn't ask where he had been.

"Here," I said. "Take one of these. My feet are killing me." I handed him one of my grocery bags.

"How'd it go?" he asked. We made no reference to the strangeness of our meeting; not that there should have been anything strange about my running into the man I had lived with for so long within a mile of our shared home.

"It's over," I said. The wind and the bright sun and the silence were disorienting. I pictured myself posing for a photograph atop an Alpine glacier in summertime: was Stuart my ski instructor?

"I know, you think your life's all of a sudden supposed to change. Thank God it doesn't." A caravan of fire trucks and police cars parked below us; burly men in uniform walked the open metal grid of the roadway. "It was inevitable," Stuart said.

"Please, it's only been a few hours." I was hardly prepared to play up the dramatics of the change to which I thought Stuart referred.

22

"More like almost a century of neglect." He was talking about the bridge. "You know, they never bothered to galvanize the steel in the cables; the whole thing began to rust before they had even finished building it. When it came time to dedicate the bridge, no one involved wanted the credit." His eyes climbed the square open tower of the Manhattan landing, and he wagged his finger in the air as if to scold those early builders for their lack of foresight. "Doomed from the start, that's what it was."

"They probably did it on purpose." I had never once crossed the bridge without the idea of its collapse entering my mind, and I found the possibility of its creators intentionally fostering such thrilling fear highly plausible, although I was admittedly granting them a profound penchant for dark humor.

"Of course they did." Stuart interpreted their carelessness as a kind of moral failure. "What would they care if the bridge rotted to pieces fifty or a hundred years later. They're all dead now anyway. Washington Roebling, on the other hand; he was a man with a vision of the future." The Gothic brown arches of the Brooklyn Bridge glistened in the tangled distance, majestically spanning the hundred years since its creation as much as it elegantly vaulted the once bottlenecked passage of the East River into New York Harbor.

"Come on, let's go home." I found the fresh air exhausting and felt hungry for a nap. Stuart ran ahead of me, like a child testing the limits of his freedom; I caught up to him running in circles under the train tracks. The tide of people crossing had grown heavier as rush hour approached, but the plaza at the Brooklyn end was nearly deserted, with traffic to and from the BQE completely cut off. From Broadway the bridge loomed strangely static, the reflective silvery ribbons of aluminum darting through the open steel framework replaced by heavy immobile shadows. I studied the flat patterns of light and dark, foreground and background shifting unsteadily back and forth, and felt the consequences of my isolation: how would I survive the bridge's falling out of commission?

Stuart opened the door and dragged me distractedly in after him. He greedily snatched my bag and set out my purchases on the kitchen table, and after approving the ingredients of my little menu followed me into the bedroom, where he pushed me from behind onto the bed. I collapsed windless on my stomach, suffocating from his weight. He kissed me gently on the back of my neck: "Congratulations, Tom."

"Get off me," I groaned. "Please." Stuart just laughed and pinned my arms to my sides with his elbows. He bit me in the shoulder. "Ouch!"

"Mmmmm," he sucked on the wound.

"I'm not kidding, Stuart." My voice sounded gravelly and uneven; was I making myself clear?

"Me neither."

"You're hurting me." He didn't move, only relaxed his hold on me a little. I wiggled his arms loose and spun over on my back, my knees pressed to my chest. Stuart loomed over me. I was panting heavily, my heart racing, ready for a fight, certain he was about to hit me. He grinned and bumped his chest off the soles of my raised feet, rested against me before slapping my thigh loudly with his open palm and standing at the foot of the bed. His face was red and distorted, his trapezoidal head the warped apex of his retreating body viewed from a triangulated perspective.

"Fine," he huffed from the doorway. He raised his arms over his head, swung from the lintel, landed with a thump, and kicked the door shut behind him.

I crawled under the covers and from a peephole in between my blankets stared obsessively at the bedroom door, waiting for Stuart to return. I listened for his footstep, for the refrigerator door to open and close, a cabinet door to slam shut, a radio to turn on, but I heard nothing. Cautiously I rose and tiptoed toward the door. I stood beside it, leaned against the frame, and with my X-ray vision pictured Stuart standing like my mirror image on the other side, sneakily waiting for my hand to grasp the knob, attempt to turn it, only to recognize in the faint resistance of its catch the counter pressure of his own hand locking me in. Like a prisoner obliged through the hopeless force of habit to repeat his daily ritual of checking that his guards have properly performed their job, I reached for the knob, catching myself before I had touched it with the realization there was no safe exit this way. I let my hand drop to my side and retreated to the comfort of the bed, where I lay stiff and acutely aware of the silence in the next room, until the reassuring rush of water from the kitchen faucet, like a waterfall in an urban park blanketing all other noise, followed by the click click click of the automatic pilot on our stove as Stuart set the kettle on to brew himself a cup of tea, convinced me the danger had passed, and I relaxed into the sleep I had initially craved.

Stuart was gone from the apartment when I woke up. He had set the table for dinner, and the vegetables lay washed and clean on the kitchen counter, but there was no note or other sign of explanation for his whereabouts. I had grown more than accustomed to his unexplained disappearances, felt almost grateful at times for them; I never fully trusted he would return, but I had become inured to the nagging anxiety of his waywardness and learned to dismiss the gnawing itch of my irritation as some self-feeding defect of my own character.

I assumed he would be home in time for supper and set about the task of fixing our meal. Not until I had put the finishing touches on the salmon steaks did he bounce breathless and sweaty through the door in T-shirt and short pants, a cheap bottle of red wine under his arm. He handed me the bottle and kissed me on the lips, his cheeks ruddy and his eyes glistening satisfied with the results of his exercise. He kicked off his shoes, sent them twirling into the bedroom, and followed after them, peeling off the rest of his clothes in the process, arriving naked at the end of this trail of laundry in the bathroom. He turned on the shower, put a hand to his crotch, and waved himself happily at me before disappearing into the mist. I sat nibbling at my salad, waiting for him to join me.

"Well." He poured himself a glass of wine and sat down; a droplet of water traced its delicate path from behind his ear down the side of his neck. "You did it." What exactly had I done? "There's something weird going on in the neighborhood." Stuart began to report the observations of his run. "I think there must have been some big bust on South Second Street. Police cars and ambulances everywhere; I think several people were shot. You know the crack house in the middle of the block?"

"You mean they finally closed it?" This would indeed be big neighborhood news.

"Strange, isn't it, same day as the bridge. It's like they cut off their escape route."

"I can't imagine life without the daily shootouts, the cars honking, and people screaming at you while they wait in line. Why bother living in Williamsburg?" I intended no sarcasm. I removed the fish from under the broiler and carefully lifted them with a flat spatula onto our plates.

"Perhaps we should reconsider that split-level ranch home in the suburbs. I could paint in the garage while you fix supper for the kids, right, dear?" Stuart tore into his dinner. "Delicious, as always." We finished the rest of our meal in comparative silence, the wine working its sedative effect. Stuart proposed a walk afterward. "I'll do the dishes later." He grabbed my plate from my hand and led me out to the street. The sky was a creamy peach color, the river mulberry, the downtown skyline like a distant field overgrown with wild-flowers, thistledown and dandelion fluff seeming to rise off the tops of the skyscrapers in velvet swirls. I was pleasantly tipsy, imagined myself swimming in the cottony breeze. We walked south along the abandoned waterfront past the burnt-out hulks of the area's once thriving industry to the Navy Yard, where the granite façade of the Old Naval Hospital, the blind sockets of its windows boarded over with plywood, straddled the top of a grassy slope behind a high barbed-wire fence. A group of young men, soldiers perhaps, played soft-ball on the darkening field. We dipped under the BQE and strolled through the Hasidic section, lights bright in every window. The sun had set but the sky was still light, pink now like the edges of a ripe peach where it touches the pit, when we passed over the highway at Marcy Avenue, almost home.

I went to bed immediately and fell asleep with an uncom-fortable presentiment of absence, a mild dread of the new-found quiet in my life. Stuart must also have fallen prey to the disturbing failure of sound, unable to work perhaps with-out the regular rumble of the subways to punctuate his thoughts. I could sense him through my sleep climbing into bed, rolling and folding me over, tucking his knees securely in behind my own, pulling the sheet tight around his neck, his head sunk in the down of his pillow, his body radiating extraordinary heat, an overpowering organic furnace at full blast. In my dreams I was being chased by soldiers in a terrible war, bloodshed and murder and torture everywhere, fires raging, bombs exploding, each of my successive hiding places exposed, my life a perpetual, harrowing series of nar-row escapes. I watched myself maneuver from forest to field to town to city as if viewing a black-and-white documentary, the grain of the film depressing and inescapable. I was running through abandoned bombed-out streets, air-raid sirens wail-

ing, when the war suddenly seemed to end and the scene
quickly changed, as if a new reel of film had been loaded,
in Technicolor this time, and I was running now up a wide,
vivid green, grassy hill, the sky cobalt blue. A voice whispered in my ear, urging me not to look back while lamenting
the eternity of souls who couldn't have been saved. I gained
the top of the hill, shuddered from the horrific burden of the
pastoral scene and what I felt to be its mocking invitation to
view my own future, and awoke in a panic.

"Stuart." I sat up straight and nudged him. "Wake up,
Stuart." I looked at my alarm clock; the night was still early.
I was shivering.

"Hmmm?" he groggily asked.

"Please, wake up. I'm afraid."

"What's the matter?" He muttered the words.

"I don't know; I'm frightened." My teeth were rattling, my
legs heavy and numb like a pair of wet sponges, my pulse
racing at an uncontrollable speed.

"What are you afraid of?" Did he sound like he
cared?

I thought for a minute, embarrassed now to answer him.

"Dying."

"So?"

"I don't want to die." I began to cry a little.

"It's your fate, Thomas." Comforting words. He rolled over
and closed his eyes; was he really asleep or just pretending?
I jumped out of bed and pulled on my pants. I felt I was
suffocating, would choke to death if I didn't get out of the
house immediately. I hobbled into the kitchen and phoned
Oscar.

"Hello?" She was on the verge of hanging up before I could
find my voice; I announced myself in a terrified whisper.
"Thomas, is that you? What's the matter? You sound horrible."

"Can I come over?" My legs ached, felt like they would implode if I didn't find somewhere to run.

"You want me to come and get you?" She swallowed any irritation or bother, her voice instead full of open concern.

"No." I hung up the phone and flew out the door. I raced up Bedford Avenue at marathon speed, passed the Orthodox Cathedral at Driggs and Twelfth, slowed to a brisk walk in the boxy Italian neighborhood under the expressway where Oscar and Blythe lived. When I buzzed, Oscar leaned out the window and threw down the keys, and I let myself in. She stood waiting for me at the top of the stairs in a bathrobe.

"God, Tom, Blythe still thinks I'm on the phone with you." I had gained the landing and felt like I had just run a four-minute mile, as if my legs were made of butter and melting under me. I was wheezing, unable to speak. "Come on in; you need a glass of water." She sat me in one of the three carefully clustered Corbusier chairs in their white-painted living room and fetched me my drink.

A dog barked in the bedroom and Blythe called out. "Is that you, Thomas?" Something hard thumped to the ground. "Naughty dog," Blythe shouted, evidently peeved at the animal's leaping from the bed. Tulip the Chihuahua scampered into the room, her nails clicking merrily on the wood floor. She danced joyfully around my feet, pranced on her hind legs, and leaped about my ankles like a rhebok muscularly vaulting over savannah grasses. I reached to pet her, and unable to control her excitement, ecstatic at the scratch of my index finger along the top of her rib cage, she relieved herself in a submissive yellow puddle. Oscar, always one step ahead, handed me my water and wiped up the spill with a bunch of paper towels she held ready in anticipation of just such an emergency.

"Boy, is she happy to see you." I lifted Tulip into my lap;

her tiny body seemed to shiver from the energy of its own
pulse. She blinked her eyes at me and licked my wrists.

"Come in here," Blythe hollered. I followed Oscar into the
bedroom, set Tulip on her pillow, and sat myself on the edge
of the bed. "What happened?" she asked.

"I guess I had a nightmare." I sipped my water. Oscar
climbed onto the bed and sat with her back against the wall.
She bent her legs and her bathrobe slipped under her knees,
opened at the stomach, revealing the nacreous flesh of her
belly, where I spied a deep maroon X, a fibrous cicatrix
stitched with white, the zippered tattoo left from what I assumed must have been an appendectomy. She pulled the folds
of fabric around her waist and the scar disappeared from
view.

"Bad, huh?" I nodded yes to Oscar's question. Already
the worst of the fright had passed; I was left to sort out its
disorienting effect on my memory. She held my hand,
squeezed it in both hers. "You feel better now?"

"I'm okay." I felt the sensation return to my limbs, my
lungs fill with air. Tulip circled the bed, nestled her muzzle
on my hip.

"Tulip will take care of you." Blythe massaged the dog's
hind legs with her thumb and forefinger. No one spoke, and
the awkward question of my presence filled the room: what
was I doing here?

"You're doing fine." Oscar let go of my hand and I pressed
it against Tulip's fleshy little black nose. I plucked at her
whiskers. The skin lifted off her jaw at the pointed follicles,
but she remained placidly in place and let me abuse her,
only scraped in lazy irritation at the side of her mouth with
her grainy tongue. I absentmindedly banged my leg on the
side of the bed; the whole apartment shook from the rhythm
of my restless tapping, the armoire across the room audibly

rocking on the not quite level floor. I was exhausted but wide awake, knew that sleep remained an ambitious goal still hours away, and dreaded how I would pass the interval. Oscar sensibly spared me the embarrassment of having to explain my uncomfortable limbo by suggesting, "Let's go for a drive."

"Sure," I mumbled, grateful to follow wherever they might lead me. Oscar readied herself in the bathroom while Blythe threw on a shirt and pants over her nightgown, then sat beside me on the bed, a tuft of flannel poking through her open fly.

"What exactly is going on with you and Stuart?" I found her directness encouraging.

"I don't know." Why did I always say that? Of course I knew. "I think about breaking up all the time."

"And?"

"I mean every day I think about breaking up with him, and I imagine spending my whole life thinking about leaving him and never doing it." Like a caged animal I paced the perimeter of the mental trap I had set myself. "Is that what people do? Is that why people stay together?"

"Frankly, Thomas"—Blythe looked at me hard and laughed—"that's really pathetic. This may come as a surprise to you, but lots of people stay together because they want to; it is possible to be with someone and wake up every morning glad that other person is there." She lifted Tulip and shook her in both her hands, kissed her wet nose. "Maybe your subconscious is trying to tell you something."

"Like I've been living in daily fear for my life with a homicidal maniac for the past three years?"

"You guys talking about Stuart now?" Oscar poked her head out the bathroom door; she had slicked her hair back with a wet comb and her temples gleamed in the fluorescent bathroom light.

"Look, aside from the fact that he has the moral sensibility of a reptile, Stuart's an absolutely charming creature." Blythe

lowered Tulip to the floor, held the dog's belly in her palm
so her miniature paws just ineffectually scraped the well-
sanded surface. Tulip's tiny limbs revved like the gears of
an engine in neutral, and her beady eyes hungrily scanned
the dusty corners of the room, until Blythe dropped her hand
like a clutch the final quarter of an inch, the gears engaged,
and Tulip sped off in a frantic dash through the living room.

"He's a sadist, and he preys on weakness. That's the fun of
it." Oscar took the empty glass from my hand and chased the
dog into the kitchen. "Let's go." She tucked the dog into her
open leather jacket, turned out the lights, and stood in the
shadow of the front door. I found the darkness, the creeping
trails of light from the streetlamps, the wavering silhouettes on
the reflective floor unnerving. Danger seemed to lurk wherever
I turned; was there nowhere I was safe? I felt more myself again
out on the street, only astonished at the night, how efficiently
the earth's rotation moved me along, heedless in its creaking
and groaning of my own puny, desperate state of affairs.

I sat in the front between Oscar and Blythe, the world
reduced in my view to a parallelogram of swerving sky, dangling streetlamps, and warped tenements. "Actually"—I
gulped—"maybe this isn't such a good idea." I had forgotten
what a maniac Oscar was behind the wheel; even on the best
of nights her driving was likely to put the fear of death in
me. "Can we just go to Kellogg's instead?"

Oscar turned left through a red light onto Metropolitan
Avenue. The neon of the local truck stop flashed just the
other side of the highway. "You sure?" she asked. I was. She
parked at the corner of Lorimer and I scrambled out after
Blythe with the eerie sensation I was perpetually half a step
ahead of myself, living in a spliced second of time, my body
like some futuristic sculpture dragging after itself, my eyes
forever peering over the cliff's edge of the present into the
uncannily familiar future. I was living in parallel universes,

haunted and comforted by my own ghost, as if I were wistfully peering in at my own life as it slipped away, yet reluctant to gain entrance, grateful even for what I termed the excruciating exclusivity of my soul.

I sat by the window next to Blythe in a roomy mauve booth. The green globe of the lamp by the entrance to the subway station loomed large in the glass; I stared at it, transfixed by its double reflection shifting in the imaginary distance. I heard Oscar order me a grilled-cheese sandwich without my asking. She and Blythe petted the dog under the table and whispered conspiratorially their plans to acquire a budgie to keep her company. They pleasantly ignored my trance-like condition, patiently accepted the responsibility for seeing me safely through the aftershocks of my fright. I mechanically ate my sandwich, the food settling in my stomach like an anchor mooring me within easy grasp of reality, and took a turn holding Tulip in my lap. The time seemed to pass lazily, my body settle into the oily vinyl banquette, my mind float in a fuzzy haze of recovering sensibility. I enjoyed sitting there blankly absorbing whatever tidbits of conversation Oscar and Blythe threw my way, was disappointed when I found myself somehow back in the car, the two of them looking at me curiously, slightly exasperated, wondering what to do next.

"I can go home now." I felt the last of my panic pass as if a timer had tripped, neatly raising the dimmed lights of my vacant mind to their usual high voltage.

"You can sleep over if you want to," Blythe offered.

"No." I felt a wave of homesickness sweep over me. "I just want to go home, please." The radio played softly and Blythe serenaded Tulip. The short drive seemed to last a painfully long time now I was ready to return, as if each red light were stubbornly timed to my disadvantage. We turned onto Broadway.

"You can't go on like this, Thomas." Oscar finally broached the unspeakable subtext of my unscheduled visit.

"If you don't do something we will," warned Blythe.

"Yeah, like kill you," Oscar added. She thought a moment: "One of you, anyway."

"I know." I slid to the sidewalk and kissed Blythe through the open window. "Thanks, guys. Good night." I slipped through the front door, felt myself like a spirit seem to pass right through the hollow steel and float to the back of the apartment, where my limp body curled on the mattress received my consciousness back to itself as if the previous hours had been just one more in a series of entirely normal out-of-the-body adventures, my somnambulist self up to the same old tricks, another mysterious night on the town fading fast to the dregs of memory, only a twitch in my nose, a heavy sigh beside me suggestive reminders of what was, what might have been, what yet remained to be.

I continued to live my double life throughout the following summer, as if I were outside myself watching horrified the deteriorating state of my world, curious at times how it would all end. Michael I hardly ever saw. News would occasionally reach me—Lucas spotted at the museum, Michael waved to on the subway—and the few rare times when I actually ran into him myself were like those transfiguring moments described by Wordsworth: "Rushed in as if on wings, the time in which / The pulse of Being everywhere was felt." I knew my romantic imagination was making much of him, selfishly, unfairly so; still, I could not help myself, he had so effectively excluded me from his illness, and thereby left me free to fantasize what I would of his decline. There were fleeting odd moments when the question rose in the back of my mind—is he still alive?—and all I could make of the agonizing, unknowing uncertainty was to wonder how and when the end would ultimately announce itself.

I last saw him that same summer, on an overcast day in August. The early scent of autumn was in the air and I was in a strange mood, as if I had been living three years of endless summer in New York and winter was finally approaching, leaving me hopelessly unprepared. I had rushed irritated from the law library, fed up with the futile search for some academic journal, my part-time job carried over from school the bitter pittance on which I lived, and was surprised to discover Michael hunched over at the corner peering into the sunken ground-floor windows of the reading room.

"What exactly are you doing?" I asked. He straightened his narrow back, startled.

"Thomas." He smiled, and I thought he looked rather well, almost unchanged from his former self; only his long-sleeve shirt was suspiciously loose at the elbows. What if I had him all wrong, what if he wasn't sick, his fancied fate nothing but the putrid product of my own diseased imagination, a fantastical attempt to loose his hold on my psyche? If he should die it will be my fault, I thought. "A passing fancy. That's all." He looked at the street sign over my head. "Did I ever show you that Sullivan building down on Bleecker Street?" Michael always managed to have something for me.

"No," I answered, intrigued at the possibility I had perhaps hundreds of times unconsciously passed such a landmark. He gestured east and we began walking toward Broadway.

"Are you still with Stuart?" He sounded hopeful; I wondered what for.

"I don't know." I kept saying that.

"When will you learn, Thomas? What are you waiting for?"

"Does it ever get easier?" I felt like a train about to jump the rails, Michael the engineer I was trusting to somehow keep me on track at the last second.

"Does what get easier?"

"Life, I guess. Am I supposed to get used to this? Is there something I should be doing?" I was hungry for a reassuring answer, a simple solution.

"You're asking me?" He rolled his eyes skyward, and I was struck by their vacancy, the painful, listless suggestion of a divided self, already half withdrawn from the living world, the remainder patiently abiding the process of its own dissolution. "How should I know?" We crossed Broadway at Bleecker Street and stood in the middle of the block across from a tall narrow white building, sleek and transparently lean despite the heavy crust of terra-cotta detail grown like tree bark on the surface.

"I can't believe I never noticed it before."

"It's the only building he ever built in New York." Michael scaled the façade with his eyes. "Amazing they never tore it down."

"Benign neglect," I said; the idea struck a chord.

"Yes," he said, "how fortunate to sit here just off the beaten path, barely noticeable, causing no fuss, drawing no attention to itself." He lapsed into silence and I stood uncomfortable beside him. I wanted to touch him, put my fingers to his pale cheeks, and ask after his health, his hopes and fears for the future, hug him and hear him whisper in my ear sweet invitations to come visiting. Instead, I remained stiff, arms awkwardly held to my side in reluctant obedience to the distance I sensed he demanded, and waited for him to speak.

"What do you want me to tell you?" he asked. He shook his head and frowned, his features tensed in the reflexive scowl which had haunted my forgotten dreams on a train in upstate New York at the very outset of what was proving to be a long journey. He hunched forward as if something had snapped inside him, as if his spine like a spring had become unwound and flexed in a circle of woozy, uncertain motion. He clutched his arms to his stomach and looked at me, the corners of his eyes and mouth smooth and relaxed now, the magnitude of his self-composure awesome. "I'm only thirty-two years old," he said, explanation for everything.

"I don't know what's the matter with me, anyway," I lied, then lied some more. I felt him urging me on, pleading with me not to mar the bright surface which he held so dear. "Everything's actually fine."

"Good." He accepted my untruth. We seemed to be speaking in code, enacting some ritual of prevarication vital to both our sanities, a gentleman's agreement to tread lightly and ask for nothing. He was leaving me. The bulletproof glass which seemed always to exist invisibly between us cast in the blue August light a barely perceptible shadow, a reflective hint of the vast gray canyon which separated us. I was perched on the edge of a deep gorge and Michael was waving to me from the other side, the earth ripping apart between us, rolling and rising like a great tidal wave until he had disappeared entirely from view and all I could see was the exposed sandwich of loamy topsoil streaked with sand riding the crust of the planet, the upper and lower mantle, the liquid sea of the outer core crashing against the solid center in the unimaginable distance. Without a further word Michael had gone.

I scanned the street for his retreating figure and felt the sting of his rejection as forcefully as if he had fled screaming obscenities, railing against my selfish interests, relentlessly accusing me. I had had him there before me and foolishly let him slip between my fingers, like some sylvan sprite often heard from but never seen, glimpsed at last in a shadowy glade, frightened away and lost forever by the stupidity of my clumsy, overeager step and heavy breath. Perhaps if I hadn't knocked so loudly, instead simply waited patiently and presumed entrance, the doors locked to me would have opened of their own accord. I stopped, slapped myself mentally on the wrist, ashamed of my morbid curiosity, my thrill-seeking instinct and wounded pride; it should have been enough to know I wasn't wanted. Hadn't I deliberately driven him away?

Solace: I turned the corner of Broadway in blind search of comfort, some fortifying simple pleasure to carry me through the next few difficult hours, courage and a reason to want to go home. A sweet memory entered my mind, and I strolled downtown with a renewed sense of purpose and the image before me of a dark green box glimpsed in a crowded display. Prince Street loomed and I hastened my step. The precious gourmet grocery on the corner was bustlingly busy; an arty crowd, arbiters of the local ton, were gathered, wispily sipping espresso, in the enormous plate-glass window opposite pyramids of golden fruit and bins of spartanly arranged, well-preened produce. I navigated my way to the candy counter in the middle of the store as if by echolocation and selected a box of Frango mints. The line at the cashier was long and a crazed woman in black kept pushing me from behind with her shopping cart full of daintily wrapped packages and long loaves. I balanced the box in my jittery fingers; several times I reached to set it among the gourmandising gewgaws piled on the counter, as if it were some pornographic appliance drawing unwanted speculative attention to myself. Was my needy hunger so embarrassingly obvious? The cashier lifted the box in her limp hands and turned it over in listless search of a price; her droopy eyes apparently saw nothing, and after enduring several long seconds of her deliberate torture, I was forced to point out to her the white sticker on the narrow side of the cardboard cover.

"Ooooh, 'rango mints," she rudely exclaimed, returning my

own look of tart displeasure while counting my exact change. She handed me back a nickel and asked, "What's this?"

"It's Canadian." I dropped the coin to the counter.

"We're not living in Canadia, you know." The woman in black impatiently scraped my ankles with the front wheels of her cart. I was trapped in hell, fighting to give away my money. I found another dime in my pocket and flicked it at the cashier. I fled the store without waiting for my receipt or the nickel due me, although I was not quick enough to avoid her calling after me with sniggering emphasis on the final word, "Don't you wanna bag, sir?"

The afternoon had turned blustery and cold and I clutched my present to myself in a daze, wondering at the trouble it had so far caused me. I walked north back to Houston Street, but my legs hurt and the thought of riding the subway in my frazzled condition seemed borderline dangerous, likely to set me reeling over the edge. So I unwrapped my candy and lingered on the corner waiting for lightning to strike, inspiration to hit, my next adventure to begin. A taxi pulled to the curb without my hailing it, one of the sleek new fleet just introduced, and with a fateful shrug I settled into the tinted-glass respite of the back seat.

I told the driver my destination. He had never heard of the Williamsburg Bridge and snorted his disapproval at my directions, but I ignored his wayward glances and devoted my full attention to the Frango mints. The box lay open on my lap, the creamy brown cubes huddled together in rows, their crinkled white wrappers absorbing each shock of the road. I popped the first into my mouth; delicious, but not quite as I remembered. The initial shock was the same, the firm thin coating and the smooth milky texture beneath, the subtle building flavor of mint. Then the sweetness gave way and my now more sophisticated taste buds detected a tingling acid

aftertaste, almost a burning sensation at the back of my throat,
chemical peppermint.

A second chocolate, and again the burning, flagrant and
cutting, not at all what I expected. I ate three more in rapid
succession anyway, waiting for the old taste to return. So
it's been a few years, I told myself; they were still delicious.
One more for wishful thinking and I dropped the cover back
on the box, happy after all with my supply, certain despite
my tentative disappointment it would be all gone by the end
of the day. The taxi swerved into the left lane at Chrystie
Street and pulled up next to another cab. The driver rolled
down his window and aimed a barrage of incomprehensible
insults at his fellow hackman, until the light changed and he
threw his hands up over the wheel as the other car sped off.

"I know him in Pakistan," he said. "I no see him in ten
years." We were moving now, turning onto Delancey Street,
the bridge in full view when I realized the depth of my stupidity. "Asshole," he muttered. I ordered him to pull over at
the corner; he was blind to the flashing lights ahead, completely unaware of my mistake and irritated at losing his fare.
I foolishly tipped him far more generously than he deserved
and once again walked over the bridge, this time with my
Frango mints tucked tightly under my arm. The roadway was
teeming with painters and welders and structural engineers,
but the promenade was mostly empty, only a lone figure on
a bicycle or casual stroller left from the initial tide of people
that had long since devised alternative routes.

I hardly minded the walk, enjoyed as I always did the sight
of my dirty little corner of Brooklyn spread before me: a plume
of black smoke rose from the sugar factory, where a huge
ship was unloading its international cargo; the dome of the
Williamsburg Savings Bank shimmered in the western sunlight like the first time I had seen it; a woman sat painting

by an open window of the loft building on Berry Street; a fleet of school buses, parked in a row on Kent Avenue, awaited its cargo of religious students. I rather regretted having to descend to shore, to the stinking mess of Driggs Avenue, the fancy cars with Jersey plates parked on Broadway across from the steakhouse, the obnoxious pounding of a drum from the blue building at the corner of Bedford Avenue. I clutched my Frango mints to my chest.

I inserted my key in the lock and listened before turning it; already I knew something was wrong, someone was there with Stuart. I could see it all happening, my future unfolding before me, my mind cloudy with cursed visions. I opened the door and entered. Tony and Stuart sat together at the kitchen table. The radio played softly, sexy black love music. Stuart had a shoe box full of old photographs before him, was walking Tony through images of his childhood and adolescence. They hardly looked up at me, and I could feel myself repelled as I passed them, as if they existed in an opposing magnetic field, a frictionless buffer of energy forever preventing our collision.

I sat on the bed, eating a handful of chocolates and watching them through the open door. Tony laughed quietly at some whispered joke and looked up. His eyes met mine and he shrugged. I felt the look in his eyes reduce me to the most tired cliché, their vapid indifference a gloating, unsympathetic reminder of my irrelevance. Had they no shame? Stuart rose to use the bathroom. "Just one second," he said to Tony, then grinned self-satisfied at me as he maneuvered through the bedroom. I moved to the sofa and faced Tony.

"So," I began, and rose from the sofa unable to finish. I gathered Stuart's photos together and returned the box to his studio shelf. I sniffed the air; it smelled like nothing, absolutely nothing.

"What?" Tony said, leaning forward and tilting his head

to render his feeble joke intelligible. Stuart returned. I looked at them both and all I could see was two corpses, a pair of dead bodies lying stiffly side by side in matching pine coffins, eyes milky and sunken, their powdered skin blackening while I watched. I tried to picture them together in bed, their smutty frames locked in joint-cracking contortions, grunting and moaning like some disgusting pair of a rutting mammalian subspecies, but I saw nothing. How long had it been since Stuart had touched me?

I didn't see them leave, or remember hearing their faint goodbyes until long after they had slammed the door shut behind them. I paced the apartment, dazzled at how quickly and thoroughly I had become a stranger in my own home. The prescient sense of exclusion which had been haunting me for months had finally reached a climax; my divided life had at long last broken in two: one part lay devastated on the sofa, dissolved in a puddle of aching tears, groping blindly with his bare hands at the thousand pieces of his broken heart strewn like cut crystal smashed against an open hearth, palms gritty and bleeding raw from pathetically attempting to gather the glass dust, while the other part brewed himself a cup of tea, ate another Frango mint, breathed a series of long, easy, grateful breaths as if deeply satisfied with the results of a full day's labor, and savored a hard-earned feeling of accomplishment, looked forward to his enjoyment of the rewards accruing to a job well done.

I remained deeply divided throughout the solitary summer night. My crying half crouched insensate most of the evening on the sofa, refusing food or drink, waiting for Stuart to come home. My practical half, however, convinced the day of my liberation was at hand, carefully plotted my long-sought escape, and with impressive efficiency and sureness packed my life into a pile of suitcases, boxes, and shopping bags ready to move out the front door. Neither portion spoke to the other; they simply ignored each other and occasionally stole a sly, disapproving glance in the other's direction, the one shocked at the other's coolheadedness and grim acceptance, he irritated and impatient with his counterpart's seemingly self-indulgent, stubborn refusal to face the facts.

Not until the following morning had my fractured self begun the slow process of reconciliation, both portions mindfully— albeit wordlessly and full of suspicion—sitting together enjoying a cup of coffee when Stuart walked whistling through the door. He eyed my heaped belongings and looked at me wearily sipping my hot drink. After removing his T-shirt and wiping his dirty face with it, he crumpled it into a ball and threw it underhand against the tin ceiling.

"What's going on?" He looked at me as if he had just run to the corner for a quart of milk, unsure what to make of the practical joke I was playing.

"You tell me." I think that was the crier speaking, hungry for the sordid details.

"Just one of those things, I guess." Stuart was hardly forthcoming; he seemed determined not to make this easy for me. "We can still be together, maybe just be roommates for a while."

"Listen, Stuart"—the plotter now. "This is the end. I'm leaving."

"Just like that?" He sounded pathetically unaware of how meaningless his words had become.

"Just like you went and fucked Tony!" the jealous crier shot back.

"On your recommendation, wasn't it?" He removed his pants, stood temptingly before me in his underwear.

"Once I did it. Once." Who was it staring bleary-eyed at his square hips and shoulders, whispering hoarsely, "Please, Stuart, please, just one last time," clinging on bended knees to his tan thighs? He sat on the sofa and pulled my shirt off over my head, slid his hands under my arms, and raised me on top of him, his tongue on my neck, behind my ears, lips pulling against my own, reducing me to a flood of uncontrollable sensation. I no longer knew who he was, no longer cared, simply drank at the fountain of his body like the thirsty traveler I was, accepted the fleeting hospitality and comfort he offered, not minding the consequences, not caring how extravagant the cost might be. He had become a total stranger to me, every square inch of his flesh exotically new and unbearably desirable, the density of the desire and despair he physically embodied so great we were like a black hole at the end of the universe greedily sucking in the entire history of creation; only I knew in the tiny corner of my imagination set apart that my mind was playing tricks on itself, wanting at last what it couldn't have, dangerously associating this exquisite passion with the not necessarily related physical presence in which it took place.

"You realize this changes nothing," I said. We were in the shower and he was washing my hair, and I felt myself in control again, like the captain of an ocean liner navigating through a series of unfamiliar shoals in the night who must fight to ignore the magnificent distraction of the aurora borealis, burdened not only with the responsibility for my own future but with the future of the hundreds of unsuspecting travelers who placed their confidence in me; I must steer this ship to deep waters, ignore all physical pain and exhaustion, postpone the luxury of collapse until the safety of morning, when I can make the phone call which I know will end everything.

"Let's get married." He handed me a towel. I felt his touch through the cotton and pulled away. He stood in the doorway drying himself, blocking my passage. I was too familiar with his sadistic humor, yet I balked, considered for a moment his proposal. "When you're rich and famous," he finished.

"Excuse me." I squeezed past him, always apologizing for something.

"Think about it, Thomas." He followed me, watched me dress, remained naked himself.

"I am," I answered. My hands shook as I filled a plastic bag with my toothbrush and sundry other toiletries. I picked up the phone and dialed Oscar's number.

"Who are you calling?" I ignored his question. Oscar had been waiting to hear from me and I gave her the signal.

"I'm all set," I said, staring at Stuart as I spoke. He sat on the edge of the bed, legs spread wide, one hand raised gripping the back of his neck, the other fondling himself. I cradled the receiver between my shoulder and ear and listened to the dial tone. I watched Stuart grow hard again. He was using sex as a weapon, determined to leave me bleeding, mortally wounded if at all possible. I dropped the phone and looked at my watch; there was still time.

A knock on the door. I swallowed hard and wiped my mouth with the back of my hand. It was over.

I learned of Michael's death on Thanksgiving Day. I was home for the holiday and my father called me to the phone in one of his many mildly dismissive tones of voice, not so much irritated at the intrusion as uncomprehending why any-one should call me in the first place. The voice at the end of the line was unfamiliar and I struggled to place it. Whoever it was had launched an intimate inquiry into my health and well-being without bothering to introduce himself.

"Who is this?" I asked, suspecting some sort of unappe-tizing joke.

"It's me—Mark. Don't you remember?" He sounded hurt I hadn't recognized his voice, as if I were supposed to feel a particular thrill at having heard from him after so many years.

"Why are you calling me?" I had no patience for pleasantries, no interest in chitchat, felt certain anyway of his purpose; his was just the sort of call I had been expecting.

"Jane's idea," he explained, the simple facts following, Mark no longer attempting to bathe in a softening light the truth of my having been reduced to an afterthought, or explain how it was that Michael had already been dead a month. I returned to the table and resumed my meal. No one asked who had called; no one cared. I felt only a minimum of grief. What right, after all, had I to mourn Michael's passing? He was perhaps less a stranger than I had realized, but he was gone now, and I felt ashamed of my grief, ashamed of the multiplicity of losses I so easily substituted for his death, my mourning what never was. There had been moments when I felt Michael knew me better than I knew myself, and I wondered, was this nothing more than the final in a long series of necessarily missed opportunities, the ironic conclusion of what had always been our fate, as if Michael had from our first meeting deliberately held me at a distance from his heart equal to the distance I lived from my own, cradled me there in my swaddling clothes, confident I would come in the fullness of time he had himself been denied to an understanding, feel a gratitude and a debt which can never be paid to the living?

That night I enjoyed a perfectly sound sleep, undisturbed by the suburban quietness. In my dreams I was standing again with Michael on Bleecker Street, and he was turning to leave, just as I remembered, only my mind, like some clever editor who through the careful insertion of a comma, the deletion of a pair of dashes, irrevocably changes the meaning of a crucial final couplet, added a brief pause, just long enough for Michael to stop at the corner and wave at me, his lips mutely molding the word I had until that moment not even realized I had longed to hear: "Goodbye." I awoke crying, glad he was dead.